The Enodia Enigma

Christopher J Wright

Cover by ambient_studios through fiverr.com

ISBN: 9798564308007

For Karen

Part 1. Amber

1.

"You are absolutely sure, Doctor Fryer?"

"Beyond a shadow of doubt, Your Grace. The figures cannot lie."

"So, it falls upon us to meet the challenge after all. Let us hope we are a match for it. Go and make your preparations. I shall do likewise."

Fryer did not move.

Sighing, Duke Edrik placed his quill back in its inkwell. "There is something else that you wish to discuss?"

"It's the Off Worlders, Your Grace. They have untold knowledge. Perhaps we should seek their assistance with our endeavour? It might be prudent to have – "

"I mistrust them, Fryer. They say that benevolence and curiosity are their motivations but I see little to back that claim. They drop from the skies and herald a new era, then ignore us for almost a year. And now they send a 'scientist' to study us. Even that halfwit Zandis is suspicious of them – "

"Your Grace, you speak of the king."

"No need to look so shocked, Fryer. But, for once, I agree with him. No, we shall not allow the Off Worlders to interfere."

"What of the woman? She will remain after the sky-ship has gone."

"She must be watched closely until we can decipher her intentions. She is a complication, one that cannot be allowed to become a hindrance."

* * * * *

"This is the last chance to change your mind."

"Good," Amber said. "I'm hardly going to come all this way and turn back now, am I?"

Norton gestured towards the three-hundred strong crowd behind her, and to the sprawling city beyond.

"But look at the place. I can't leave you here."

Amber followed his gaze. It was true that the city was backward by the standards of their home planet of Vindor. Denford was a motley collection of mostly wooden buildings, many of which looked as if they wouldn't survive a strong storm.

"I'm not going to let that put me off," she said. "Something unusual is going on here, and I'm aiming to get to the bottom of it."

The engines of Norton's courier ship rumbled into life, the low roar drawing cheers from the crowd.

"So you say, but do you really need to be abandoned here alone? Why not wait a couple of years until things are a bit more civilised? Or at least till a proper team can be organised?"

"If I wait that long, things will already have changed. I want to study this world as it is, before it's civilised out of all recognition. By then, it'll be too late."

Norton shook his head. "I'm not going to change your mind, am I? But I had to try." He reached to the holster at his side, drew his laser-pistol and held it out. "Look, I know you said no weapons but, please, take this. I'd feel a lot better if I don't leave you completely defenceless."

"All right," she said, taking the pistol, its cold metal making her shudder. "I'm sure I won't need it. But thank you." She checked the safety catch was on and put the weapon in a coat pocket out of sight.

When she looked up again, Norton was receiving a message in his earpiece.

"We're ready to launch," he said. "I'll be back to pick you up in a year. I'll try to get a freighter to drop by and check on you, but I can't guarantee anything. This is such a backwater."

3

"The whole point was to get here first," Amber said. "There'll be an emissary from Vindor here before too long as well, I imagine, but the longer I have the place to myself the better. Don't worry. If I need help, I can always use the Astracomm. Somebody'll be here in a few weeks."

"Till next year, then. Go careful." Norton turned and walked up the access ramp into the ship.

As the ramp withdrew into the bulk of the craft, completing the perfection of its streamlined shape, Amber retreated the fifty metres or so to the edge of the watching crowd.

After a minute of waiting, the engine noise grew and the ship lifted, to a chorus of excitement from the watchers. It rose to a hundred metres. Then, a brief glow from the main engine array at the rear of the ship pushed it away from the city. As it hung in the air, the main engines fired. Then the craft accelerated before disappearing into a glowing dot in the sky.

Drinking in the atmosphere of a genuine pre-industrial world, Amber threaded her way towards her new home, the Beacon Inn.

The city was a jumble of bustling interconnecting streets. The road from the gates to the inn was paved but most of the side streets consisted of nothing more than mud. Routes would have to be planned in bad weather.

Horse-drawn carts took produce into the city, slowly edging their way through the tangled masses of men and women. As she walked, she was acutely aware of the looks she was receiving from the townsfolk and the conversations that paused and then restarted with more vigour as she passed. It was no wonder. The colours and cut of her clothing made her stand out. They were a world away from the simplicity of most of these townsfolk.

She began analysing some of the surface layers of the culture about her. The majority of women were accompanied, and all who she could see wore skirts. Her own outfit would appear masculine.

Hats seemed to be the preserve of the poorer groups – probably a practical side-effect of a limited access to personal hygiene. The pungent aromas that assailed her nostrils supported her theory.

Amber smiled. She was doing what she loved.

Since her last expedition, she'd spent more than a year in the staid atmosphere of academia and had found the experience draining. It was a necessary evil, comprising conferences and publishing papers the university required to justify her funding. But throughout, she had set her sights on the next expedition to a newly re-discovered society.

She'd scoured each of the monthly reports from the Navy's Exploration Service. The planet of Enodia stood out as significant – small language drift and a skew in scientific development. The university hadn't agreed with her, though, and refused to fund a full expedition. So, she'd had to go it alone, as she often did. Truth be told, she preferred it this way. It meant she was in full control.

She reached the Beacon Inn.

It was timber-framed, as were many of the buildings in the city, but it was the best place to stay. It was one of the few that had electrical lighting, having its own steam-powered generator in an outhouse.

Amber stepped into the large common room. Three men, including the innkeeper Joram Travis, were taking chairs down from the tables. Joram walked towards her.

"Welcome back, Miss Stefans," he said. "It all went well, I hope?" Before Amber could respond, he continued, "We'll be serving lunch in about an hour. Will you be coming down or should I send something up to your rooms?"

"I've a lot of unpacking to do, Mr. Travis," Amber said, "so send something up, please. But I'll definitely be down for dinner," she added. "After all, I want to meet the people of Denford and your public rooms seem an excellent place to start."

Joram smiled. "Very good, Miss Stefans. We'll be powering the generator up at five o'clock today. There's always a number who come in for the lights."

The innkeeper led her up a flight of stairs and along a narrow passageway.

"I've put you in the suite, Miss Stefans. I thought you'd appreciate the extra space due to your long stay."

He opened the door at the end of the passage, entering and holding the door open for Amber to follow.

"That's very kind of you," Amber said as she surveyed the room. The furnishings were simple. It wouldn't be what she was used to at home, but they were sturdy and more comfortable than she'd had to endure at times.

"If there's anything you need, please let me know," Joram said. "Otherwise, I'll get on."

Amber thanked him again as he left and set about unpacking the trunks that had been delivered earlier.

By mid-afternoon, she had her rooms how she wanted them. As well as her personal effects and clothes, Amber now had a small library of books on archaeology and cultural anthropology. Although old fashioned, it was more convenient to have actual books. They helped conserve power for the computer equipment.

The lounge was a combination of office and storage room, with her computer and hand terminal, holo-recorder, scanner, spare parts and power cells.

Once Amber had unpacked everything, she took Norton's laser-pistol from her coat pocket and stored it away safely. She wouldn't be needing that.

2.

Bayl Groms picked his way down a narrow side street, carefully avoiding mud patches remaining from the previous night's rain. This quarter of the city was not one a gentleman would normally visit and he had forgotten how bad it was. Placing a perfumed handkerchief to his nose, he vowed he'd take a carriage next time.

Finally, Bayl reached a properly paved street and came to the Beacon Inn.

He went into the common room. It took a moment for his eyes to adjust to the gloom and, in that time, he was approached by a rotund man, dressed in garb whose cut and material suggested it had once been fashionable. Now it was old, worn and soiled.

"Good day, gentlesir. Might I provide you with food or wine?"

Bayl looked around the room. A single customer sat at one of the simple wooden tables, tucking into a bowl of soup.

Bayl pressed his handkerchief to his nose once again. "I've not come here to eat. I'm seeking one of your guests… the Off Worlder, Professor Stefans."

"I didn't think it would be long before she started getting visitors. She's in her rooms, sir. Up the stairs and farthest door on the right."

Bayl nodded his thanks and made his way up the narrow wooden stairs. When he reached the door, he took a moment to compose himself. He must not allow his personal enthusiasm for this assignment to overcome the need for prudence.

He knocked on the door. As he waited, he realised he was about to enter the rooms of a woman without a chaperone. He flushed. A glance down the corridor confirmed that nobody was watching.

The door opened.

A young woman, her long dark hair tied back in a ponytail, stood there. She wore outlandish clothing: blue trousers, a white buttonless shirt and a small blue waistcoat. In short, she was dressed like a man. But she was anything but.

"Can I help you?" she said, grinning.

His mouth was gaping open. This couldn't be Professor Stefans. The woman wasn't even thirty years of age, far too young for such a high position.

"Ah… I'm here to make the acquaintance of Professor Amber Stefans. Could you let her know that Bayl Groms of the Royal Counsellors is here."

Her grin turned into a smile.

"I'm pleased to meet you, Mr Groms. I'm Amber."

"But… Forgive my rudeness, I expected somebody a little – "

"Older?"

Embarrassed, Bayl nodded.

"It's all right. I get that a lot. I assure you I am quite old; forty-one years by my calendar, which would be forty-three by your own."

"But you –"

"Don't look that old? Why, thank you." Professor Stefans smiled again. "Please, come in and sit down."

He entered and took a seat close to the door.

"Actually," she continued, "I almost expect that reaction now. We have medicines that slow the effects of ageing. Most people from my world would look young to you."

"You can *slow* ageing? How long do your people live?"

"A hundred and thirty years isn't unusual. But I'm sure you didn't come here to discuss my age. How can I help you?"

Bayl looked around the room as Professor Stefans spoke. His eyes alighted upon the writing-desk. At first glance, there seemed to be an assortment of paperweights, but some had buttons upon their surfaces and there was no sign of any papers. He realised the woman was still waiting for him to speak.

"Actually, Professor, I'm here to see if I can be of help to you. I am in the employ of the Royal Counsellors and, while we're aware you're not here in an official governmental capacity, we still wish to ensure your stay here is a success."

"And perhaps find out why I'm here?"

Bayl shifted in his seat.

"If you wish me to be direct," he said, "then, yes, this has puzzled us. You describe yourself as a scientist, but we are at a loss to imagine what knowledge you could gain from us when you have ships that float in the sky and travel to the stars."

There was a school of thought that held that this Off Worlder woman must be a spy, come to gather information in preparation for an invasion. He didn't subscribe to such a theory. With the power they had, they would have no need for subterfuge if they truly harboured ambitions of empire. But still it left the question of what such an advanced people could learn from Enodia. Was there, perhaps, a more subtle deception at play?

Professor Stefans looked at him, holding his gaze for a moment too long. To Bayl's relief, she rose from her chair and walked to the desk. She picked up one of the palm-sized paperweights, turned it over a few times in her hands and faced him again.

"Let me answer you with a question of my own, Mr Groms. Am I right in thinking that you're finding this meeting a little difficult?"

"Indeed, Professor," he said, blushing. "There are aspects to this situation which break the social norms, quite aside from the fact that you hail from another world."

Stefans nodded. "I thought as much. At a guess, I'd say a lot of it stems from my being female?"

"It is not the done thing for a man to visit a woman alone in her rooms," he said. "And some of my discomfort stems from your manner not being what I am used to from a lady."

"Forgive me," she reassured him, smiling. "Every world builds up its own social rules and the roles of male and female here are not uncommon on newly re-contacted worlds. It's such things I've come to study. I want to immerse myself in your culture and investigate why it's developed the way it has."

"You want to study our culture?" he said, leaning forward. "Why would you travel so far for this? What can you possibly learn from us?" The espionage theory suddenly seemed more plausible.

Professor Stefans returned to her chair, still holding the paperweight. She looked directly at him.

Bayl held her gaze.

"I'm impressed, Mr Groms. You're an open-minded man."

"Would that indicate that I have passed a test?"

"You have," Stefans said. "If we're to work together, then I needed to know how well you could deal with uncomfortable situations."

"I don't recall making a suggestion that we should work together."

"True, but it would suit both our purposes. You're under orders to keep an eye on me and what better way to do that than accompany me. I need somebody with knowledge of this world to help me direct my work. It's perfect."

"If you would have me be your colleague, I would appreciate an answer to my question. Why have you travelled so far to study our culture?"

"Of course. Although I don't know how satisfactory you'll find the answer. My people have the luxury of being able to pursue scientific study out of curiosity rather than practical needs. My own studies are a good example. We learn a lot about why societies develop the way they do and get insights into our own culture as a result. But the real reason I'm here is that I'm fascinated by studying new peoples."

"So you visit all the new worlds that are discovered?"

Stefans smiled. "Me? Good grief, no. I've only been to a dozen or so worlds myself. There are far too many for them all to be studied in depth."

"Then why did you choose to visit us in particular?"

"Because your world is unusual, Mr Groms."

"How so?"

"Two reasons," she said. "Your knowledge of the sciences is quite uneven. Most worlds go through a series of advances in roughly the same order, if at different speeds. Your knowledge of electricity is more than a hundred years ahead of most other areas. I've seen variations, but never quite this pronounced."

"And the second reason?"

"The ease of our conversation. I've studied the recordings taken by the scout ship which came here a year ago. Of course, I've had to spend time learning some details of your language, but mine is surprisingly similar. According to the records, Enodia has been out of touch with the rest of humankind for roughly a thousand years. It should have changed much more in that time."

"And you've travelled all this way because of those two peculiarities?"

Stefans smiled again. "Yes. It may seem unimportant to you. But I want to find out why things have worked out this way. Often it's the unusual that tells us the most."

Bayl shook his head. "I will not pretend to understand your motivations, but they seem harmless enough. As you have correctly deduced, I have been charged with monitoring your activities here, so I will accept your invitation to accompany you. Perhaps I may understand your aims more clearly in time. Now, if you could give me some idea of what your studies will entail…"

Stefans held up the paperweight.

"This will be the key to most of what I'll be doing."

Bayl leaned forward even more. It was a dull, black substance with several raised areas on one side of its oval. "What is it?"

"It's a recording device. I'll use it to interview people and then collate the information into a rounded view of your society. Would you like to see it in action?"

Bayl nodded. Seeing this Off Worlder technology was one of the main reasons he had volunteered for this post.

Stefans pressed one of the raised areas and a green light appeared on the side facing him.

"Oh," Bayl cried, pulling away.

"Don't worry, Mr Groms," Stefans smiled. "It won't hurt you."

He leaned forward again. "What is it doing?"

"It's recording images and sounds so that I can replay and analyse them."

"Can I see these images?"

"Of course." Stefans's hands moved across the recorder and the green light turned to blue. A moment later, another light formed above the device and coalesced into writing, hanging in the air, and facing her.

As Bayl reached forwards to touch the writing, his hand passed straight through, distorting the words. He pulled back.

"It's all right," Stefans said. "That won't damage it. Now watch."

Some of the writing glowed brighter, faded, then was replaced by an image of Bayl himself, leaning back, then forwards as he had done earlier.

"What is it doing?" the device said.

"It's recording images and sounds so that I can replay and analyse them."

"Can I see these images?"

"Of course."

Bayl's mouth fell open.

Stefans chuckled.

His image was replaced by the writing. It too vanished, leaving the recorder as it had been, a dull, black paperweight.

Bayl sat in silence for a time. Then he said, "What do you intend to record with this machine?"

That's where your help will be appreciated," Stefans said. "At first I just want to get a general sense of things. I'd like to wander the city, speak to a few of the citizens. But I'd also like to record any special occasions or events, things like weddings, funerals, holiday celebrations – that kind of thing. Hopefully, you'll be able to suggest some good places to start and help me avoid causing any offence when I work."

"That shouldn't be too difficult. In fact, your arrival is timed fortuitously. There is a festival taking place next week that's just the sort of event that you are seeking."

"Excellent," Stefans said. "That'll give us a few days to explore the city and help me get a better feel of the place. Now, if you would excuse me, I have some notes I'd like to write up. Perhaps we could meet in the morning and begin our work?"

Bayl left the Beacon Inn and traced his way back to the Counsellors' offices. Though the meeting had been brief, he had seen enough to be certain that his instincts were correct. The Off Worlders were going to bring unimagined changes. One small device, that seemed almost magical in its working, had proved that.

The woman herself seemed to be genuine, but not all Off Worlders would be scientists. There would, no doubt, be others of a more dangerous disposition. Still, she would be a useful source of information both for his work and personal curiosity. This promised to be the most intriguing task he had ever been set.

As he made his way down a side street, he grinned, not noticing he walked through a puddle he had sidestepped less than an hour earlier.

3.

Doctor Karl Fryer took a copper disk from the laboratory bench and placed it in the cylindrical space between three vertical glass rods. Next, a circular piece of cloth, dipped in brine, followed by a zinc disk. Time and again, he repeated the process until the stack filled the length of the rods. Finally, he touched the contact wire to the top of the stack and a bulb on the desk glowed, more brightly than in the previous experiment.

Fascinating. More discs did lead to a greater current. As he had suspected. If only the ancient journals had said more about this.

"My greetings, Doctor."

He looked up from his bench.

Duke Edrik had entered the laboratory, with that vagabond Medda in tow.

Fryer always felt uneasy in Medda's presence. Without being unduly large or powerful, there was menace in his bearing. He was a man capable of violence without pity. He had never understood why the Duke needed such a man in his employ.

"Your Grace," Fryer said. "Is it prudent to be seen together today?"

"What? Oh, there's nothing amiss in a benefactor visiting the university to see the fruits of his donations, is there? You worry too much, Doctor."

The Duke examined the apparatus on the bench.

"This will be of use to us in our – project?"

"No, your Grace. This is but a curiosity for the moment. However, it has a great potential. If we can power electrical devices without the need for a steam generator, then – "

"You must not allow such frippery to divert you from the matter in hand. Have steps been taken to safeguard your men?"

"Of course," Fryer said. "They have all been given tasks that will keep them away from the festival. There was discontent but they will be safe."

"And your preparations?"

"Continuing apace. We will be ready at the due time."

The Duke nodded in satisfaction. "Good. You have done well, Doctor."

"What news of the Off Worlder Stefans?" Fryer asked.

"Maybe, Medda, you will respond for us."

"Yes, Your Grace," Medda said. "She's harmless, I'd say. Spends her time walkin' the city, talkin' to folk of little worth in the main. She's done nothin' to say she'll be a problem. The King has put one of his minders on her but that's no surprise. I'm keepin' an eye on her too, just to be sure, mind you."

"So, you see, Fryer," the Duke continued, "it seems we had no need for concern. By the end of the day we will have reached the final stages of our vocation... assuming your calculations can be trusted."

"Of course my calculations can be trusted," Fryer exclaimed.

"Then everything will go according to plan," Duke Edrik said. "Come, Medda."

After they had gone, Fryer unlocked the desk where he kept his papers. It wouldn't do any harm to check the figures one last time.

* * * * *

Amber drank in the view of the street, a bustle of activity. Men and women, arrayed in a hundred different shades and hues of the most garish colours, milled along contentedly, browsing the myriad different stalls.

A mix of heady scents filled the air, far more pleasant than the usual Denford fare: spices from tropical climes; women wearing perfumes too expensive for everyday use; the rich aroma of meats cooking at a dozen fires. Even the fresh hops smell of the frothy ale that was being freely distributed from strategically positioned barrels made a change from its usual stale cousin.

Bayl was beginning to lighten up a little, thank goodness. During the first couple of days he had made his distaste for the common people quite obvious. He had tried to keep the greatest physical distance possible from the more pungent of those she had interviewed, and he always had a perfumed handkerchief ready. Matters improved through the week, though, and Amber had every confidence he'd come through. She suspected he might learn as much about his own world as she would.

She picked her way through the crowds, Bayl hovering by her side. He'd warned her of the risk of cutpurses and viewed her safe negotiation of the Founder's Festival as his personal responsibility. But as her holo-recorder was her only possession of value, she was at ease. The crowds were good natured, intent on enjoying the day.

Her eyes swept over the mix of faces, lingering on a young couple walking arm in arm towards a space set aside for dancing. It had often struck her that peoples who were regarded as backward knew how to enjoy themselves more than those on Vindor. While the technological wonders that she took for granted drew people together from a great distance, they got in the way of people actually enjoying each other's company – one of the reasons she sought out worlds like this.

"So, who was this founder, Bayl?"

"King Arthur," Bayl said, "was our first and most distinguished ruler. He brought peace to the warring tribes of the time and established the university here in Denford. He was a remarkable man." He looked at her. "What? Did I say something amusing?"

"Did you really have a king called Arthur?"

"Why, yes. Is that so strange? Arthur is a common name, though no other kings have used it in deference to our Founder."

"It's odd how names resurface in unexpected places," she said. "There's an ancient legend of a king of that name. He was a good ruler if I remember correctly."

"Then it sounds like the perfect name for a king."

"Yes it does," she said. "Whether it was chosen or just a coincidence."

The street along which they were walking came to an end, opening up into the Founder's Square and a thronging crowd.

On the opposite side, the square was dominated by the Royal Mausoleum, a recently rebuilt stone palace housing the tombs of the previous rulers of Enodia. Typical of similar structures Amber had seen on other worlds, it was an expression of Denford's growing confidence and strength. Large, perfectly cut blocks of stone gave it a feeling of permanence.

The windows of the upper story were interspersed with small alcoves containing life-sized statues of former monarchs. Amber counted thirty-eight of them and the lower story had the same number of empty alcoves, awaiting their future residents. The builders obviously expected this building to last for some time.

As it was difficult to get a sense of the occasion from within the crowd, Amber pointed to some steps leading up to another building that gave a better view. She and Bayl jostled their way through the good-natured crowd, climbed four steps and turned to take in the view.

"So, Bayl, what am I looking at?" she said as she used her holo-recorder to take in the scene.

"I'm afraid this could all be a trifle disappointing for you if you're seeking for deep meanings. Most of what you see speaks for itself," he said, grinning.

He pointed at the mausoleum where a raised wooden platform had been constructed.

"That will probably be of most interest. At noon precisely, the King will arrive and address the crowd, giving honour to the kings who have gone before and to the nation. It'll be quite brief, though some might venture that it will not be brief enough. There'll be some traditional dancing and other entertainment. After that, the crowds will be left to their own devices while the King and his nobles retire to the palace for a more sophisticated celebration."

Amber continued to record the scene. "Don't underestimate it, Bayl. There'll be more than enough to keep me busy for a good while. You might even get some time to yourself."

Sometime later, they heard the sound of drums beating a steady marching rhythm over the noise of the crowds, signalling the arrival of the King. Amber hadn't noticed that time had passed so quickly. She glanced at the sky. The Sun was near its zenith, but without its usual power.

From her raised position, she saw two files of uniformed figures come into view as they entered the square to the left of the platform. Each man wore a blue army tunic and marched with a musket over his shoulder, a sword hanging at his belt, keeping time to the drums. Twenty soldiers were followed by four drummers, then an ornate open coach drawn by four horses and, at the rear, another twenty musket men.

The crowd broke into cheering. As the procession got closer, Amber made out something of the coach's occupants. An older man and woman rode, facing forwards – presumably King Zandis and Queen Olma. They had the bearing of royalty Amber had seen on other planets, waving to the crowds with reserved politeness but remaining firmly aloof from the occasion.

The coach halted beside the platform, the soldiers taking up position to form a cordon between it and the crowd. The King and

Queen were helped down by officials, then climbed the stairs to stand before the crowd.

Zandis raised an arm, gesturing to the crowd to quiet.

Something didn't feel right.

Amber wasn't the only one to feel it. The cheering died more quickly than it should have. The guards were shifting about, shuffling from foot to foot, their eyes darting around the crowd, ready to take up their weapons. The sunlight was dimming, some corners of the square already in darkness.

Amber looked up to the sky for heavy clouds. But it was almost clear. The Sun was losing its brightness.

"Bayl," she said.

But he was lost in his thoughts.

Amber touched his shoulder, causing him to start. "Bayl, it's getting darker. Is a solar eclipse expected?"

He looked skywards, turned an ashen white. "Gods, no." He looked down again, his eyes hard and focused. "We have to get out of here, Amber."

"But it's just – "

Bayl grabbed hold of her arm. "Trust me, please."

Others had now looked skywards, an anxious murmur spreading everywhere.

On the platform, King Zandis was now shouting. "My people, please be calm. There is nothing to fear."

Amber and Bayl were no longer the only ones trying to leave the square. The bulk of the crowd was now trying to reach the exits and Amber was buffeted by the people trying to get past her. Bayl was being pulled away and losing his grip on her. She grabbed at his hand, glad of the reassuring contact, and managed to pull herself closer to him.

As the light continued to fade, the murmuring of the crowd turned to a clamour. Behind her, she could hear a deep voice barking out orders. Then there was a sharp crack – gunfire, followed by a second. The crowd surged around them as panic spread. Again, Bayl was pulled away.

She could see the road they were aiming for about ten metres ahead. It was a bottleneck. People approached from all directions, with she and Bayl being funnelled towards the right-hand edge of it where a stone building stood at the corner.

The pressure from the bodies around her was growing. So was the pull on Bayl taking him away from her. The joy and excitement of the folk from a few minutes earlier were now replaced with wide-eyed terror – mothers clutching young children; men and women searching for lost loved ones; everyone shouting; names being called.

One was her own.

"Amber, keep hold," Bayl called.

But she could feel his fingers slipping away until they were gone and the surge took him around the corner while she was pushed against the stonework of the building, held fast by the throng of people around her.

She had been here before. As a young child, she had played at the bottom of a small waterfall near her home. She had toyed with the falling water, feeling its weight on her hands. But then her brother Lars had pushed her in. The waterfall had hit her with its full force, pushing her under, holding her powerless and unable to move until she thought she would die. The memory was vivid. She could feel the icy water around her. Then Lars's hands were on her arm, pulling her out of danger.

This time there would be no such rescue.

The pressure on her body was crushing the air out of her lungs. She had to relieve it. She pushed against the wall, crying out with the effort, her desperation freeing her a little. But the weight was too great and her strength gave way, leaving her still pinned against the hard stone. As her breath was squeezed from her, tears ran down her face.

There was nothing she could do.

The flow of bodies shifted. A man careered into her from the side causing sharp pain in her arm. She was shoved along the wall, around the corner, stumbling over a step, nearly losing her footing.

Seconds later, a strong grip was upon her shoulder and Bayl was there once more.

"Amber, thank the gods you're safe," he gasped. "We have to get away from here."

The press of the crowd was easing now that the street was channelling them away from the square.

Bayl used this little extra freedom to push her into an alleyway. With concerted effort, they reached it, finding a few others who had escaped from the madness. They edged a dozen or so paces along and rested against the wall of a single-storey house.

As the eclipse reached its totality, the fading light dimmed and the temperature cooled. Everything fell still and tranquil. Even the noise of the crowds in the road was quietened.

As the emotions of the last few minutes washed over Amber, tears streamed down her face. She looked at Bayl.

He was in no better a state than her, his face ashen with shock. He looked down and saw he was still holding her hand. He pulled away. "I'm sorry."

"It's nothing," she said. "Thank you for coming back for me."

They leaned against the wall, silent, lost in their thoughts.

At last, Amber said, "Why did that happen? You must know about eclipses here, but even you reacted."

"Yes, we do know of them," he said. "It was the timing of it. The histories have warned us of this day. An eclipse of the Sun on Founder's Day is a portent of great troubles ahead. It is a children's tale." Bayl rose to his feet. "Or so we thought. I will tell you of it soon, but I must make sure my parents and sister are safe. I'll take you back to the inn, then I must go to them."

Part 2. Yorvin

4.

Sharna hurried to Luran's hut, her bag of healing herbs slung over her shoulder. She pushed the leather drape aside and went in. It took a moment for her eyes to adjust to the lack of light, despite the small fire burning at the hut's centre. It made the room uncomfortably warm on a spring day, but light was a necessity.

Luran lay on a bed near the far wall, being tended to by his wife. Sharna approached and knelt so that she could examine his leg wound. He grimaced as she pulled his torn trousers away from an ugly cut.

"You've made a good job of this, Luran," Sharna said. "I'd have thought by now you would have learnt not to stand in front of a charging boar."

"I know, I know," he replied. "This will make a tale of great amusement for the women." He glared at Sharna and his wife.

It pained Sharna to be so abrupt, but she had to tread a thin line, having lost her husband in battle against the Utani four summers ago. Despite her position as the village's healer, it was not easy to be a widow in a male world and two things gained her the respect she deserved: her reputation of having a harsh tongue and her healing skills.

Taking a needle and some twine from her bag, she sewed the edges of the wound together. Luran must have felt the stitching despite the herb paste she had put on the area to dull the pain. He returned a thin smile as she looked over to check how he was doing.

"Couldn't you use the Aydoc?" he said. "I'd be up again in no time and it would hurt a lot less."

"Luran, I said you'd made a good job of getting injured, but you'll have to do a lot better than this before I even think of using it on you."

"All right, woman, I was only asking. Inflict your pain on me and be done."

He crossed his arms in front of him.

Smiling, Sharna bent over the wound again. Once she was finished, she handed some herbs to his wife. "Mix these with hot water. Give them to him morning and evening for the next four days. He needs to stay off that leg for a day or so but don't give him too much sympathy." She turned to Luran, "I'll look at it in two or three days, but you should be fine."

As she left, a light drizzle was turning to rain. She quickened her pace, picking her way through mud that lay between the assorted huts. It was then she saw Adran, her adolescent son, stumbling into the village.

Sharna knew at once that something was badly wrong. He was dishevelled, his tunic smeared with mud and ripped in places. He was disoriented, his grey-blue eyes darting around, searching.

As she made her way towards him, he saw her. Relief swept over him.

"I think he might be – he fell – he wasn't moving – we never – "

"Adran, stop blathering. Who is hurt? What happened?"

"It's Tobin," he said. "He was hit by the magic. We went to the clearing in the Old Forest. Tobin's still there." He lowered his head. "I'm sorry. We should have listened."

"That will wait for later. Come, we must tell Dornis of this."

Tobin had been Adran's closest friend since childhood and was also Chieftain Dornis' son. He had to be told, not just because he was Tobin's father, but also because he was the only one who could help.

Sharna made her way to the Chieftain's hut, Adran following behind. Dornis was resting, but she still moved swiftly to the point.

"Dornis, Tobin has been hurt. Our sons have been playing the hero in the Old Forest and Tobin has been hit by the fire bolts. From what Adran tells me, it's serious."

"We must leave immediately," he said, jumping up. "Sharna, get what medicines you need and meet me at the edge of the village."

Sharna raced home, a single room hut that served as sleeping, eating and living areas all in one, and made straight for a small wooden table.

On it rested a soft leather roll and a store of herbs and ointments. She opened her bag and checked the herbs, bowls and mortar and pestle. She then unwrapped the roll to check her tools: some small iron blades, delicate bronze needles, thin twine and the Aydoc, a smooth rounded object made of a silvery metal. All were in special pouches sewn on to the leather.

Satisfied, she rolled the leather up and tied it securely before gathering it up and slinging her bag over her shoulder. As she left the hut, she grabbed a water skin by the door and rushed out, Adran following in a silent daze.

"Shouldn't we bring some of the warriors?" he said as they waited for the Chieftain at the edge of the village.

"No," she said, shaking her head. "They could do little to help and would most likely die in their efforts."

Dornis arrived at a jog. He was dressed in his Chieftain's robes, a huge cloak of furs that added to his already formidable presence, and had a long iron sword hanging at his belt.

Sharna knew the sword would be of little use against the magic they would face. But the robes had a magic of their own, for underneath the furs was a hard but light material impervious to swords and arrows. These had been handed down from each Chieftain to the next since ancient times, when it was said that men could fly among the stars. Without their protection, the clearing would be a death trap.

The three set off in silence. The Chieftain could have outpaced Sharna and Adran, but he jogged with a slow loping stride that allowed them to match him.

After an hour, they came to the Old Forest.

"I'm sure I can remember the way to the clearing," Adran said.

"There is no need," Dornis said, coming to a halt. "I know the way well enough."

Sharna rested her hand on Adran's shoulder. "You are not the first to be young and foolish, my son. Not by a long way."

A thousand paces into the forest, Dornis signalled them to stop. Sharna scanned the forest. The trees were well spaced and she could see the edge of the clearing ahead.

Dornis ran from the cover of one tree to the next. She and Adran followed in his path.

Sharna brushed the rain from her eyes. It had been falling for over an hour and had left her clothing soaked through and her hair matted to her head.

It had been many years since she had been in this forest. She had barely been out of childhood then, a new apprentice to the village healer. With only a few months of training she had been much too confident of her abilities. Dornis had come to her, telling of a friend being hurt by the magic of the clearing. Swearing her to secrecy, he had asked for her help. The wounds had been beyond her skills. The boy had died.

This time was different. Adran had come straight to her. Her skills were much greater.

What must Dornis be thinking, though? He had already lost a friend to this place and now he risked losing his son.

Dornis signalled to Adran and her to halt. They were close to the edge of the clearing and Sharna could see the grey stone hut at its centre, about a hundred paces away. It was six-sided with straight-edged walls, twice the height of a man and with a flat roof. A doorway was on one side. Everything was the same as all those years ago.

"There," Adran said, pointing.

Ten paces in were the remains of part of a fallen tree trunk and, beyond that, Tobin lay under the cover of a rise.

Dornis called out, "Tobin."

All they heard was some faint groaning.

"Thank the gods. He's alive." Dornis said. He turned to Sharna and Adran. "Wait here. I'll bring him to you."

The Chieftain positioned himself so the fallen tree trunk was directly between him and the stone hut. After steadying himself, he sprinted into the clearing, eating up the distance to the trunk in four long strides, before diving for its cover. As Dornis dived, a bolt of blue fire shot from the nearest wall and flashed towards him, crashing against the top of the trunk, sending a shower of wood chips spraying behind him.

Sharna let out a gasp. It was the first time she had seen the fire-bolts and she knew only too well the sort of wounds they could cause.

Dornis sat against the wood, taking a few seconds to ready himself again. Pulling himself up to a crouch, in one fluid motion he vaulted the trunk and landed at a run on the far side. After three strides, he threw himself to the ground close to Tobin. More fire streamed from the hut, narrowly missing Dornis, slamming into the earth.

He examined the boy's shoulder, then glanced over towards Sharna and shook his head.

Keeping as low as he could, Dornis got to his feet and, with difficulty, gathered his son into his arms. Tobin cried out. Hardly waiting until his son's cries had subsided, Dornis lumbered with his burden.

He zigzagged as more fire streamed past him and Tobin's head. Then, as Dornis slid over the trunk, another bolt hit him square in the back, catapulting him forwards. Tobin fell over the trunk while his father tumbled beyond. Smoke rose from Dornis's furs and an acrid smell filled the air.

Crying out, Adran sprang towards them.

"Stop," Sharna shouted.

He turned towards her, despair on his face. "But we can't – "

"Wait," she said. "Wait and watch. There is still hope."

She prayed she was right, that the magic of Dornis's robes was stronger than the firebolts.

Cursing, Dornis pushed himself up on to his elbows. Behind him, Tobin was groaning in pain – a good sign. Sharna let out a sigh of relief.

Once again, Dornis got himself into a crouch and picked up his son. He set off in a slow run, keeping as low to the ground as he could. The trunk gave better protection and the two were safely behind the first trees before another blue firebolt shot out. It sped past them, hitting a tree some distance into the forest, taking a fist-sized chunk out of the bark.

"We must move away from the clearing," Dornis said. "A few hundred paces should be enough."

With that he set off in the direction of the village, Sharna and her son close behind.

They continued for a couple of minutes. Then Dornis lay Tobin on the forest bracken, so the wound on his shoulder was visible. Sharna bent over and pulled his tunic open.

It was grim viewing. The fire had burned a large area of his shoulder, but had also broken the skin and seared the flesh within. She could see his collar bone was broken in at least two places and splintered. It was quite likely his shoulder blade had been broken too.

Without the Aydoc, he would never have proper use of his arm again.

She looked at Dornis. "This is beyond my own skills. I'm going to have to use the Aydoc or his arm will be crippled." She knew he would be troubled by what she had said. The Aydoc was nearing the end of its life. Each use could be the last. "None would judge you harshly for this, Chieftain. If it were anyone else, you would ask me to use it without hesitation. Your son deserves no less."

Dornis looked at Tobin for a moment, then nodded his agreement.

Sharna reached into her bag and pulled the Aydoc out, settling the silvery metal into her left hand. She then held it out about a foot above Tobin's wound. When she had the right position, she pressed two faint markings on its surface. Segments of vivid colour appeared on it, forming indecipherable symbols. A pattern of light appeared above, coalescing into an image of Tobin's shoulder.

Sharna pressed one of the coloured areas on the Aydoc, causing the image to show Tobin's bones in blue. She shook her head. The collar bone was so shattered, it could never heal by itself. Sharna touched another segment and a brown mist descended from the object on to Tobin. In the image, the bone fragments moved slowly into alignment with each other.

As the mist performed its miracle, Sharna glanced to the bottom of the image where a short red line blinked on and off. It was the Aydoc's heartbeat and, although it beat steadily, the line was faint. Every time she used it, she feared the life force would give out. But how could she not use it when faced with an injury like Tobin's?

Once she was satisfied the bones were healed, she made the Aydoc show the burn damage in red. Then she set the mist to work again. This time the effects were more visible. She watched as the angry burns of the wound healed and the shape of the flesh was restored to normal. As soon as she was sure the wound was healed enough for there to be no lasting harm, she pressed the coloured segment that recalled the mist and it rose back to the Aydoc. A second later she dismissed the image, thankful that the Aydoc's life force had lasted once more.

Sharna examined Tobin's shoulder. He would experience discomfort from the remnants of the burn, which still showed pink, but he would be able to use it normally within a few days.

She turned her attention to Dornis. "Let me look at your back now, Chieftain. We had best make sure all is well."

"It's nothing, Sharna," he said. "I would have felt it if it had pierced the robes." He made no serious efforts to stop her from checking, though. The furs had a hole about the size of a man's palm burnt into them, but underneath was a blackened but still intact hard layer.

Tobin was stirring now, struggling to pull himself to a sitting position. His father helped him up against a tree. The boy felt his injured shoulder and smiled in surprise. He grasped it more firmly.

"Careful, Tobin," Sharna said. "The wound will need time to heal. You won't be going on trips into the forest for a week or two yet."

He and Adran exchanged guilty glances.

"I don't need to tell you of your stupidity, then?" Dornis said. "You're lucky you both weren't killed. Others could have died trying to rescue you. You were trying to prove you are worthy of being warriors, no?"

Tobin and Adran exchanged glances again and nodded.

"A warrior does not take risks without reason. He has wisdom as well as courage. All you have done today is prove that you are not ready. Until you are, the women will find plenty of work for you in the village. Perhaps that will keep you from any more foolishness. Now let's get going, we have a way to travel."

Adran helped Tobin to his feet and the pair trudged through the forest back to the village, Sharna walking with Dornis a few paces behind.

The rain began to ease and stopped soon after they left the forest. Sharna looked at the two boys – almost men now, despite their foolish actions. They had been chastened by Dornis's words and the prospect of more domestic chores but, as the journey progressed, their mood lightened. They were talking together, no doubt Adran filling Tobin in on what he had missed.

"They seem to be recovering," Dornis said.

"You should have been harder with them," she said. "They must never try anything like that again."

"They won't. The scare will be enough. It was for me. And though I couldn't tell them now, they've shown bravery that might save their lives when used in better ways."

"Or get them killed."

"True, but they have shown strength today. For that, at least, I'm glad and so should you be."

Dornis was right. Adran would be a fine warrior – as his father had been. But a warrior could be taken in death at any moment and Adran was nearing the day when that could happen to him. The loss of her husband had been hard; she could not face the prospect of losing her son too.

"How is the Aydoc?" he said.

"Its heartbeat is still strong, but the line of light that shows its life-force is almost gone. It was many times longer when I was first shown how to use it. In another two or three healings, I fear it will be gone and the magic will be spent."

Dornis placed a hand on her shoulder. "The Aydoc was of great service today, but I have seen you perform wonders without it. If it dies, you will still be the most skilled healer in all the Corini. We will have the robes which save lives in their fashion. The village will grow and we will prosper."

5.

Adran crept along the edge of the forest.

A hundred paces into the grasslands, a small group of deer chewed on the rich summer grass. One of the does raised her head, sniffing at the air, searching for signs of predators.

Adran froze, not daring to move further until the doe relaxed and returned to her grazing.

For two long months, he had been forced to endure the work that marked him as a child. It had been hard to bear, but he and Tobin had borne it without complaint, knowing they had brought it upon themselves.

As Adran was beginning to wonder if the Chieftain would ever relent, Dornis allowed them to join on the occasional hunt and be numbered among the warriors. They were given the lesser tasks, of course, but were able to wear the furs that showed their new station.

A loud bird call came from his right. Adran knew it was Dornis or one of the others, signalling the start of the hunt. He looked to the left, where Tobin was hidden in some tall grass. He would make the first move. The deer had their heads aloft, alert to danger. After a moment, Tobin rose from the grass and ran towards the herd, shouting, waving his spear.

Adran hefted his own spear in readiness.

The animals turned and bolted for the forest, straight towards Adran. He ran straight at them, making as much noise as he could. The startled creatures veered away, running parallel to the trees. Adran followed to keep them from turning once more.

They were much faster than either Adran or Tobin. Two deer got far enough ahead to bolt for the safety of the trees. Adran pushed on as fast as he could, his lungs burning. The remaining four deer held their course.

At the right moment, the Chieftain and six hunters rose from their hiding places, a spear's throw in front of the fleeing animals. The deer turned away, one tumbling to the ground as it tried to change direction, not getting the chance to recover as two spears hit it. The other three turned for the forest, bounding once more towards Adran. One fell from a spear thrown by Dornis.

Adran's mouth dried as he realised the last two were coming towards him. This was his chance to prove himself.

Readying his spear, he ran to where the two animals would pass him. The deer sped towards him, splitting as they approached so one would pass on either side. For a second, Adran was unsure which to target and, by the time he had chosen, the moment was gone. He flung his spear, grazing the rear haunches of one, and then they were within the forest, disappearing out of sight.

"You nearly had her, Adran," Tobin called as he moved closer, still jogging. "For a minute, I thought you were going to beat me to the first kill."

"I still will," Adran breathed. "You'll see."

They headed over to the fallen animals which were now surrounded by the other hunters. Two of the men were bleeding the deer with precise cuts to their necks. Then they slit the carcasses open and pulled the innards out.

The stench was overpowering, making Adran want to retch. He turned away from the sight and approached Dornis. "I'm sorry, Chieftain. I hesitated."

"You did, lad," Dornis said. "At least you know what you did wrong. Which is more than some do. Almost nobody gets one on their first try. Some don't even manage it on their fifth, do they, Nerac?"

"No, they don't, Chieftain," one of the hunters said with a wry smile while the others let out loud chuckles. "But, Adran," he continued, "I got one in the end."

Soon, both deer were tied securely to long poles and the group were ready to move on.

As the newest members of the hunt, Adran and Tobin had the task of carrying one of the carcasses, the other taken by two of the warriors who had missed their throws. As Adran took the front of the pole, they hoisted it on to their shoulders and, although the doe was heavy, months of water-carrying had prepared them well. It was half an hour's trudge back to the village. But it was worth it.

After they had walked a third of the way, Adran realised Tobin was slowing down.

"Hey, Tobin, hurry up," he said, craning his neck to look round.

Tobin was looking over his own shoulder, intent on something off in the distance. Adran stopped and looked in the same direction.

Not far above the horizon, a small light burned in the sky. It was like one of the brightest stars at night. But this was here in the afternoon, when the sun was still high.

"Father," Tobin called, "there's something in the sky."

Tobin lowered his end of the pole. Adran did the same, taking a step forward to look at the light.

It was coming closer, the light intensifying. Adran could hear it now, a low rumble of distant thunder.

As he watched, the light dimmed, leaving a trail of black smoke. But the noise kept growing, becoming a deafening roar. Adran covered his ears and dropped to his knees to cower before the wrath of unknown gods.

It was coming straight for him.

He could make some detail out now. It was a bird, but vast and unlike any he had seen before. Blue in colour, light glinted off its rounded body and stubby wings. Smoke poured from numerous small holes along its length.

He saw the creature scream overhead and head away into the grasslands, its black tail of smoke hanging behind it. It reached the top of the next rise before hitting the ground with a force that made the ground shudder. The earth sprayed around the bird as though from a rock hitting water.

Then there was silence.

Adran looked about to see that, like him, everyone else was on the ground.

Chieftain Dornis rose first. "Bring the carcasses towards the bird. The rest of you, come with me."

Dornis set off at a run, followed by the four most experienced warriors.

Adran, Tobin and the other two warriors hefted their poles once more and followed as quickly as they could. The older warriors outpaced them, reaching the bird before Adran and Tobin had crossed even half the distance. The Chieftain and the warriors stopped, sizing up what they could see of the fallen bird.

There was a furrow in the ground like that a plough would make in a field, but it was huge, as though made by giants. As Adran and Tobin drew closer, they saw pieces of metal of varying sizes scattered about on the ground. Some were still glowing as if heated in a blacksmith's fire. The air was obscured by the remains of the black smoke, but Adran could make out the bird's bulk at the far end of the furrow. It had to be over a hundred paces in length, dwarfing even the largest huts in the village.

Adran, Tobin and the others followed the lip of the furrow and finally reached Dornis, who, with the older warriors, was crouching about thirty paces from the bird.

"Wait here and guard the meat," he ordered. "If we are attacked, you must warn the village and the rest of the Corini. Do you understand?"

"Yes, Father," Tobin said.

Adran nodded.

Dornis approached the side of the fallen bird, the four other warriors fanning to left and right of him. Their readied their spears but they were so small next to the bird.

A clanging came from the bird's belly, the sound of metal against metal.

The warriors froze, their attention focused on the spot from which the sound came, twenty paces along the body and ten feet above the ground. The sound rang out again, like a hammer striking the shell of the creature. The warriors edged towards the source, maintaining a distance from the bird.

As the sound rang out for a third time, that part of the body fell away revealing a doorway. Smoke streamed outwards through the new opening.

A figure appeared there. It paused for a moment, then tumbled to the ground.

Nerac approached, prodding it with the shaft of his spear. But there was no reaction.

Dornis bent to examine the fallen creature. It looked like a man. Its clothes were torn, and it had many small cuts on its face and body. One of its arms was broken.

After a few moments, Dornis looked up from the prone man to the bird. "If this one is anything to judge by, we are not in danger, but what manner of man comes out of a metal bird?"

"The old stories tell of men flying to the stars," Luran, one of the older warriors, said. "Maybe they're true."

"You've always been too keen to believe those tales, Luran."

"What else could this be? He might even have knowledge of the old magic."

"You could be right," Dornis said, "but we know nothing of this man, not even if he is friend or enemy."

"But if he is a sorcerer," Luran said, "and we help him –"

"Perhaps. Nerac, what do you think?"

"He has power, wherever he comes from. We can't allow him to become an enemy. Either we kill him now or we offer all the help we can. I'd say killing him would be the simpler way. We might not get another chance."

The Chieftain knelt, fingering the edge of the smooth material that formed the man's clothing.

"We help him," Dornis said, rising to his feet. "Otherwise we are no better than the Utani. Tobin, Adran, come here."

Adran raced over to the Chieftain with Tobin not far behind, taking the opportunity to look more closely at the man. He was tall, but thin, and though he wasn't a boy, he didn't wear a beard.

"Yes, Father?" Tobin said.

"Run to the village. Tell them we'll need oxen to carry any wounded. You'd better get your mother, too, Adran. We'll need her skills."

* * * * *

Sharna, Adran and Tobin had set off for the fallen bird as soon as Sharna had gathered her bags, leaving the oxen to follow.

"You're sure it was a man?" she said.

"Yes, Mother," Adran said. "He wasn't like any I've seen before, but he was definitely a man. Do you think he might be a sorcerer?"

"If he lives in a bird made of metal, then it's likely, but we don't really know what that means. If he had truly powerful magic, then he wouldn't have fallen to the earth and been hurt."

"What if a more powerful sorcerer had beaten him?" Tobin said.

Sharna shuddered. "I doubt that could be true. We've seen nothing of such men before, let alone a battle between them."

As they came in sight of the metal bird, Sharna gasped. A huge tear in the ground cut across their path, with the bird itself at the end of it. The three hurried to where two of the warriors guarded the deer carcasses. Beyond that, eight unfamiliar people were laid out in a row on the grass, with Nerac standing beside them. He saw Sharna and the boys coming and shouted for Dornis.

Dornis came to the mouth of an opening on the side of the bird. "Sharna, we needed you sooner. Two were dead already, and three are close. The other three should live."

With several in need of her aid, she hurried to the nearest of the injured. None were conscious. She soon discovered four were dead. Three would survive, although their wounds needed attention. Another, a woman barely out of childhood, was hovering on the edge of death from a gaping wound to her side. Sharna reached for the Aydoc and held it over her.

"Sharna," Dornis said, "what in Corin's name are you doing?"

"Would you have me let this woman die?"

"If it means the death of one of our people, yes. What if Adran is the next to need the Aydoc and it is gone?"

Whatever she did, lives would be lost when the Aydoc eventually failed. She looked down at the young woman. The skin of her face was perfectly smooth and beautiful, but pale. Blood poured from the abdominal wound. "Dornis, this woman is dying in front of me and I have the power to stop it from happening. Besides, they are sorcerers. If we do this for them, they will be grateful and they might have Aydocs of their own."

The Chieftain shook his head. "You haven't seen inside the bird. If they have such things, they're likely broken or burnt. They won't be able to help in that way."

"I have to do what I can," Sharna said. As she touched the Aydoc, it sprang into life, the familiar image of light forming above it, this time showing the girl's abdomen.

Dornis moved closer and hovered. "You go too far, Sharna. We will speak of this afterwards." Then he turned and was gone.

She didn't hesitate any longer. She had to use as little of the Aydoc's life as possible. It didn't take long to find the damaged tissue causing the loss of blood. She set the Aydoc to repair the cuts and boost the blood. The brown mist descended into the girl. As the wound was severe the mist stayed down for some time, as Sharna expected. The red heartbeat flashed. When the mist rose, the bar of light had disappeared and the flashing had ceased. The light above it still showed the woman's body. She was healed.

The woman's eyes flickered open. "Where am I?" she said. "Who are you?"

"I am Sharna. A friend."

"The others —"

"You'll see them soon. Now rest."

The woman's eyes closed again.

When the oxen arrived, Sharna arranged for the survivors to be put on litters and pulled behind the beasts. The dead were draped over the backs of two of the others.

By the time they started the journey back to the village, the afternoon was drawing to an end. But they would make it before nightfall.

6.

Lieutenant Yorvin Bandrell of the Sattorian Navy awoke.

The light was dim. He could make out little of his surroundings. His left arm throbbed with pain. It was in a sling with crude wooden splints holding it in place. That was right. His arm had been broken in the crash and it had made opening the hatch almost impossible. There had been some tribesmen with spears and he'd prepared to defend himself, or was it to run – he couldn't remember.

He sat upright and strained his eyes to get a better idea of where he was. The sudden movement made his head ache and it took a few moments for the pain to ease. He was sitting on an uncomfortable bed in a large circular room. There were three other beds, each with their own occupants – three of the crew. That left four unaccounted for. He wondered who was with him in the room. It was impossible to make out any distinctive features in the low light.

He knew the Captain wouldn't be one of them. He had died in the crash. The ship had been a mess. The mission was in tatters. How had things gone so badly wrong? Only three days ago, they'd been on the verge of success.

* * * * *

"Lieutenant Bandrell, please report to the bridge."

Yorvin paused the recording he was making for his wife and pressed the comm badge attached to the sleeve of his left arm. "On my way."

He re-started the recording. "Sorry, Jan. I've got to go now. That's probably the first response from Minerva. I'll tell you more next time I get a chance but things might get busy."

He terminated the recording and instructed the computer to send the message home to Sattoria. The Astracomm would get it there in two months, the same time it would take a ship to travel there, and that made keeping track of the conversations at times tricky. But keeping in contact was one of the things that kept him sane. They'd been searching for a year now, and it was a long time to be away.

Throwing his uniform jacket on, he made his way through the narrow corridors to the bridge.

Captain Weng glanced round as he entered. "We've got an incoming signal from Minerva. Take the helm while I deal with it."

"Yes, sir." Yorvin took his place at one of the stations while the Captain stood before the main viewing screen. Weng looked over at the weapons officer who, on a small ship, also doubled up with communications.

"All right, Garcia, let's do this."

After a few seconds, the communication link was established – the Searcher was three light-seconds from the Minervan main world. A stern middle-aged man appeared on the screen.

Following established protocol, Captain Weng allowed the hailer to speak first.

"Sattorian starship Searcher. You are not to approach any closer to our planet."

"Understood, Minerva." Weng turned to Yorvin. "Full stop, Lieutenant."

"Yes, sir."

"As you can see, we are holding our position," Weng continued. "We are here on a mission to re-establish diplomatic and trading links between our worlds – "

"That is a worthy cause, Captain, but you will forgive me being suspicious of such a claim. For the past decade, the only ships to visit our system have been raiders and pirates."

"Of course," Weng said. "We have experienced the same ourselves, but we want to change that. So many worlds have fallen into barbarism since the Great Conflict and those of us that remain struggle to survive. If we reopen trade between our worlds, we will both be stronger for it."

One of Yorvin's screens showed two ships closing in on their position. They each matched the Searcher for size. He transferred the sensor images on to a corner of the main screen so the Captain could see it.

"It strikes me things are simpler than that," the Minervan said. "You are near collapse yourselves and so you seek to be a parasite, feeding off our strength."

Yorvin winced. It wasn't true, of course – but not far off. Building the Searcher and her two sister ships for this mission had consumed most of the limited stockpiles of several rare raw materials.

"Please allow us to –" Weng then saw the approaching ships. His face hardened. "Minerva, please identify your incoming ships and their purpose." The Captain cut the outgoing channel. "Lt Bandrell, I need to know how much time we've got and a full capability scan of those ships."

"We have two minutes to weapons range, sir. They're non-jump vessels, both outgun us."

"It's standard procedure," the Minervan said. "Our cruisers will ensure that your intentions are honourable."

"They are entirely honourable. The trade we seek will benefit both our worlds. As you can see by our presence, we still have working jump technology. That alone makes us potentially valuable allies."

The Minervan man paused for a moment. "Yes, it does," he said. "I must contact my superiors. Please hold your position for a few minutes." The link was terminated and the screen went black.

"What are those ships doing, Bandrell?"

"Still on an intercept course, sir."

"Are they slowing?"

"Barely, sir. Unless they've got very powerful engines, they'll overshoot."

"Damn," Weng said. "Bandrell, about face and get us out of here." He pressed his comm badge. "Engineering, we're going to need to jump soon. Prepare the engines."

"Yes, sir. Commencing the initiation sequence now. Ninety seconds to availability."

Yorvin turned the ship and put the sub-light engines on full thrust, all the while concentrating on the chasing ships. The Searcher wasn't going to stay far enough ahead.

He turned to the Captain, who was working at his console, calculating a course. "Captain," he said, "they're going to be in weapons range in 25 seconds. We need to engage the jump engines."

Weng glanced at his screen. "And we've still got sixty seconds till we can get out of here. Let's hope my instincts are wrong or this could get messy."

The seconds dragged by, Yorvin staring at the screen, the chasing ships closing in. Why were the Minervans reacting this way? Everywhere they had gone, they had found peoples desperately seeking their aid or jealously guarding what they had. Maybe the mission had been doomed from the beginning. Already one of the Searcher's sister ships, the Explorer, had lost contact and now it wasn't hard to guess why.

"Ten seconds to weapons range," he said.

"Evasive manoeuvres, Bandrell. Garcia, ready laser batteries and two mines. If they shoot, hit them hard."

Yorvin initiated the automated process of rapid minor course adjustments that would make the Searcher harder to hit, although at the cost of a reduction in speed. He had been through this drill countless times, but this was the first time he might be shot at by a dangerous foe.

The Minervan ships were now in range.

"Lead ship has fired and missed, sir," Garcia said.

"Return fire," Weng ordered, "and launch the mines if they hit us."

The Searcher's laser batteries fired on the lead ship in a two-second burst, hitting and causing its energy shields to flare. The battery started its recharging. It would be another seven seconds before they could be fired again.

The ship lurched.

"Hits from both ships, sir. Our shields are down to twenty percent. I've released the mines."

It was an old tactic. A release of general debris would make it look as if laser fire had got through, but would also contain self-powered mines with small nuclear warheads. At a signal from the Searcher, the mines would power up their thrusters and home in on the Minervan ships.

If it worked it could cripple or destroy, but only against chasing ships – as now – and unsuspecting opponents, as the mines would be easy targets until they got close.

There were only twenty seconds left till they could engage the jump engines.

The laser batteries flashed into life again, as Garcia sent another volley at the Minervans. Again, the lead ship's shielding flared in response.

"I think we've caused some damage, sir," Garcia said. "There's some debris."

"Well done, Garcia. Keep at them until they break off."

It could be a ploy, but there would be no sense in them using the same trick. The Minervan debris would never get anywhere near the Searcher.

Without warning, the bridge was filled with a shower of sparks. Yorvin was thrown from his chair, landing hard on the floor. It took a few seconds to get back on his feet and regain his console.

"Garcia, activate the mines," Weng ordered, picking himself up.

"Yes, sir."

Back by the chasing ships, the mines would be coming to life, calculating the intercept course in a split second and firing their thrusters.

"Engineering," Captain Weng said over the comms, "are we still ready to go?"

"We briefly lost power to the charging, sir. We'll need another twenty seconds."

"The course is laid in. Activate the jump as soon as you're able."

The chasing ships were adjusting their courses. They must have spotted the mines. A huge blast engulfed the Minervans' second ship, while the first let fly with its lasers at the mine that chased it. A few seconds later, the ship began to move back on to an intercept course with the Searcher.

They'd bought valuable time. It should be enough.

Yorvin sat, eyes glued to the screen, watching the chasing cruiser close the distance once more. A brief loss of balance and the Minervan ship was no longer there.

Searcher had made the jump. They were safe.

* * * * *

"Safe" had been a relative term. They had escaped with their lives but in a ship that was badly damaged and which had lost the bulk of its fuel as a result.

Captain Weng had set a course for the nearest habitable world, a backwater planet which had been heavily bombarded early in the

Great Conflict. The remaining fuel had been enough to reach the system but not for a controlled landing.

They'd run the simulations over and over again, but it hadn't looked good. The Searcher wasn't designed to glide in an atmosphere. They'd exhausted the last of the fuel to slow the descent and Yorvin had used every ounce of piloting skill he had. But still the approach had been way too fast and the ship had begun to break up.

At least he was alive. Now he needed to find out how the rest of the crew were and the extent of the damage to the ship. He looked around the room once more – his eyes had become accustomed to the dim light – and he could make out the figures on the other beds.

The one immediately to his right was Junior Engineer Cobannis. The ones to his left were two of the marines, Corporal Rowan and Sergeant Prason, the ranking NCO of the three onboard Searcher. That left the four others unaccounted for, including the Captain. He was probably dead. With any luck, the others would be in another room nearby.

As he rose to his feet, the pain in his temples surged back, but this time duller. A small amount of light was coming from what must be the doorway in the far side of the room. Yorvin made his way over. It was a hanging piece of leather.

With his good arm, he pushed it aside and stepped into a primitive looking village. Although it was night, a near full moon gave enough light to see an assortment of circular huts, all single storey and with thatched roofs.

"Wait."

Yorvin turned to face two burly tribesmen. They had long dark hair, black beards and wore heavy furs. Each dipped a sharp, silver-shining spear straight at his heart.

As Yorvin began to raise his arms, he winced at a new wave of pain.

One of the tribesmen nodded to the other, who ran off towards the largest hut.

"Am I a prisoner?" Yorvin said.

"That is for the Chieftain to decide," the tribesman said, lowering his spear.

Three people approached. The other guard was accompanied by a man and a woman.

The man, dressed in a tunic and trousers, had as much hair as the guards, and was clearly a leader. Who the woman was, was not obvious. But if the man was the chief, then she would have a say in what went on in the village.

"I am Dornis," the man said. "a Chieftain of the Corini tribe. Welcome."

"I'm grateful for your help and hospitality, Chieftain. I am Yorvin Bandrell of Sattoria, a place far from here."

"I do not know of this Sattoria," Dornis said, "and I have travelled far. Do you fly among the stars, as the old legends say men did?"

"Yes, Chieftain. My ship can fly between worlds, or at least it could."

The Chieftain and the woman exchanged glances.

"Only three of my friends were in the hut with me," Yorvin said. "Are the other four safe?"

Dornis looked to the woman who said, "We found four others with you, but all were dead before I could help them. The young woman was also injured but we were able to save her."

"May I see those that died?" Yorvin said. These people were not advanced. Perhaps they were mistaken.

They led him to a nearby hut where the four were laid out.

"We do not know your burial ceremonies," Dornis said, "so we placed them here."

Yorvin approached Chief Engineer Gildoman. He felt for a pulse, but Gildoman's body was already cooling.

He stood for a moment, head lowered, to compose himself. The mission was over. Now, the most he could hope for was to get back home to Jan and to his two young daughters. His very being ached for that simple comfort.

Part 3. Amber

7.

With a measure of reverence, Bayl carried the tome through the hushed aisles of the library. A few scholars were browsing the shelves as he passed, or were seated engrossed at the reading desks.

The original copies of the ancient histories had long since been lost, but the volume he carried was more than three hundred years old. It had required the blessing of the Master Librarian to gain such access which, in turn, had required all of Bayl's arts and position to obtain.

He placed the volume on the desk at which Amber sat, amply lit by the sunlight streaming in from a nearby window. He turned the pages to the period relating to the establishment of the kingdom.

Finding the section he sought, he handed it to her.

She read:

> With the might of the nearby tribes crush'd and their challenge dismiss'd, Arthur took the mantle of the kingship upon himself to the great joy of his people. The city of Denford was found'd at his behest and there he was crown'd on the twenty-fourth day after the vernal equinox in the year five of the new era.
>
> This day must be remember'd through the ages for its import is greater than that of the kingship alone. In the year that the Sun surrenders its light on the day of celebration, know that Enodia will face a time of ferment and danger. A conceal'd host of creatures, great in power and malice, awaits its opportunity to strike and swarm across the land.

But know also that Arthur and his Guardians will
act to foil them. Arthur must rise again and guide
his people to vict'ry.

Amber sat back, rubbing her forehead. "I thought you said this
was a historical text. That's not exactly what I think of as history."

"I understand," Bayl said. "Look at any other portion of the book
and you will find a purely factual reporting of the events of the time.
This passage stands out as a striking anomaly."

"I'm afraid that this 'anomaly', as you put it, casts quite a shadow
over the authority of the rest of the text. It's nothing more than
superstitious nonsense." She stood and walked to the window,
looking out across Founder's Square. "Eleven people died out there
because of those words. It's unforgivable."

Bayl joined her. The square was almost empty – a few people
making their way across it, going about their daily tasks. In his mind,
however, Bayl could still see the wild fear in the eyes of thousands of
people as they sought to escape an unknown danger. He could still
feel the crush from all sides, squeezing him till he thought he might
never take another breath. It was something he would never forget
and those ancient words had indeed been the cause. However, it was
far from unforgivable.

"You dismiss these words all too easily, Amber," he said. "I
confess I had my doubts about them, as did many others, but the
eclipse did occur on the day of the festival, as the book foretold. It
has to be taken seriously."

"Rubbish," she exclaimed, disturbing those seated at nearby desks.
"If you have a moon of the right size," she continued in a whisper,
"eclipses will happen, and Enodia has one. If you wait long enough,
you'll get one on pretty much any day of the year. What's to stop me
writing a prophecy like that for this date? It may take hundreds of

years, even thousands, to come true but eventually some poor innocents would get trampled to death because of it."

"I'm sorry that we disappoint you so," Bayl said. He turned and strode out, his footsteps on the polished wooden floor echoing, drawing disapproving looks from the scholars. How could she be so dismissive? The eclipse had happened. There was at least a possibility the other words were true as well.

He reached the door and went into the entry foyer. Hearing the sound of footsteps behind him, he left the door open. He walked on, past the broad stone stairs leading to an upper floor.

He heard the door close.

"I'm sorry," Amber said. "What angers me is that people died because of those words. I realise this wouldn't have been the writer's intention and that you hold it in high regard. I shouldn't have been so quick to judge."

"I'll escort you back to the inn," he said, marching through the foyer out into the square.

After a few paces, Amber said, "What are these creatures it speaks of?"

Bayl stopped, looked her in the eye. Was this an opportunity for another jibe?

"We don't actually know," he said. "Fear of the unknown is part of the power of the words. Of course, there have been all sorts of theories and stories from packs of wolves to fire-breathing dragons, but there isn't anything that's known for certain. Children have been frightening each other for centuries with the speculation. When the eclipse began, everybody in the crowd would have remembered the wildest of those theories. That's why the effect was so dramatic."

"There must have been some encounter with them even if it's just a myth. The writer must have had something in mind."

"I agree," Bayl said. "But there's no hint in that or any other writing. There have always been wild animals, of course. Our people have hunted them for centuries, but there's nothing capable of organised behaviour."

"I still can't believe it's genuine, Bayl," Amber said. "I've been looking into that mythical king called Arthur. It was pretty much as I said. He was even supposed to return after his death when his country was in its direst need. Obviously, it never happened, though it left a story that has endured for thousands of years. That passage in the book mentions Arthur's return, as well. It's too much of a coincidence."

"It would seem so."

"There she is," a raucous female voice called out.

Three women stood about ten paces away. They were obviously of the lower classes, dresses cut from the cheapest of cloths, a film of dirt covering their over-exposed skin. Probably barmaids in the least salubrious of taverns. He pressed his perfumed handkerchief to his nose

"She's the cause of it, I tell you," the woman continued

The other two nodded.

Amber walked towards them. "Please, I had nothing to do with the eclipse. How could I have done?"

"Well, all I know is that till you got here things were all right. Now you're here, this happens. It don't take a lot to work out what's going on, does it?"

"My good woman," Bayl said, stepping forward to Amber's side and a little beyond. "You should know better than to make such ridiculous accusations. Are you saying that Professor Stefans can control the Sun?"

"What?" The woman stared at him for a moment. "I don't know about that, but you shouldn't be standing up for her 'gainst your own people." The woman spat in Amber's direction. It missed Bayl's arm and landed at Amber's feet. "Go back where you came from, love. It'd be better for all of us."

Bayl placed himself in front of Amber. "You will turn and walk away now. Otherwise you will be spending some time in His Majesty's custody."

As the woman glared at him, Bayl could see several other people watching the spectacle. He held the woman's gaze until she broke eye contact.

"You should know better," she said, turning away.

"The eclipse would have happened on Founder's Day whether this woman was here or not," he told the onlookers. "Just remember that." He turned to Amber. "Come on," he whispered, "let's go."

They walked in silence for a while, aware dozens of eyes were following their path.

"It might be best to stay away from public scrutiny for a few days," Bayl said. "I can only apologise for the manner and nature of that woman, but I suspect that there will be others who will sympathise with her views."

"You're right," Amber said. "It'll be better to stay out of the way with the people feeling like this. Do you think it will last long?"

"Not for too long. I fear it will be difficult for a week or two at least. After that, it will take time for the impact of events to lessen and you will have to work to overcome their suspicion."

Amber forced a half-hearted smile. "I hope you're right. It's a waste, though. I'm probably only going to have a year here and already two weeks have gone by without much to show for it."

They reached the doors of The Beacon Inn and were greeted by Joram, the innkeeper. He always knew when Amber was about to return and was there to meet her. If this had been on the core worlds, she'd have said he must have some cameras to warn him of her impending arrival. His goodwill, at least, was intact, which something. Amber wondered if his business might be suffering because of her. If he were to join the opinion of the masses, then she might find herself looking for new lodgings. Maybe it was time to get right away from the view of the people.

Bayl readied himself to leave. "Is there anything we need to discuss before I go?"

"Not right now, Bayl, but I have decided on the next step," she said. "Further trips around the city are pointless for now, so I think it's time to venture outside. Tomorrow we'll begin to organise our first dig. If the people of today won't talk to us, then we'll ask those from the past."

She made her way upstairs. It was the perfect answer. It would get her away from the people's superstitions while they calmed down, and help get some clues about the planet's past. If she could find a suitable site close by, then they might even be on their way in three or four days.

Powering on her computer, she sought out the scans of Enodia she'd had Norton take of the planet before landing and transferred them to the holographic displayer. A few seconds later she was sitting in front of a glowing half-metre diameter sphere, a perfect representation of the planet in the visible spectrum. She took a few seconds to admire the image. The mix of blues, greens and browns that made up a fertile planet was always a thing of beauty. She would show it to Bayl tomorrow. It would make his eyes pop out of his head.

Turning to the search for a dig site, she located the city of Denford and magnified the display to a hundred-kilometre radius. As she cycled through the various scans, the colours changed. She focused on areas as features caught her interest, then drew out again and moved on. It took a few hours to settle on some prime targets.

Three showed promise.

One was probably the old spaceport from before the Fall — judging from the size of it and the match with old maps that had survived on Vindor. But the size of the place made it a much larger project than she wanted to take on.

The second site was smaller but located deep under a hill, therefore unattractive for the same reason.

The third site looked right. It was more than thirty kilometres away – which would mean a trip of almost a day with the transport available – but it was small, near the surface and had very high metal concentrations which meant it would be interesting. Although it could be a vein of metal ore, local geology suggested otherwise.

After making some notes, she switched the computer off, sat back, stretched and yawned. Standing, she walked over to the window. The Sun was lowering in the sky, the street was quiet. It was late and she was hungry. She hoped Joram would have a meal ready for her.

Smiling, at peace, she made her way downstairs.

8.

"Are you sure this is our destination?" Bayl said.

Amber looked out at the grasslands stretching off into the distance, dotted here and there with copses and woodlands. A hundred metres ahead, the natural undulations of the landscape had joined to form a small hillock. She glanced down at the map displayed on her hand-terminal and compared it to the scene before her.

"I am," she said. "Though I agree it doesn't look like much."

Four days had passed since Amber has settled on the idea of venturing out of the city. Bayl had readily agreed. Indeed, his eyes had popped when he saw the holo-scans of his homeworld.

He arranged the transport and manpower with an efficiency that showed he was very good at his usual post in the government. As well as ten labourers and three wagons full of equipment and supplies, he had even arranged for two soldiers from the city garrison to accompany them. She had protested they weren't necessary, but Bayl had insisted. They could be attacked by outlaws or wild animals.

After a long day's journey from the city, they pulled the wagons to a halt. The afternoon was drawing to a close.

As Bayl set to organising the tents, food, latrines and the lighting of a fire, Amber examined the hillock. On the surface, there was nothing to suggest anything unusual. Her portable scanner said differently. She crossed the hillock a couple of times, homing in on the strongest metal readings. They were in the right location. In places, deposits were only a metre or two below ground.

After a time, Bayl came over. "Are you still convinced we are in the correct location?"

"Yes," she said. "Everything fits the scans. We should start to see some results tomorrow."

"What do you believe is down there?" he said, inspecting the ground, hoping to see some clues.

"It could be any number of things. That's one of the things I find fascinating about a dig. If we're really lucky, it could be parts of the original colony ships that arrived here ten thousand years ago. That's unlikely, though. It was probably taken to pieces and reused. We might find parts of a settlement from before the Fall or a crashed vehicle from the same period. It might be a monument from the past thousand years or even a weapons stash." Amber looked over the hillock, picturing each of the possibilities in her mind. "Who knows…"

Bayl was silent for a moment, then raised his head upwards. The first few stars were glistening in the deep blue of the darkening sky.

"Did I say something?" Amber said.

"Why, of course you did," he said, looking straight at her. "You – but that wasn't what you were asking."

"No. You seemed distracted. I was wondering if I'd said something to cause it."

"You speak of Enodia being colonised thousands of years ago. We have been of the belief that men have always lived here, that we were the pinnacle of civilisation. There were legends from long ago that men could fly between stars, but we thought they were stories to keep simple people amused. Although it became clear that was not the case the moment your first sky-ship arrived last year, somehow a casual statement from you brings home its implications a hundred times over."

Amber placed a reassuring hand on his arm. She'd grown used to Bayl's intelligent curiosity and forgotten that he must be experiencing a cultural shock. Most of Enodia's inhabitants could put the larger issues to the back of their mind. After all, there had only been two visiting spaceships which had soon departed. Bayl was being forced to deal with much more immediate evidence of the change that would sweep across his world.

"I know it must be difficult to come to terms with," she said. "I'm sorry if I've loaded more on you than I should."

"I must admit to a strange mixture of excitement and concern," Bayl smiled. "I've already seen the great benefits your people might bring us. But I can't help wondering if sometime ahead we will regret the day the sky-ship arrived. What will happen to my world?"

Amber sighed. She wanted to reassure Bayl that everything would be all right but, she also knew that was over-simplistic. "There will be changes," she said, "and mostly for the good. My government has a policy of technological elevation, but we've learnt from experience that this should go slowly to cause the minimum disruption."

"There have been ill consequences?"

"On some worlds, yes. It's a similar reaction to the one I had after the eclipse. People are naturally suspicious of new things and this can lead to unrest if things change too much, too fast. So, things will happen slowly to give your people time to grow accustomed to the new situation."

They looked over to the camp. Some of the men were sitting by the fire, talking and laughing. Another was tending a pot of stew on the flames.

"This sounds so benevolent," Bayl said. "I would like to believe your people come to help us, to make the lives of these men better. However, my experience of human nature makes me loathe to accept this at face value." He looked back to Amber. "What does Vindor gain from this?"

"Eventually we get a trading partner and, hopefully, an ally. Humanity has been through a very difficult thousand years since the Great Conflict began. For a time, my ancestors feared that Vindor was the only world to have survived with any degree of strength.

There were a handful of others, but we learnt that civilization is a fragile thing and we must do what we can to spread and secure it."

Amber broke her eye contact with Bayl. She was making it sound more noble than it was.

"You're right about human nature, though," she continued. "There will most likely be unscrupulous individuals who will try to take advantage of a new opportunity. But there's not many rare minerals here to attract them, and you have the advantage of being one of many rediscovered worlds. Enodia won't stand out to them."

"We stood out to you."

Amber smiled. "My interests are obscure. I don't think you need worry on that score. Let's go see how that meal is doing. I'm starving."

* * * * *

The morning was overcast with a light rain. Not ideal conditions to commence a dig, but nothing more than an irritant. Amber had pinpointed the location of the strongest metal readings and marked out a rectangular section of the turf, two metres by five. The men had been digging for a couple of hours. The trench was now a metre deep.

Amber watched, anxious. According to the scans, this was the depth at which the first discovery would be made.

Part of her concern was due to the diggers' inexperience. They were farm labourers from a primitive world. They had no concept of archaeology or the fragility of anything that might be buried here. Of course, she had tried to explain the importance of taking care but, as far as they were concerned, they were digging a hole in the middle of nowhere.

She paced along the edge of the trench, hoping to catch a glimpse of anything that might look out of place, ready to intervene.

As she turned, she saw Bayl grinning at her. She smiled back. "The first hours of a new dig are always a bit special," she said. "If there's going to be something significant, there'll be clues to it early on."

As usual, when the first breakthrough came, she was at the wrong end of the trench. The sound of metal against metal brought the digging of the four men in the trench to a halt. Everybody stopped to look.

Pushing the man out of the way, Amber jumped into the trench and began scraping the loose soil away with her hands, much to the amazement of the surrounding workers.

Soon, she had moved enough earth to see a gleam of metal. She slowed down, pulling the soil away from around it. It was a narrow, curved fragment, about a quarter of a metre long, obviously from a high-level technology – certainly beyond anything that Enodia would have had since the Fall. She held it up for all to see.

"This is what we're after," she announced. "I'll need to test it, of course, but I'm convinced this has been here for more than a thousand years."

Her words were greeted with a murmured response. Some of the men made comments to each other. She let them settle before continuing. "There will be more like this, so go carefully from now on. There will be things down here that will break easily."

She climbed out of the trench and headed for her tent.

Bayl moved over to join her. "This is obviously what you were hoping for," he said. "How can you be sure it is so old? It looks in too good a condition to be that age."

She held the fragment up. "You're right, it does look too new. But that's part of the reason I know it must be old."

"I don't understand," he said.

"Unless it was made of gold," she said, "anything made on Enodia since the Fall would be prone to rust or other degeneration. So, either this was made in the last few years or it is very old indeed."

"And since we found it buried in undisturbed ground it's unlikely to be new," Bayl said.

"There's more, though," she said, reaching for her scanner. "I'm willing to bet this isn't iron, steel or anything else that could have been manufactured here."

She passed the device over the surface of the metal. At this close range, it could give a detailed summary of the chemical elements in an object. Analysis software could then give a layman's summary of what this meant. Amber looked at the readout.

"As I thought. It's made of a complex alloy that would need a high technology to manufacture. Whatever is down there is very old. I think we can say this trip will definitely be worth the effort."

Bayl reached for the fragment and turned it over in his hands, studying it. "So, what is it?"

"I'm not sure yet. It's curved, so could be part of the outer casing of some sort of vehicle. Or it could just as easily be part of something very ordinary like a gardening tool. We'll find out soon enough."

The rest of the day was taken up with the discovery of a vehicle. It was of significant size, with appendages suggesting it had been designed with atmospheric flight in mind. By the end of the day, enough was uncovered to reveal the top of a hatch into an interior, which, Amber decided, would be the focus for the second day's digging.

Overall, the vehicle was in poor condition with many small holes in the chassis. How much was due to the passage of time and how much was due to its original condition was, at this stage, impossible to tell.

9.

Ayrus Medda waited at the edge of the copse, watching in the darkness. He was a kilometre from the camp, far enough away to avoid being detected but close enough to see the lights and judge when most of the group were asleep.

The woman Stefans had so far been no trouble to the Duke's plans. Medda had advised him she could safely be discounted, and his grace had been on the point of agreeing, when she decided to leave the city with a party of labourers and a couple of soldiers. That had changed things, obviously, and Stefans was firmly back under consideration.

Of most concern was that she had travelled thirty kilometres to a remote location, dug a hole in the ground and, within a couple of hours, found what she was looking for. Somehow, she had known where to come. Medda had to find out what was going on.

All but one of the camp lights were out. Given two military men in the camp, Medda knew the last light was for the watch.

He walked towards the camp. At this distance, there was no need for concealment. His black tunic and trousers melded into the darkness of the cloud-covered night. His soft leather boots made no sound on the turf moistened by the day's rain. The only risk of detection was his bullseye lantern, but that was a necessity if he was to see what was causing Stefans so much interest.

As he drew closer, Medda circled around to put the hillock between himself and the light from the camp so his approach would be undetected. He listened for activity, but the quiet of the summer evening was only broken by a cricket chirruping nearby. As the ground rose, Medda followed it upwards until he was at the same level as the excavation.

Again, he circled the hillock until the camp came into view, now only a hundred paces away. A small fire burned at its centre, with six tents arrayed in a semi-circle facing the hillock. Several wooden benches were around the fire, one of them occupied by a uniformed man who sat, leaning forward with a musket on the bench by his side. At first, Medda wondered if the soldier might be asleep but after a few moments he pushed his weight backwards, stretching his arms and yawning. Not asleep, perhaps, but far from alert. That would do.

Medda continued around the hillock, until he reached a pile of earth, the dig site. He edged forwards, feeling for the lip. Then he positioned himself so he was crouching at the edge nearest the tents. Maybe it was wrong to turn his back on the guard but it was necessary – the bullseye lantern would give off a tight directed beam. He could use his body to hide any reflected light that could be seen from the camp.

With a final glance at the seated guard, Medda pointed the lantern into the hole and lifted the shutter. As light streamed into the depths of the hole, the sight took his breath away. The hole was two metres deep. Near its bottom, sheets of metal reflected the beam upwards. Medda pushed the lantern's shutter down and turned to the camp. The guard still sat, once more leaning towards the fire.

He aimed the shutter higher to examine his find. It was a large, curved, pock-marked sheet of metal – part of something much larger. The only things he had ever seen on this scale were a steam engine and the Off Worlders' skyships. Why would either be buried here in the grasslands?

"Stand and reveal yourself!"

Medda flinched. The guard was closer than he thought – he must have walked towards the dig site. Medda stood slowly, risking a quick look over his shoulder. The guard was about forty paces behind him with his musket levelled straight at him.

"Reveal yourself!"

It wouldn't do to get caught. The Duke would have to negotiate his freedom, the consequences of which would be awkward.

Turning, Medda held the lantern away from the guard – let him think he was in control.

"Come forward."

Medda turned the beam straight into the guard's face, holding it there. The guard raised his trigger hand from the musket to shield his eyes. Dropping the lantern, Medda dived to his right, landed in a roll, got up and raced off into the darkness.

A sharp crack of musket fire sent Medda into a crouch. As he didn't hear the musket ball pass by, the shot must have missed by a distance.

Getting the news to the Duke was the priority. With a final look back at the camp, Medda disappeared into the night.

* * * * *

Amber awoke with a start. As she came to, her thoughts were slow. She heard a male voice shouting outside. The sound of a musket firing brought her to. She switched on a small portable light and put on a coat and some shoes. She hesitated, then reached for her laser-pistol, hid it in her pocket and left the tent. Outside there was a confusion of people reacting to the gunfire.

She made for the dig – the direction the shot had come from – and soon reached some men standing at the edge of the camp.

Bayl was talking to one of the soldiers.

"Yes, sir," the soldier was saying. "There was somebody out there. I shouted for him to show himself and then fired a warning shot over his head when he ran. "But he got away off into the night."

"You're sure it was a man?" Bayl said. "Couldn't it have been an animal? It's dark out there."

"No, it was a man all right, sir. He had a lantern. I reckon it was one of those fancy bullseye ones. There weren't much light, and then he turned it straight into my eyes and blinded me. Should still be out there. He dropped it and it went out."

Amber followed them to the trench where they found the lantern the soldier had described.

"Well done," Bayl said to him. "I'll see that your sergeant gets a good report."

Setting the guard back to his duties, Bayl arranged for a labourer to join him for the remainder of his watch.

"This troubles me," he said, approaching Amber. "We're a good distance from any villages and the local residents would have no reason to be poking around. This has to be somebody from Denford who is interested specifically in what you're doing."

Amber grimaced. "It might mean the opposition to my being here is more organised than we thought," she said. "A few disgruntled individuals might spread some rumours, but they wouldn't follow us all the way out here."

"When we get back to Denford," Bayl said, nodding, "I'll have this investigated."

* * * * *

"Right," Amber said. "That should do it."

There was now a gap large enough for someone to crawl through in the vehicle's hatch.

The labourer moved out of the way. Amber descended three metres down a wooden ladder to the base of the trench.

It had taken most of the day to get to this point where a large section of the side of the hull, four metres in length and two metres in height, was now visible. It was composed of the same silvery metal that had been discovered the day before. To Amber's mind it was clearly the side of a ship.

Kneeling, Amber shone a powerful flashlight into the darkness. There were mud and debris inside but she could see, for at least some distance, that it opened out into a sizable space.

Bayl reached the bottom of the trench and looked in. "Are you sure it's safe to go in there? If it's over a thousand years old, it might be ready to collapse."

"I can't be absolutely sure," she said. "But these old ships were well built and their materials don't decay much."

She handed a second torch to Bayl. "You coming?"

Bayl stared at the torch before flicking the switch. A bright beam shone out. "How could I not?"

Attaching her torch to her belt, Amber eased herself feet first through the gap and edged down the earth slope until she reached the harder floor of the deck. Then she adjusted the torch to a diffuse setting to get a broader look. She was in a short corridor that, after a few metres, split left and right. The air had a musty smell.

Bayl reached the bottom of the slope. "So, which way do we choose?"

"Left, I'd say. We should try to get to the bridge or cockpit."

They walked along the corridor, passing unopened doors on either side. Everything was covered in thin films of dust but, other than that, everywhere was pristine.

A small object off to one side caught Amber's eye. She picked it up and brushed off the dust. It was a clasp made of a silvery, but tarnished, metal.

"We're not the first to have been here since the Fall," she said. "From the workmanship, this comes from the past you know about."

She passed it to Bayl.

"Now this does look old," he said. "So naturally you tell me it's quite new. This doesn't get any easier, you know."

"New is a relative term here. I'd guess it's several hundred years old but newer than the ship. This thing was discovered a long time ago and then forgotten again."

Amber put the clasp in a bag. They continued down the corridor, following a right turn before reaching a door on the left.

The door looked as if it opened by sliding it from the centre. A defunct button panel to its side had a small handle which, when Amber twisted it, opened the door enough for her to get a finger hold. Bayl helped to prise it open.

Beyond the doorway, the Bridge opened out, with several control panels, though most were damaged and broken.

Bayl gasped at the sight before him. "Men would have flown this ship from here?"

"Yes. And from the number of consoles, I'd say this is a spaceship. This would have been able to fly to other star systems."

He shook his head. "To think, this has been here all this time and we had no idea."

"I told you this could be interesting, didn't I?" she smiled.

While Bayl wandered around, Amber examined one of the consoles. Although it appeared to be intact, it had been stripped of some of its parts to leave a half-finished look.

"Amber," Bayl called. "I think this might be important."

He was standing by a plaque on one of the walls. He had cleared the layer of dust from it and uncovered some writing: SNS Searcher.

Part 4. Yorvin

10.

Blazing, ferocious flames climbed high into the sky. They weren't like the cremations back home on Sattoria, sanitised and out of sight.

Yorvin could make out his four crew mates on the pyre and the smell of roasting flesh was unmistakable and sickening. It was, however, the closest to their customs that could be achieved on this world.

The two marines, Prason and Rowan, stood silently, continuing their usual impassive reaction to events. Yorvin knew this was only for show and that they were going through the same sort of turmoil as he was. Still, it was good to know they were sufficiently in control for him to be able to rely on them. His real worry was Cobannis. She was young and, with Chief Gildoman dead, a lot would rest on her shoulders.

Who was he kidding?

His biggest worry was himself. Captain Weng's body burned before his eyes and responsibility for what was left of the crew was now his, not to mention the hopes of his home world. It had taken the concentration of failing resources to build the Searcher and her two sister ships, the Seeker and the Explorer. When the Explorer had stopped sending reports two months ago, the burden of expectation on the Searcher had grown, focused on the Captain.

Now that focus was intense, and his alone. He had to find a way to repair the ship and either continue the mission or limp home.

The four Sattorians stood for some time by the flames, saying their farewells to their comrades, watched by the Chieftain, the woman, Sharna, and some of the villagers.

At length, Yorvin approached Dornis.

"Once more, Chieftain, you have my thanks. We'll repay you as we're able. I need to discuss with my crew what we're to do next, but I think we'll want to go out to the ship to see what we can recover. Would you be willing to have somebody guide us there?"

"As you wish, Bandrell. I'll have two of the warriors go with you when you are ready."

Yorvin walked into the village and made for the hut that had been assigned to them. The village was small but there must still be more than two hundred living here, judging by the bustle of activity and the number of huts. The people, all mirroring Dornis's simple dress, showed a reserved interest. They were obviously curious but unwilling to catch his eye. The children were a different matter, though. They openly stared at him; two of them, about ten years of age, even being bold enough to follow him.

"Can you really fly?" one said.

"No. I wish I could, though" he smiled. "I have a ship that can, but it has to be mended."

Yorvin went into the hut, taking a seat on his bed to wait for Prason, Rowan and Cobannis. After a few minutes, they returned and sat on their own beds. None of them said a word, the silence growing until it felt like a tangible presence in the room. Yorvin wanted to scream out, curse the universe and everything in it for the hand it had dealt them.

But that would be petulant, self-indulgent. It was a weakness he could not allow.

He stood, waiting until the eyes of his three crewmates were on him.

"This is where we start fighting back," he said. "We've suffered one blow after another but now our luck has changed. We're among people who want to help us. So our first job is to go back to the ship and see what we need to do to repair it. We leave first thing in the morning."

"What if the ship's beyond repair?" Cobannis said. "What if it needs replacement parts we don't have?" Her eyes were wide, pleading, asking what if I'm not up to the job?

"If it looks hopeless," Yorvin said, "then we'll have to rethink. But we won't know till we look. There'll be the remains of the old starport as well. That could provide parts or, if we're lucky, maybe even a ship. I have a family back on Sattoria and I'm damn well going to see them again. We all are."

Cobannis nodded, forcing a smile through her tear-stained face.

"Good," Yorvin said. "Anything else?"

"Sir," Rowan said. "I've looked everybody over for injuries as best as I can without my medi-scanner. We need to get that and some drugs off the ship when we go back. But the point is Cobannis, sir."

"What's wrong with me?"

"No. No, Cobannis, it's nothing bad," Rowan said. "It's just that the rest of us have obvious injuries that have been treated by these tribespeople. The Lieutenant has his broken arm, Sergeant Prason has cracked a couple of her ribs and we all have cuts and bruises. Except for Cobannis. Take a look at that rip in her uniform, sir. From the size of it and the amount of blood, that must have been a major wound. But there's only a scar and that looks old. Even with regenerative drugs, it would take over a week to heal like that."

"So, what are you saying, Rowan?" Yorvin said.

"She's been healed in a way I can't explain, sir. I know I didn't do it and we had nothing on Searcher that could do that sort of job, anyway."

"Cobannis," Yorvin asked, "do you remember anything about this?"

"No, sir, not really," she said. "I remember waking up near the ship. Their healer, Sharna, was there. I think she told me to rest and the next thing I remember was waking up here in the hut."

"That's interesting," he said. "When they were telling me about how they couldn't help the others, they did say they'd saved you Cobannis. No mention of you other two." Yorvin made for the door. "I will speak with Sharna."

* * * * *

One by one the strangers left the fire and returned to their hut. It was odd to Sharna that sorcerers gifted in the ancient magic should choose such an ordinary and simple death ritual. She had expected something stranger or more complex, but then the four of them had shown no signs of being anything more than human. Perhaps that was all they were.

Sharna returned to her own hut to collect her healing bag and herbs. The strangers' wounds needed checking again. Without the support of the Aydoc, Sharna was nervous of performing her work, almost as much as when she had been a young apprentice. What if she made a mistake or her skills were inadequate? It was no more than the healers in the twenty other villages of the Corini had to bear, but for Sharna it was new and disturbing.

To her surprise, Adran was waiting for her. He had been spending most of his time with the warriors lately.

"Adran," she smiled, "to what do I owe the honour? Shouldn't you be off hunting or something?"

"No, Mother," he said. "The Chieftain has only sent a patrol out today. I think he wants to keep a few more warriors around the village in case there's any trouble with the sorcerers."

"I doubt they mean us harm," Sharna replied. "But I suppose Dornis is right to be cautious until we know more. And I hope they really are sorcerers. But they are as easily hurt and killed as we are."

"Oh, they're real, Mother," Adran said. "You should have seen the bird they flew in while it was still in the air. Even though it was about to crash, it was actually flying." He scratched his head. "Why do you suppose they came here?"

"I don't know. It may be they don't mean to be here at all. I'm sure it was not their intention for their bird to crash."

"This could be a good thing for the village, though?"

"Yes, it could," Sharna said. "It is my hope they may use their powers to help us, but we should be wary of them until we know their true intentions."

Sensing that somebody was outside the hut just before hearing a knock on the wall, she pushed the leather drape back and saw the leader of the strangers. Perhaps he had heard what she and Adran had been speaking about?

"Come in," she said, regaining her composure.

He stooped as he entered the hut – he was several inches taller than any in the village.

"This is my son, Adran," she said.

Adran stepped forward and bowed. "You are welcome in our village, Bandrell."

"My son," Sharna announced, "was the one who ran to the village to bring aid to your ship."

"Then you have my thanks," Bandrell said. "Your efforts saved our lives."

"I had better see if I am needed," Adran said, hurrying out.

"The young are the same everywhere," Bandrell said. "They want to be in control before they are ready."

"True enough," Sharna said. "It's my task to hold him back while I can, in the hope he will have gained enough sense by the time I cannot."

"Sharna," he said, "there's something I want to ask you. It was you who tended to our wounds?"

"Yes. In fact, I was about to come over to see how you were all doing. Do any of your friends need further treatment?"

"No, it's not that," he said. "It's Cobannis, the younger woman in our group. She seems to have recovered a lot more quickly than we would have expected. My medic thinks she's very lucky to be alive."

These sorcerers would know the woman had been healed by magic. Sharna should have thought of that. And if she told him of the Aydoc? Would he help or would he claim it as his own?

"Is something wrong?"

She took a deep breath. "It's over there," she blurted out, pointing at the table. "Please, don't take it from me."

He frowned, then nodded. "Show it to me," he whispered. "I won't steal it."

She reached for her leather case, unrolled it, lifted out the Aydoc and held it up for him to see.

He took it from her.

"Be careful," she gasped, shaking. "This is the first time ever someone else – "

Bandrell turned it over in his hands, examining it. "Interesting. You've had this for some time?"

"It's been in the village for generations."

"And you used it to heal Cobannis?"

Sharna nodded.

"You didn't use it on the rest of us, though?"

"No. I only use it for the most serious injuries and illnesses. But now the magic within it has died."

"Died?"

"It will still show the picture of the wound but will no longer heal."

Bandrell handed it back. Sighing with relief, she took it and placed it back in the leather case.

"I'd like to let Rowan and Cobannis have a look at it, if that's all right," he said. "We might be able to help."

"I'll bring it with me now," she said. "As I said, I want to check all your wounds."

She gathered her things and followed Bandrell to the strangers' hut. The other three were inside, waiting.

"Rowan, Cobannis," Bandrell said, "there's something I want you two to look at."

As he looked over to her, she took out the Aydoc. The eyes of the other man, Rowan, lit up.

"May I?" he said, coming towards her, Sharna allowing him to take it from her. "They have a couple of these in the medical museum back home, sir," he said. "They weren't working, though. They're from before the Fall, and way beyond our technology to fix. There are doctors on Sattoria that would kill to get hold of one of these. Metaphorically speaking, of course, sir."

"I don't understand," Sharna groaned. "Does that mean you cannot restore life to the Aydoc?"

"Aydoc?" Rowan said. "That makes sense. We know it as an AutoDoc. As for restoring life to it, it depends what went wrong with it."

The young woman, Cobannis, spoke up. "If it's outright broken, we probably can't help. But if it's a power problem, then we might be able to rig something up with a cell from the ship."

Sharna shook her head several times, then looked at Bandrell.

"Forgive us," he said. "We're using words that are unfamiliar to you. If the AutoDoc is broken then our technology, our magic, is not strong enough. If it has run out of… life, then we might be able to help."

Sharna smiled. "Over the years, the life has ebbed away from the Aydoc. If you can revive it, many lives will be saved."

11.

Two of Dornis's warriors led the way towards the Searcher. With a pair of oxen in tow, it was slow, frustrating going for Yorvin and his crew.

"I've never seen you so animated as when you saw that AutoDoc, Rowan," Yorvin said, as they walked along. "What do you know about it?"

"Like I said, sir, they're museum pieces these days. They were top notch technology before the Fall. AI and nano-technology allowed an untrained person with a bit of instruction to match an experienced surgeon. They were expensive, though, and we only had a few dozen on Sattoria. The loss of technology and surgeons after the Fall meant they were used constantly. When the power cells were used up, they managed to put lower tech cells in to replace them, but gradually they failed and we had to rely on human skills again. Like I said, sir, they'd be falling over themselves to get hold of one."

"They were expensive, you say?"

"Yes, sir. Not sure how much, but it must have been millions of credits."

"Then what would one be doing on a place like Enodia? This planet has always been out of the way. I wouldn't have thought they'd have been wealthy enough to afford something like that, even for their main medical facility."

"I don't know, sir. Maybe somebody important was visiting?"

"Maybe. Though if they were that important, you'd have thought they would have got away and taken it with them. It might mean there's some higher tech stuff here than we'd expect."

After another half-hour, the fallen Searcher came within sight. The furrow made in the crash was huge and the hull was covered in breaches of varying sizes, no doubt caused by the entry into the atmosphere.

"Cobannis," Yorvin said, his heart sinking. "I need an assessment of the state of the ship. What would it take and how long to make her spaceworthy again. Don't be alarmed. I know it won't be pretty – and I'm not expecting miracles – but I need the facts straight up before we can decide what to do."

"Yes, sir."

"Prason, you and Rowan, go through the ship and hunt out anything that could be of use to us. In particular, there are still two mines in there I wouldn't want any of the locals to get their hands on. We don't want the tribespeople playing with nuclear warheads, even if the chances of them activating one are zero."

That left him to check the bridge to see what was working and what could be salvaged.

Leaving the two tribesmen outside minding the oxen, Yorvin climbed through the escape hatch he'd opened two days ago and made his way forward. Although the emergency lighting came on when he accessed the controls, that meant there was just enough light to see the disarray. Anything not fixed down had been flung across the room. Every console was damaged. It was a complete mess.

Yorvin cleared the debris from the chair by the communications console and, sitting down, tried to bring the Astracomm to life. An indicator light showed it had power, but the display showed no link to the transmitter. Communication with Sattoria might be their best hope. He'd need Cobannis to look at it.

It wasn't long before it became clear there wasn't much he could do on the bridge. The next priority was to see if any of the personal computers had survived the crash. The Captain had downloaded as much data to them as possible and placed them in locations that would give them a chance of survival. As one was in clothing in

Yorvin's own cabin, he made his way there. It would give him the opportunity to pull together some of his own belongings as well.

Although the room was in disorder, the locks on the drawers and cupboards had held. With his broken arm in a sling, getting them undone was painful. But he soon had the computer out of its drawer. It had survived the impact, thank goodness.

As he pulled out a bag for some of his own things, he noticed the picture of his wife and daughters on the floor.

The cover was cracked, the image damaged. It was the only hard copy picture of Jan and the girls he had. His daughters, only five and three when the picture had been taken, smiled broadly at him as they sat on either side of his wife.

Gathering it up, he picked the picture out of its broken frame, trying not to damage it further. He shoved it into a pocket. Now was not the time to get emotional.

He collected his clothes and personal effects together and put them into the carry-all, then made his way to the other computers. All four had survived.

He found Cobannis in Engineering. "What's the verdict?"

"I haven't even finished checking the systems, sir," she said, sweat running down her face, "and already I don't know where to start. You'd be talking about a month with a team of engineers in a spacedock. We're not going to get off the ground at all here. We need too many replacement parts."

"If we could find the parts, could you do it?"

Cobannis looked around the room. "I don't know, sir. We'd need some heavy lifting gear for starters, and I'd have to perform some procedures I've never done by myself before."

"All right, Cobannis. Concentrate on finding anything valuable that's small enough to take off the ship, especially tools, hand devices and power cells."

Guessing he'd find Prason and Rowan at the weapons locker, he made his way through the ship's corridors. He found the two marines going through the cache of weapons and armour. The store was mostly intact, though there was some damage near a small hull breach at the far side.

"Not looking too bad, sir," Prason said. "We can put together two full sets of battle armour, which is all we need since only Rowan and I are trained to use it. We've got three sets of Sieve Armour, three laser-rifles and five pistols that are serviceable. Add in about a hundred weapons-grade power cells and we should be able to handle anything on this planet."

That meant all four of them could be armed and armoured. Civilian Armour would be effective against arrows, though swords and spears might be another matter.

"Have you checked the mines?"

"Yes, sir. We've got them ready to go in their secure cases, so they'll be safe from prying cavemen."

"Good. Start getting things together. I'll meet you outside. And both of you – be careful what you say. These people aren't stupid. They won't take remarks like 'prying cavemen' too well. We need to keep them onside."

Yorvin made his way out to supervise the loading of the oxen.

* * * * *

Cobannis, took what looked like a thin dagger to the Aydoc.

"No," Sharna cried, reaching for it.

Yorvin caught her arm. "Careful, Sharna. Cobannis knows what she's doing."

He held up a device of his own showing a picture of the Aydoc.

"Look," he said, "we found some information about the AutoDoc in our own records. It shows us how to bring it to life again." He tapped some buttons and the picture of the Aydoc flipped over. Then part of the picture's shell came away to reveal a hidden compartment.

Sharna looked at Cobannis and then back at Yorvin, her suspicions still not dispelled. "But you said that the Aydoc's magic is stronger than yours and that you have none that work. How do you know you will not damage it?"

"This was how it was done when our AutoDocs were used and it caused them no harm."

A metallic sound pulled her back to the Aydoc. Cobannis had opened it to reveal a compartment like that on Yorvin's picture. She removed a small rectangular object and replaced it with another. She then snapped the missing part of the shell back into place and held the Aydoc out to Sharna. It had taken a minute.

"Is that it?" Sharna said.

"I hope so," Cobannis smiled. "Start it up and we'll see."

Sharna took the Aydoc and pressed against its surface in the way she had done so many times before. The coloured segments sprang into life – which meant it had not been damaged – but then it had still been able to do this much. She looked at the line of light forming in the air above it. It was wider than she had ever seen it before.

"I think it lives again," she laughed. She beckoned Yorvin over and held the Aydoc over his broken arm. An image of it coalesced above the Aydoc as she pressed the colour sequence which, long ago, she had been taught would heal bones. With another press, the brown mist descended from the Aydoc to his arm. She watched the image as the bone knitted together once more. As the mist returned, she pulled the Aydoc away.

As Yorvin took the sling and splints away, he flexed his arm.

"That's incredible. It feels as if it had never been broken. Magic is a good description for it."

Healing Yorvin's arm had been as exhilarating as the first time she had ever used the Aydoc. She was grinning like an adolescent girl. There were so many in the village she could now help. Daynor had been sick for years but, as his life was in no danger, Sharna had shied away from using the Aydoc on him. As long as its life could be restored more than once, she could now help him, too.

"Can what you have done be done again?" she said.

"Yes," Cobannis said. "Probably many times. With heavy use, it'll fail in a way we can't fix, but that will be many years away."

"Then there are some of the people that I must go to."

"Of course," Yorvin said. "But when you're done, will you look at Prason? Despite her efforts to hide it, her ribs are causing her pain."

"Of course I will."

* * * * *

Yorvin walked to the Chieftain's hut. It had been a couple of days since their arrival and he could now move through the village without everybody watching him.

The trip to the Searcher had made it clear that, while Cobannis had much she could work on at the ship, it was never going to fly again unless they could find a stock of spare parts. Analysing the records of Enodia had shown that the planet's primary starport was located only sixty kilometres away. That would be the best place to start.

Yorvin had decided to ask Dornis what he knew of the starport. A dot on a four-hundred-year-old map was only so useful after all. He hoped that seeking the Chieftain's counsel would help to build relations with the villagers. So far, and particularly because of re-powering the AutoDoc, that had been going well. The villagers had shown themselves to be friendly with a tinge of awe for the sorcerers that had come from the stars.

84

Yorvin had described technology as magic a few times and he didn't like it. He didn't want to fuel superstition, but it was simpler than trying to explain the complex concepts of his devices. There was no denying that the respect it generated was quite beneficial to him and his crew.

Sharna, though, might be open to the concept. His initial instinct had been correct: she was a prominent figure in the village, even if officially all power lay with Dornis. She had used technology, knowing it didn't make her a sorceress, and she had seen the AutoDoc with the case off. If he did it carefully, without disturbing her model of the world too much, then her trust in him would grow. She would make a valuable ally.

When he reached the Chieftain's hut, Yorvin knocked on the wall by the side of the doorway.

Dornis pulled aside the flap. "Bandrell, come in. I heard about what your young woman did to the Aydoc. Sharna is raving about it, and she'll now be trying to heal every child with a cut knee."

Yorvin stepped inside the hut. It was larger than the others in the village – but not by much – and there was little ostentation in the simple possessions within. Pride of place was given over to the warrior's furs placed on a wooden stand and the sword that hung from it on a belt.

"You have shown us great kindness," Yorvin said, "and we were in a position to help."

"You wished to speak with me?"

"Yes, Chieftain. We're hoping to make repairs to our ship, but it is badly damaged. We need to look for items that might help us. Long ago, there was a great city about a day and a half's walk to the east." Yorvin gestured in the direction. "We need to visit it to see if it has anything that might help us. I wanted to let you know of our intentions and ask if you know about this place."

85

"I know the place of which you speak," Dornis said. "I have seen it twice. It is an eerie place, a ruin that men avoid. It is said that the ghosts of men long dead haunt it but, almost as bad, it is in the territory of the Utani."

"Who are the Utani?"

"We are of the Corini tribe. This village is a small part of it and there are more than twenty others in our tribe. The Utani are our enemy and we have fought them for generations. What you propose is dangerous, for the Utani will not welcome strangers, especially ones who travel with our people."

"In that case," Yorvin said, "it might be best if we went alone. I was going to ask if you could spare us a guide, but we should be able to find it ourselves from the maps we have."

"But there are only four of you, and only two of you are warriors. You could meet a band of twenty or more."

"You're either underestimating me or Prason," Yorvin smiled. "Prason is the most skilled warrior I know, and we have a few surprises if we're attacked. We'll be all right."

12.

Yorvin fastened his Sieve Armour into place.

Made from a black material, it would stop projectiles, absorbing their impact energy. Underneath, a crystalline layer could dissipate laser fire to some extent. It covered the whole of his body and limbs, which would unnerve the people of Enodia and help avoid the conflict Dornis had mentioned.

And if the armour that Cobannis and he were wearing didn't do the trick, then Prason and Rowan would surely do so. To a tribesman used to furs, swords and spears, the sight of a marine in battle armour covering every part of the body in a hard, protective shell would seem unworldly.

Setting out from the village, Yorvin put Cobannis in charge of navigation. She steered by an inertial mapper that measured distance travelled and so could mark current position on a map.

As scouts, Marines Prason and Rowan fanned to the right and left to warn of anything that might present a problem. Their equipment and training made them ideally suited for this. Chameleon technology helped them to avoid being seen, while broad spectrum scanners allowed them to see in infra-red as well as other frequencies and so spot concealed animals or men. The armour gave power-assisted movement that allowed the wearer, with training, to keep up a running pace for hours while feeling he was only jogging. Add to this a fully integrated communications system that allowed the tracking of other friendly units, and the battle armour provided a formidable capability that was godlike to the inhabitants of a low technology world.

They had a long journey ahead of them. Initially across grassland, they would reach some forested hills towards the end of the day, and then descend into a valley to the old starport.

"How are you holding up, Cobannis?" Yorvin asked as they walked.

"I'm all right, sir," she said too quickly, forcing a smile.

"It's okay to feel overwhelmed."

"I'll manage, sir. You won't have to worry about me letting you down."

"It's not as simple as that, Cobannis," Yorvin said. "I'm far more worried that you feel you have to be perfect and claim you can do the impossible. I'm in the same boat as you. For the last year, the Captain's been in control of everything. Now he's gone and the rest of you expect me to fill his shoes. It's ironic, really. The job is the toughest it's been and the person best able to do it isn't here anymore."

Cobannis nodded. "It's hard not having the Chief around. When you spend all that time in engineering, you get used to them being there, talking about all sorts of stuff like home and family as well as the job. I knew he'd be there to bail me out, stop me from making any mistakes. Now he's gone and we've got a ship in pieces. I'm not sure I can fix it even if we find the parts we need. I don't want to let you down, sir. I don't want to let the Chief down."

"And I don't want to let the Captain down either," Yorvin said. "All we can do is give this our best shot. Of the four of us left, I'm the one best placed to command, and you are far and away our best engineer. Just give me your honest opinion of what can and can't be done and I'll try to make the best decisions based on it. Understood?"

"Understood."

Early afternoon, they entered Utani territory and increased their vigilance. There wasn't much to indicate the change. The grassland was as open and rolling as it had been when it belonged to the Corini and there was no sign of any tribesmen.

After an hour or so, Prason reported from her position to the left. "I think we have a contact, sir. I'm getting something on the infra-red on the edge of the rise, about a kilometre north of my position. It could be an animal but its movements are too deliberate. Shall I investigate?"

So, they were being watched. That was to be expected and didn't necessarily mean the watchers were hostile.

"No, Prason. Just keep an eye on them and let me know of any changes."

They continued onwards, shadowed by the infra-red contact which occasionally came into view, leaving no doubt it was intelligent and deliberately tracking them. As the afternoon wore on, the grassland gave way to a sparse forest and a steady upwards climb.

Yorvin activated his communicator. "Prason, you and Rowan come in closer. It'll be easier for our shadow to slip inside a wide cordon in these trees."

"Yes, sir."

Prason reported further sightings, but their pursuer always maintained a distance.

They made camp in a shallow cave near the top of one of the hills. The marines set up a perimeter at a twenty-metre distance around the cave that would detect movement by anything larger than a small rodent and then sound an alarm.

At Sgt Prason's insistence, she and Rowan took the watch shifts for the night. They were trained to stay vigilant for long periods and function for several days on minimal sleep.

Cobannis and Yorvin settled down near the back of the cave.

He slipped into a restless dream. The Searcher hurtled down into the atmosphere. Yorvin fought with the controls to keep the ship somewhere near a safe course. The fuel warning light had been on since before the descent had begun and each time Yorvin made a correction, he feared it would be the last. The Searcher's hull temperature kept rising until alarm klaxons sounded. Hull breach was imminent.

"Lt Bandrell."

Yorvin awoke with a start. Rowan was leaning over him, calling his name. The harsh blaring of alarms sounded from outside the cave. Someone – or something – had tripped the perimeter.

"Shut that noise off, Rowan, then help Prason."

"Sir." Rowan ran out of the cave.

Yorvin fumbled in the dark for his laser-rifle. It would be unwise to switch lights on and become an obvious target. After a few moments, the alarms went quiet and he activated his comms link. "Prason, report."

"We have a group of five contacts, human, who tripped the perimeter sensors. They ran at the alarm. Should I pursue, sir?"

"Track them, Sergeant. I need to know if they have any friends. Don't engage unless you have to. Leave Rowan on guard here."

Yorvin took up a cover position near the mouth of the cave. He could see Rowan ahead, making a token effort to stay hidden as he scanned the forest nearby, looking for any signs of life.

"Can you see anything, Rowan?"

"Nothing, sir. Everything has been scared off by the noise. I'd say they'll think twice before coming back."

Prason's whispered voice came through on the comms.

"Lieutenant, I've tracked them to a small camp about two kilometres from your position."

"Well done, Sergeant. What's their status?"

"The five who ran look to be the entire group. It must be a patrol, sir. They're having an animated discussion. We have them rattled. They don't look up for an attack, sir, and they don't have the numbers to cause us any problems as long as we're alert."

"Understood," Yorvin said. "Watch them for a little longer to confirm and return to base at your discretion."

Yorvin relaxed. His worst fears were, at the moment, unfounded. He'd had visions of their presence attracting a mob of the Utani. While he was confident the two marines could deal with it, there was a real risk to Cobannis and himself. He also didn't want to be responsible for mowing down dozens of men armed with nothing more than bows and spears. That possibility was unlikely, thankfully, but there was always the chance these five might fetch reinforcements.

An hour later, Prason returned to camp and reported that two of the tribesmen had departed.

The rest of the night passed without incident.

* * * * *

Next morning, they were descending out of the hills into a wide grassy valley, with a broad, slow-moving river at its centre. It was an ideal place for human habitation but, after scrutinising the valley, Yorvin could see no signs of it.

The reason became obvious when, about four kilometres distant, he caught his first view of the spaceport.

A ruined city is a disconcerting sight. Yorvin had seen his fair share of these over the past year and still it was difficult not to be affected. Part of him imagined what this place must have looked like in its prime. A darker side imagined his own hometown in this sort of state.

Dismissing such thoughts, he soon got down to the task of assessing its condition. The taller buildings were in a poor state. Without exception, they were in ruins. The Great Conflict had touched this world, as it had so many others. Many of the smaller buildings did seem to be intact, though, which included many of those in the spaceport proper – which was clearly visible at the northern end of the city.

They continued their approach and reached the outskirts by noon.

It was an eerie place. A city in the middle of the day should have a bustle about it and the absolute silence made the place feel wrong. It was no wonder such places often gained the reputation of being haunted in the minds of those who succumbed to superstition. It was difficult to ignore the feeling, even when one understood the psychological processes behind it.

Any remaining members of the Utani patrol would be unlikely to follow them into the built-up area, at least, so they could explore in reasonable safety.

Yorvin split the four of them into two groups. Prason accompanied Cobannis straight to the spaceport while Rowan teamed up with Yorvin to move from building to building, searching for vestiges of the old technological society that had once dominated this world.

What they found was a mixture of empty rooms and useless junk. The city and spaceport had been picked clean in the intervening three hundred years – probably near the start of the period when people would still have known what would be of help to them. Cobannis did find some parts she might be able to adapt for use on the Searcher, but nothing to help with the sub-light engines or jump drives.

By the middle of the next day, they knew nothing more of real use would be found. They gathered all the portable parts they had found and noted a couple of larger items for later collection.

And so they began the long trek back to the village.

13.

The strangers had been gone for two days when a young warrior ran into the village. Near exhaustion, he stopped for barely a moment before running to the Chieftain's hut.

Sharna did not recognise him. He must have come from one of the other Corini villages. She grabbed her herb bag.

Dornis came out of his hut.

"Chieftain Dornis," the young man said, collapsing at his feet. "Utani warband – to north – hundred men – "

A hundred men was a huge force; their own village could only muster about forty warriors. For the Utani to move so many into Corini lands, there was a strong chance of war.

Dornis reached down to the man, helping him to his feet with a strong arm. The Chieftain guided him into his hut, Luran and Nerac following. Sharna joined them.

"A hundred?" Dornis said as he sat the man down. "That can't be right. Are you sure?"

"Scout who saw – counts well – my Chieftain believes – "

"Dornis," Sharna interrupted. "Let the boy recover his strength. You'll get more sense out of him, then."

"You can perform your arts on him in a moment," he said, not looking at her. "I need more news first. Warrior, what does Chieftain Varril request?"

"He thinks Utani – making for fallen bird – has sent runners to four villages – send all strength you can."

"There" Sharna said, pushing her way through. "You've got what you need now, Chieftain." She took hold of the young man by the shoulders, led him over to Dornis' bed-and sat him down. "He needs to rest."

"We may yet regret our decision to help the sorcerers," Nerac said.

"Perhaps," Dornis replied. "But if the bird is their goal, then it would be there whether we helped or not."

"Why would they risk war with us?" Luran asked.

"Because they are the Utani," Dornis said. "It is their way. They risk it now because they fear the magic of the sorcerers and they hope to steal some for themselves."

"And they choose this moment because they have seen the sorcerers travel through their lands," Nerac continued. "The Utani know the sorcerers cannot hinder them."

"Then they must be stopped," Dornis said. "We must not allow them to plunder the bird."

"What of the village?" Nerac said.

"It will be protected. It is time for my son to take on some responsibility. Luran, Nerac, assemble all the warriors. We have little time to waste."

The two men ducked out of the hut at a run. Dornis reached for his furs and his sword.

* * * * *

Adran paced around the edge of the village as the afternoon wore on, scanning the horizon. Tobin had been left in charge of the village, with Adran as his second, together with four other younger warriors. Here he was, with aching feet after more than a day's worth of guard shifts, bored and frustrated at still being treated like a boy. The only saving grace was, in another hour, it would be Tobin's turn to take over and he would be able to rest.

"Adran!"

The call was coming from the other side of the village where another of the warriors, Paeron, was standing guard. Adran raced over.

"Look," Paeron said, pointing.

A band of men, still some distance away, were breaking into a jog and closing in. Adran could see, from the clothing they wore, they were Utani. There had to be about fifteen of them, too many for six young warriors trying to protect women, children and the old.

"Tobin!" he shouted. "The Utani are here!"

Almost immediately, Tobin was by his side. He watched the Utani, getting closer and closer. "Ready your spears." he ordered.

Adran joined the other four warriors in a line, his spear at the ready.

Behind Tobin, the village was panicking. Some women, including Adran's mother, came up to him. Tobin turned and faced them.

"Sharna," he said, "get all the women and children and hide in the forest till my father returns. If any of the older boys or old men insist on getting their swords, let them."

Looking at Tobin, Adran's mother hesitated.

"Sharna, go!"

With a final, worried look at Adran, she turned and began gathering the villagers.

Tobin turned back and looked out at the Utani. They were still jogging towards the village and were now two hundred paces away.

"We have to buy time for the women," Tobin said, "for our mothers and our sisters. Take cover by the huts until I give the order to throw spears. Have your swords ready."

They waited for the Utani to close in. Adran watched the attackers, his mouth dry, his spear-arm shaking. For years, he had looked for the chance to prove himself and, now it was here, he was going to die in his first battle.

Two of the older boys were running towards him, swords in their hands. Three of the greyheads followed more slowly. They had fought in many battles but, if truth be told, they had seen too many. Fifteen to eleven: the odds were better but still far from good.

The Utani came within throwing range.

"Now," Tobin shouted.

The Corini warriors let their spears fly. Adran stepped away from the cover of a hut and threw with all his strength.

The Utani returned in kind, forcing Adran to duck back around the side of the hut. A spear whistled past, close to where his head had been, followed by screams ahead and behind.

Pulling his sword from its scabbard, Adran ran out again, bellowing a war cry.

Four Utani lay on the ground with wounds, the rest charging on. One made straight for Adran, crying out with a deep voice. The Utani were huge, leaving Adran feeling very much a boy. Grinning, his enemy swung a heavy blow with his sword aimed at Adran's head. Adran swayed backwards, swinging his own sword against the blow. Pain seared through his arm as his weapon was knocked sideways. It was all he could do to hang on to it.

The Utani's momentum carried his sword to the side as he arced it high and round to bring it crashing down towards Adran again.

Adran grabbed his sword with both hands and swung it up. A clash of iron on iron rang out. Adran stopped the blade but was driven down to one knee. The shock of the blow left his sword arm numb. Adran tried to lift his sword to defend himself again, but he could barely move his arm.

With a smile, the Utani raised his sword to strike a killing blow. He hesitated, then staggered forwards. Wide-eyed, Adran stepped back as the warrior collapsed to the ground, smoke rising from his back.

Adran looked around to identify his saviour. He could see Tobin ducking under a wild attack and plunging his sword into a Utani's stomach. Then the air was filled with a streaming pulse of blue light slamming into the back of a Utani who was fighting Paeron. Four figures, off in the distance, were making their way to the village. Adran's heart skipped a beat.

"It's the sorcerers," he shouted. "They've returned."

In an instant, the Utani pulled away. Seven turned and fled, leaving the rest dead or wounded along with four Corini.

The sorcerers hurried closer.

"You have our thanks," Tobin said. "That fight would not have gone well."

"I wish we had arrived sooner," Bandrell said, looking at the fallen warriors. "Rowan, do what you can for them, Corini first." One of the two armoured sorcerers pulled out a device and held it over one of the wounded as his mother did when she used the Aydoc.

"Where are the Chieftain and the rest of the warriors?" Bandrell said.

"A Utani war band was heading for your bird. My father has gone to stop them."

"I see," Bandrell said. "How long since they left?"

"More than a day."

"Then whatever's going to happen probably has already," he said. "I'll send Prason out to scout the ship."

"Bandrell," Adran said, "I did not know the blue fire could be wielded by men. Could you teach our people to use it? It would help us greatly against the Utani."

Bandrell smiled. "Yes, it would, Adran. But we don't have many of the weapons left ourselves. Certainly not enough to arm your warriors." Bandrell turned to move away, then froze. "You speak of the blue fire as though you've seen it before. Have you?"

Adran glanced at Tobin before nodding. "About three months ago in the Old Forest."

The Enodia Enigma

Part 5. Amber

14.

While Amber understood that the poor condition of the spaceship in the grasslands was more than aging, she also realised that, as it was far from the site of the old spaceport, it was very likely a crash landing.

She was puzzled by the spartan nature of the ship's interior. The few pre-Fall ships she'd come across had been more impressive, more technological – which made her wonder if the ship could be from the Fall itself. She would have to analyse the artefacts salvaged from the dig as well as research the name of the ship.

They reached Denford near the close of day.

Once she had overseen the unloading of the artefacts, she arranged to meet Bayl the following afternoon to discuss the next step. In the meantime, he would make enquiries into who would be prepared to follow them to the dig site.

After a meal at The Beacon, she set to work. Her research took her deep into the night, raising as many questions as it answered.

She slept late the next morning and had barely finished eating and dressing when Bayl knocked at the door. For the first time, he took a seat without being asked.

"It's little more than speculation," he said, "but I may have some news regarding the source of our visitor at the dig site. I don't know if you recall the precise wording of the prophecy of Arthur's return?"

"What I've got to say touches on that as well," Amber said. "Hang on a second." She took her holo-recorder from the desk and set it to display the image of the history book she'd taken at the library.

"There," Bayl said, pointing to a portion of the text. "Notice it says that 'Arthur and his Guardians will act.' For centuries, there have been rumours there is a group who see themselves as these Guardians."

"Rumours, you say? Nothing more?"

"No. There's never been anything of substance, just whispered tales in taverns. Since the eclipse, however, those rumours have been growing."

"And what do they say?"

"The Guardians are making active preparations for Arthur's return. There's still little hard evidence, but my colleagues are making strong efforts to track down the source of these rumours."

"If there is such a group," she said, "I suppose it would make sense they'd be interested in my arrival. How do you think they'd view me?"

"We must allow for the possibility they could be hostile. In light of that, and the souring in attitudes which we saw over the last fortnight, I've taken the precaution of organising a guard for you."

"All right, Bayl. It does make sense to have somebody watching after me, but keep it discreet, will you?"

Bayl nodded. "Of course."

"Now, I have some news of my own," Amber said. "I've done some analysis of the objects we retrieved from the spaceship and it wasn't what I expected. The ship isn't as old as I thought. It's more like seven hundred years old, three hundred years into the Fall itself."

"Does that make a difference?"

"My first thought was it must be a mistake with the dating. There wasn't any space travel in this region then except for a planet called Minerva, not too far from here. They didn't have the capability to travel outside their own star system, though."

"So the ship shouldn't be here?"

"That's what I thought, but then I got lucky on my search for the name of the ship, SNS Searcher. As you can imagine, most planets weren't very good at recording events during the Fall. They were too busy trying to survive to worry about that. However, our own records on Vindor mention an SNS Explorer that arrived at our system and was destroyed by our defence forces. The ship was on a mission from a planet called Sattoria to seek out new trade routes. But our navy over-reacted and opened fire. It wasn't one of our proudest moments, I'm sorry to say, but it does back up the date. It happened around seven hundred years ago."

"So you think the ship we found was another sent from the same planet?"

"It's better than that, Bayl," she said. "Sattoria is now a part of the League, so I have access to their historical records. The details are sketchy and from a document written long after the event, but they sent three ships out – the Explorer, the Seeker and the Searcher. The last contact from the Searcher said that they were severely damaged and were going to make an emergency landing on Enodia. After that, there were no further records."

"Meaning that they all died, then?"

"No, Bayl, I don't think so. The ship was in bad condition, but some of the crew may have survived. It's far more likely the communications equipment was damaged beyond repair and any survivors had no way to contact Sattoria. They'd have had to live out their lives on Enodia."

"Then why is this the first that we know of it?" Bayl said. "Surely such people would be remembered?"

"It was a long time ago and it depends how long they survived or whether they survived at all, of course. But maybe they did leave their mark. You've said already that these Guardians, who are so interested in what we are doing, are tied in closely with King Arthur. He established the kingdom in Enodia. You've not told me any dates but I bet I could make a pretty good guess as to how long ago his rule began."

Bayl nodded. "This is the year 689 after the Founding."

"That's too much of a coincidence," Amber said. "A significant advance in your civilisation is made at about the time that a technologically advanced group arrive here. They could well have made an alliance with King Arthur and given a technological boost to your people."

"And that would have allowed Arthur to dominate his enemies and establish the kingdom," Bayl continued. He ran his fingers through his hair. "Being around you has a way of turning things completely on their head, you know, Amber."

"It's not definite, Bayl," she said. "It all fits together but it's nowhere near a proof. Mind you, it does give us a direction for our future research." She took a deep breath. "This theory raises another possibility. If we accept King Arthur had the aid of these Sattorians, then that throws a whole new light on the matter of the eclipse and the prophecy."

"In what way?"

"They would almost certainly have had the necessary information and means to calculate the exact dates and locations of eclipses of the Sun – for hundreds or even thousands of years. So, they would have known the first part of the prophecy would be fulfilled in our time."

"Which would mean the prophecy is true and we are to face an invasion?" Bayl said, frowning.

"Given that it speaks of Arthur rising from the dead, that's unlikely. But it's entirely possible that there is a message in it, although I don't see what. Or maybe the Sattorians had nothing to do with the prophecy. Or perhaps they went mad exiled here and did it maliciously. I have no idea, really."

"What can we do?"

"There's not much we can do directly, we still don't know enough," Amber said. "We continue our research, but we take anything that looks like superstition or Arthurian myth more seriously. We also need to know more about these Guardians. I suspect that if we can find out their intentions then we'll get a clearer picture of what's going on."

"As I mentioned," Bayl said, "we're already investigating the Guardians with all diligence. What we shall find of an organisation that either does not exist or has managed to stay veiled for centuries is a matter of debate. I will, of course, inform you as a matter of urgency of anything that we do uncover."

* * * * *

The night was clear and cool. The stars and a crescent moon gave enough light for Ayrus Medda to move down the alley without tripping over raised cobblestones. He moved quickly and soundlessly to the rear of the Royal Mausoleum, his own near-perfect stealth making Doctor Fryer's clumsy blundering unbearable. If the night watch was within a hundred paces, they would have heard him. At least the two men accompanying Medda and Fryer were competent.

Medda couldn't fathom why the Duke had insisted on Fryer accompanying him. Yes, they had to find the correct artefact and yes, Fryer would recognise it instantly, but Fryer was a liability on a mission like this – a bookworm with no athletic prowess – which meant an extra man was needed to mind him. A group of two was now a group of four, one that would be more easily spotted.

Medda motioned for one of the men to position himself at the base of the wall. He leant against it, holding his hands cupped in front of himself. Medda jogged towards him, placing his right foot into the waiting hands and then sprung upward, grabbing the top of the wall and pulling himself up on to it. He scanned the courtyard below. Medda signalled the all-clear to his men. The second repeated the climb and in a matter of seconds he lay on the wall a few feet away.

Finally, it was Fryer's turn. Despite the practice sessions, he still approached too slowly, barely got any height and needed the assistance of all three others to scrabble on to the wall. This was the most dangerous moment. The sound of Fryer's inept attempt would attract any nearby patrol.

After waiting for a sign they had been heard – none came – the four men dropped to the ground and made their way to the Mausoleum building proper.

A double wrought-iron gate was the only entrance into the imposing stone building and Medda led the others directly towards it. He pulled out a large key which Duke Edrik had assured him would fit the hefty lock securing the gates.

He placed the key into the lock. It turned. Almost there.

Approaching from the rear of the building meant Arthur's tomb was the first they reached – the more recent kings were placed towards the front of the main hall. The gates opened on to a short corridor which ended in a T junction. To the left were the guardrooms, stores, workshops and the like. Their goal was to the right. Soon, the corridor opened into the main hall, a broad, spacious area with marble walls and a geometrically patterned mosaic floor, dimly lit by oil lamps along its length.

The first gate bore Arthur's name in gold lettering. Through its bars, Medda could see the sarcophagi of Arthur and his queen, each with a stone likeness carved into its lid.

The Duke had provided no key for this inner gate, but the lock was less robust.

"Deal with it," Medda ordered.

One of his men produced a chisel, mallet and a large piece of felt. With a knife, the man cut a strip off the felt and wrapped it over the bolt. He placed the chisel against the felt and hit it with a heavy mallet blow. The thin iron bolt buckled, slid free of its moorings and the gate swung open.

Medda picked up one of the lamps and carried it into the tomb area. "Doctor?"

"The artefact we want," Fryer said, walking to the head of Arthur's tomb, "will be located by the King's left shoulder." He dropped to a crouch. "We need to make a one-foot square hole centred on this point."

Medda shook his head. "Are you sure about this? It could take all night to get through the sarcophagus. The noise is bound to be noticed. Wouldn't it be easier to move the lid?"

"Ordinarily, yes," Fryer said, "but you must remember we are expected. The stone in this area has been deliberately thinned on the inside, as it has on the inner sarcophagus. It won't take long." Fryer turned to the man with the mallet and chisel. "Please, commence your work."

Medda and the Doctor stood by as the man covered the end of the chisel with a double layer of felt and prepared to strike the tomb. The second man was keeping guard at the entrance to the tomb area.

After a couple of blows, the first crack appeared in the stone. A third blow saw a large chip fall away revealing darkness within. The stone wasn't even half an inch thick. Maybe the Doctor was useful for something after all.

"Boss," the lookout hissed, "we've got company."

Medda snuffed the lamp out. "Are they on to us?"

"Might be. There's two down the hall, weapons readied."

Fryer jumped up. "We've got to get out of here." He turned, his eyes darting everywhere, then bolted for the gate and ran out into the hall.

"Halt!" a voice shouted from down the hall. "Hands in the air!"

The Doctor froze, raising his arms. "We're going to die, we're going to die."

"Out of here, now," Medda ordered, running out of the tomb. His men followed immediately but Fryer stayed stock-still where he was, arms stuck above his head.

"Halt, or we fire!"

"We mustn't be captured," Medda shouted, pushing Fryer forward. "Run."

They sprinted for the safety of the corridor and the outer gates, Fryer – now a champion athlete – outrunning Medda with every step.

In the same instant that Medda heard the crack of the musket, he felt a sharp pain. His leg collapsed beneath his weight and left him sprawling on the hard mosaic floor, air forced from his lungs.

Gasping, he reached for his knives. But he was too slow.

A musket barrel was aimed between his eyes.

"Don't even think about it."

Medda slumped back on to the floor. Duke Edrik was going to be furious.

15.

Settling back in her chair, Amber watched her computer power down. She had worked until the early hours and had now finished arranging her notes from the second day of interviewing.

Things were going better than she had expected. They'd interviewed citizens, focusing on King Arthur and the prophecy. Although some still viewed her with suspicion, others were now eagerly expounding their own theories on recent events.

Many envisaged a resurrected King Arthur riding into Denford at the head of a large army, ready to battle the host of creatures from the prophecy. The lack of any real clues as to what the creatures might be only allowed for imaginations to take hold: dragons sleeping in the mountains for hundreds of years; unknown creatures that might be discovered in their exploration of other continents; an army of strangers such as herself from the stars – these were just a few of the more rational theories.

If nothing else, she was getting a good set of data on the study of a collective mini-hysteria in the populace. At the back of her mind, though, was the nagging thought that this prophecy might well have been put forward by people who were no more superstitious than herself. The temptation to engage in the same sort of speculation was very difficult to resist – which was in itself an interesting phenomenon.

She was starting to think in circles. It was time to get some sleep. She had just prepared herself for bed when she heard footsteps on the stairs and a forceful knock on the door.

Thoughts of the intruder at the dig site filled her mind. Amber approached the door but didn't open it.

"Yes?" she said. "Who is it?"

"It's Private Bodis, Miss. I have a message from Mr Groms. He requests that you should go straight to the Royal Mausoleum. He says it's urgent."

"Bayl? Did he say what it was about?"

"No, Miss. Just that it was urgent."

"All right. Give me five minutes to get ready."

Why would Bayl be asking her to leave the inn in the early hours of the morning, and not come himself? This man at the door could be an impostor, a member of the Guardians, trying to kidnap or kill her. If that were the case, he'd have had to get past the real guard, and she'd heard no struggle. Anyway, if his intention was to kill, he could have burst into the room without knocking. The simple explanation was that Bayl really had sent the message and was waiting for her at the mausoleum. But that wouldn't stop her from being careful. Once she was dressed, she slipped her laser-pistol into her coat pocket.

She opened the door. He looked genuine enough. In fact, she was fairly sure she had seen him on guard the day before.

He led her through the quiet streets of the city to the square, the location of the Founder's Festival, the place where things had begun to get complicated.

On the far side, the Royal Mausoleum was an imposing sight, even in the dark – built from an ornate stonework that was quite rare in Denford. Amber could see light from several torches and activity at the entrance, a large archway with portcullis wide enough to take a coach.

Bodis led her to it. At the mention of Amber's name, the two guards on duty waved them through to a central hallway where the tombs could be viewed through ironwork gates.

At the far end, Bayl was talking to an army officer. He turned to meet her.

"Amber, I'm sorry to drag you here so late, but something has happened. Look at this."

She followed him to a tomb entrance which, unlike the others, had its gate standing open. The lock had been forced. Beyond was a side chamber dominated by two stone sarcophagi, one with the carved image of a man lying on top and 'Arthur' carved on its side. A bag of tools lay on the floor and a portion near its base had been damaged, with pieces of stone scattered about.

"Normally," Bayl said, "there's only a token guard on the Mausoleum. It's never been necessary to have more. But tonight, the guards disturbed four vagabonds trying to break into Arthur's tomb. Thankfully, they didn't fully succeed."

"What happened to the men?"

"Three of them escaped. But we have the other. He was shot in the leg and is being treated by a doctor. He should be well enough to be interrogated soon. I'd like you to observe."

"Do you have any information on him already?"

"He's refused to give a name and he's carrying nothing to identify him. The only unusual thing we have is this." Bayl held out a heavy iron key.

"What is it?"

"It was found on the man who was captured. It's a key to the rear gates of the Mausoleum."

"I take it that's not easy to get hold of?"

"Far from it" Bayl said. "There should only be two copies, one here and the other at the Palace. To obtain a copy without anybody being aware would require significant resources."

"A Guardian?" Amber said.

Bayl nodded.

* * * * *

The prisoner sat on a simple wooden chair before a simple table, flanked by two armed soldiers. His clothing, though dark coloured and practical, showed he was more than a common robber. His trousers were torn. His left thigh was bandaged. His weathered skin, well-tended hair and receding hairline led Amber to put him in his early forties.

She sat on a chair by the door of the guard chamber. Bayl sat opposite him. The prisoner watched him, then looked Amber straight in the eye. She stared back.

"By what name shall I call you?" Bayl said.

"My name is of no matter."

"Do not think that you can hide behind a cheap attempt at anonymity. We will find out who you are."

"Whatever you say."

"You can be sure of it, sir. It would, though, help your plight if you volunteer the information and the names of your three accomplices."

Grinning, the prisoner said nothing.

"Let's consider your crime, then. You were found in the mausoleum dressed in a manner that suggests you are trying to avoid notice. When challenged, you ran and were only stopped by a musket round. And worst of all, you were discovered near the tomb of King Arthur which we then find has been damaged. What are we to make of this?"

"You can make what you like of it."

"Really? Well how about this, then? You are a grave robber. You hoped to find some valuable artefacts in Arthur's tomb. You would plant them somewhere else and have them 'found' so that you could make a fortune from it. With all the interest in Arthur's reign and the prophecy, it would be lucrative."

"You have me. I can hardly deny my involvement."

"Well, I'm glad we're not going to play games around that obvious fact. But you seem remarkably calm for one who has committed such a heinous crime."

"I will accept my punishment. I was aware of the risks."

"No, sir, I don't think you were. You expect to spend time in prison for this, and I'm sure you will. But you must have a family, a wife, parents, siblings, children. Do you really think the King will allow your family to escape punishment?" Bayl pressed on. "Do you think that they will accept a life in prison as readily as you?"

"You can't do that to them! They knew nothing of this!"

Although there was anger in his voice, something wasn't right.

Then Amber spotted it. His face mirrored the anger of his voice but his eyes were calm. He was acting. Acting in the way expected of him. She hoped Bayl was playing a cleverer game than he appeared to be.

"But you've shown yourself to be a *thief*" Bayl said. "Chances are, if you're prepared to stoop to something like this, you've been thieving for years and your family are living off stolen wealth. Now, I might be able to do something for you if you tell me who your three accomplices were."

"That's an idle threat" he said. "Our laws don't work that way, as you well know. You'll not trick me like that."

"But you've stepped over a line, sir" Bayl said, smiling. "Grave robbing from a royal tomb is treason. Your family's freedom and wealth are forfeit."

"I am not a traitor," he said, raising his voice.

"So you think breaking into tombs is a service to Enodia? You must face the truth, sir. Your family will spend the rest of their lives in captivity because of your treason." Bayl said.

"I told you, I am not a traitor!" Small beads of sweat had appeared on the man's forehead.

"You Guardians are all traitors!" Bayl shouted, standing and leaning forward.

"We – " He stopped, ran a hand through his hair, let out a deep sigh. "I am not a traitor."

Bayl sat down, smiled. "Well, I'm glad we've cleared that up. You really must work on your temper, sir."

"I don't think it will be a problem again."

"So tell me, how do the Guardians think breaking into Arthur's tomb will help the situation? Were you hoping it would be empty so that you could claim Arthur had risen? Or maybe you proposed to empty it yourself for the same reason?"

True to his word, the prisoner didn't rise to this bait. Instead, he fixed a hostile stare upon Bayl.

It was a good question, though. Why would the Guardians want to break into Arthur's tomb?

Amber knew Arthur had probably been influenced by technologically advanced visitors. For some unknown reason, this time period had, therefore, been deliberately marked by the prophecy of the eclipse.

The Guardians had existed for hundreds of years. Could they reach all the way back to the Arthurian era and be part of a scheme spanning centuries?

If so, they might have their own prophecies of which this outlandish act might be part. But why?

If Arthur could really rise from the dead, that would mean some sort of cryogenics. And that would be impossible on a post-Fall world. And seven hundred years in stasis would be an implausibly long time, even at the peak of man's technology.

Then why else?

Was the Guardians' knowledge as vague as the prophecy? Maybe the tomb contained something to explain what was going on.

She rose from her chair. "I tire of this charade." She walked over to the prisoner. "You're too late. We've already opened the tomb. We have Arthur's instructions."

"No," he blurted out. "That's impossible."

Christopher J Wright

Part 6. Yorvin

16.

Yorvin was missing Jan and the girls more than ever. The Astracomm messages, despite the two-month lag, had been a frequent and regular way to see them, to know they were all right. It was more than a week since their last message. Trelena, his younger daughter, had read out a small letter she had written for him. She missed her Daddy and was looking forward to him coming home. Yorvin's smile faded. There might not be any more messages. That was why they had to repair their systems.

Hearing footsteps approach the hut, he opened the flap to see Sharna smiling at him.

"Dornis is ready to speak with you now."

Yorvin followed her to the Chieftain's hut.

"Bandrell," Sharna said as they walked, "I haven't thanked you for saving my son's life. Adran would have died and I am grateful."

"Please," he said, "I am known as Yorvin to my friends, and I hope we see each other that way now. You helped us when you didn't have to, and you saved Cobannis's life. I am grateful too, Sharna. We were in a position to help friends, what else could we do?"

Sharna smiled again. "Your magic is strong."

"We're not sorcerers."

She stopped. "What do you mean? We have seen the blue fire. You have shown mastery over the Aydoc. How could you not be a sorcerer?"

"It is only technology." Yorvin paused a moment. "I know that may sound like another word for magic to you, but it means there is an explanation for it. It means we have learned about the world and use that knowledge to do things that seem magical."

Sharna was still looking at him.

"Take an example. When you want to warm your huts in winter, you light a fire, yes?"

She nodded. "What has that to do with magic?"

"Exactly. You know how to make a fire and, because you have that knowledge, you don't think of it as magic. But, say you came across a group of people who had never seen fire and knew nothing about it. What might they think about you if you carried a lit torch when you met them?"

After a long pause, she said, "You're saying they would think that fire was magic? But all peoples know of fire. That could not happen."

"True," Yorvin said, "but I want you to imagine the possibility. They would assume fire was magical, just as your people assume the blue fire is. It's more complicated than ordinary fire and much harder to make. But it is no more magic than the fire that you use to warm and light your huts."

"Does it really matter what it is called?"

"It matters a lot. If it were magic, then I would be a sorcerer. When it's technology, then I am just a man again. One that comes from a place with more knowledge, but just a man and that is how I would have things be. I'm not comfortable with being labelled a sorcerer."

"But you are not an ordinary man, Yorvin. Your magic – your technology sets you as different, just as the Aydoc has made me different to the other women of the village."

They were drawing close to Dornis's hut.

"I will think on what you have said, though. Perhaps it will make more sense in time."

Sharna led him in. Dornis was sitting on a bench, finishing a meal and talking with Tobin, his son. "Bandrell, Tobin has been telling me of the attack on the village."

"Your son fought bravely against great odds, Chieftain. You should be proud of him."

"I am, but it still might have gone badly but for your help. You have my thanks."

"I understand from Tobin," Yorvin said, "that the Utani were making for my ship?"

"When they saw our strength, they turned and we chased them from our lands. Don't worry, your ship is undamaged and I have put scouts close by to watch for any more attempts by the Utani to reach it."

"You have my thanks in return, Chieftain." He took a deep breath. "There was another matter I'd like to discuss. When Adran saw our weapons fire, it seemed to be familiar to him. He told me there is a place in a forest where you have seen it before?"

"It is a place we avoid," Dornis said, frowning, "although the young and foolish have gone there."

He smiled at his son. "Both Tobin and I have seen it. Bandrell, it is a place of death. The blue fire strikes at anything that moves and causes terrible wounds."

"It sounds just the sort of place I should be investigating. Laser fire means technology and that might mean a way to repair my ship. I hope to be able to deal with the blue fire, as you call it."

"That I would like to see," Dornis said. "I have always been intrigued by the place, even though it has such dangerous magic. If there is a chance you can defeat it, I will lead you there myself."

* * * * *

Although Sharna had serious misgivings about the trip, she insisted on accompanying the Chieftain. She'd had no choice, really. Yorvin had heard of the clearing in the Old Forest and Dornis had agreed to lead him there. Tobin and Adran were going along too – they already knew about it. Somebody was likely to get hurt and need the power of the Aydoc.

The conversation with Yorvin the previous day had been strange, as was the idea of having two names, one for friends and one for everybody else. In the village, only Dornis had two names and one was his title as Chieftain. Yorvin had one of those as well.

These sorcerers were strange in their ways.

He objected to being known as a sorcerer. She didn't really see why. He had objects that were clearly magical, just as the Aydoc was. Even if he chose to use a different name for it, it was still the same thing. He seemed to think that, because he had a fuller knowledge, that he understood the technology, that made it less impressive. It was clear to her that a real understanding only made it more so. It meant that his people could create new magic, not just use what the ancients had left.

Halting the group, Dornis pointed ahead.

"There, Bandrell, is the edge of the trees. It is safe up to that point. Once you are in the clearing itself, then the blue fire will follow soon after."

Yorvin signalled to Prason and Rowan, who were once again wearing that monstrous clothing. They moved forward to the edge of the clearing, with the rest of the group watching from a safe distance.

A nervousness settled upon Sharna as she wondered whether the power of Yorvin's two warriors would match that of the old magic. She had seen Dornis survive a hit from the blue fire. Perhaps their clothing gave that same protection. One of them rose to a crouch, it was difficult to tell which. After a short pause, the warrior ran for the cover of a fallen tree a short distance into the clearing. A bolt of fire shot from the small building, striking the running figure on the arm. The warrior dived for the cover of the tree trunk and examined his armour.

"No problem, sir," Rowan said, his voice coming from Yorvin's arm, startling Sharna, then amusing her as he talked into his sleeve.

"What do you make of it, Prason?"

When his arm took on a female voice, Sharna had to stifle a giggle.

"It's an automated defence system, sir," Prason said. "Energy readings are pretty high, though. We could take a couple of direct hits from it, but too many would get through our armour. You don't want to get hit if you're only wearing Sieve Armour."

"Can you take it down?"

"The weapon itself is covered by holographic shielding and I'm picking up another similar area near the top of the wall. That'll be the sensor array. If we can knock that out, it'll disable the whole thing."

"Your words mean little to me," Dornis said. "Does that mean you can defeat the magic?"

"I'm not sure, Chieftain," Yorvin said. "It does mean that we have a plan." He turned to his arm again. "All right, set both of your lasers to continuous fire and try and take that sensor out."

Prason and Rowan readied their weapons and pointed them towards the building. After a count which could be heard from Yorvin's arm, blue fire streamed from their weapons focussing on a point near the top of the building. Unlike the fire Sharna had previously seen from the building and the weapons, this was an uninterrupted rod of light. It had a dazzling beauty to it.

As she stared, the world erupted in light. Bolts of the blue fire shot from the building in rapid succession, some aimed at Prason and Rowan but others shooting off in random directions. Sharna heard cries of alarm from Dornis and the others, then felt herself being pulled to the ground. Some of the bolts hit trees around them, spraying small pieces of wood everywhere.

"Are you all right?" Yorvin asked her, his hands on her shoulders.

She was so shocked by the speed of events she could do little more than nod.

"Is anybody hurt?" Yorvin called out.

Everybody acknowledged his call. Sharna breathed a sigh of relief, especially when she saw Adran was unharmed. They had been fortunate.

"Prason, what happened?" Yorvin said.

"It didn't like being shot at, sir. I reckon we upped its settings a notch or two. I don't think we were far off getting through, though. If you were to add your rifle, I reckon that would make the difference."

"Terrific," Yorvin muttered, readying his own weapon. He rose to a crouch and moved from tree to tree towards the edge of the clearing. As he moved, the building shot out some single blue bolts but none came close to hitting him. Before, it hadn't been triggered by movement within the trees.

Again, there was a pause, then the three weapons focused on the same spot. The barrage of blue bolts started up again. Sharna kept herself flat down on the ground. After a short time, though, everything went quiet.

"That's it," Prason called out. "We're through. Everybody, keep down while we make sure it's safe."

Sharna risked lifting her head to look into the clearing. What had been a smooth wall in the building now had a small hole near its top, blackened from the fire. She watched as Rowan pushed himself over the tree trunk and sprinted for the next hiding place. He was taking no chances. He dived for the protection of a rise in the ground – the one where Tobin had been injured. After a short wait, he ran for the wall itself.

"All right," Yorvin said. "We can go up there for a better look. But remember, that's only one wall we've deactivated. Go straight to the building in single file and only move round to the doorway when you're up close."

They rose and walked towards the clearing.

"Are you sure it is safe to come here, Yorvin?" Sharna said.

"To be honest, no. But I'm sure we're safe for now. This laser won't be a problem anymore. Hopefully, it's only an outer defence. Things should be better inside."

"What do you think we'll find?"

"It must be something important to have a defence system like this. I'm trying not to get my hopes up."

When they got there, Cobannis was already working on the door and a small pad next to it. She held a device up to the pad and was scanning it in the way Sharna scanned a wound with the Aydoc. The picture was flat on the device's surface rather than hovering in the air, though.

Yorvin waited until Cobannis had finished what she was doing.

"Well?"

"It's a good system, sir. It can be totally locked down from its control centre. If that's happened, then we'll have to use brute force to get through the door. If not, then I should be able to get past the system in a couple of hours or so. Trouble is, I won't know which way it's going to go till those two hours are up."

"Prason, how quick to melt the door?"

She looked at the device in Cobannis's hands. "Three to four days and most of our power cells, sir."

"Then we've got two hours to wait. Get on with it."

17.

Leaning against a tree at the edge of the clearing, Yorvin activated his comm link. "How's it going?"

"Getting there, sir," Cobannis said. "Another twenty minutes or so and we should know if this is going to work."

Yorvin noticed Sharna smiling at him – again. "Something's amusing you?"

"I've never met anybody who talks to their arm before," she said, blushing.

He looked at his arms. "I suppose it must look odd. To us, it's so ordinary we don't even notice it."

"You come from a very different world. Ours must seem primitive to you."

Yorvin shook his head. "No, or perhaps a little, in the sense of what technology you have. It's people's actions that show the most and on those grounds this world is more civilised than many."

"Because we helped you?"

"When Dornis found us, we were defenceless but he chose to assist us. You chose to save Cobannis when you thought it might be the last time you could use your AutoDoc. They were noble acts and the last year has shown me that's become a rare thing. I've been to more than a dozen worlds where people are struggling to survive. The most primitive response we got was from the most advanced people we met. They opened fire on us."

"And that's why you're here now?"

Yorvin nodded. "We limped the three-day journey here. Now, half the crew are dead and the rest of us stranded."

Sharna nodded. "It must be difficult for you."

Yorvin looked out into the forest. "This is a beautiful world but it's not my home, and home is all I really want now. I have a wife and two daughters who I might never see again. It's hard to be so far away from them and not speak to them."

"Yes," she murmured. "I think I can understand that."

"I'm sorry, Sharna. I'm feeling sorry for myself. You have lost your husband?"

"In battle with the Utani. He was a good man, one of the rare ones who could cope with a strong-willed woman. But now he is gone and I will not see him again." She looked at her son. "At least I have Adran. He is becoming more like his father each day, but I worry I will lose him as well."

"It's the cost of loving somebody, the fear we might lose them."

As Sharna nodded, lost in her thoughts, Yorvin was also left to reflect on his own words. Jan and the girls had always been the focus of his life, but only now did he realise how much. What had possessed him to leave them for so long to go on such a dangerous mission? He knew the answer, of course. It was for his family. If Sattoria was safe, then so were they. Somehow, he had to get back to them and this building offered his best chance.

Getting to his feet, he crossed the clearing to stand by Cobannis. She looked at him before turning back to work on her computer. A minute or so later, data flooded her display. She scanned through it, searching for some values or pattern; Yorvin wasn't sure what. That level of technical detail was beyond him. She smiled.

"Good news?" he said.

"Definitely looks like it, sir. They didn't lock up too carefully. I should be able to open it easily enough."

"All right. Hold on until we get the marines into place."

He called Prason and Rowan over. "Prepare to go in."

As they took their positions, Cobannis stood to one side, out of line of potential dangers from within. The others watched from the cover of the trees. Cobannis pressed some controls on her computer and the door slid slowly to one side. Using torches built into their rifles to scan what lay beyond, the two marines peered into the building.

"All clear," Prason said over her comm link. "An empty corridor leading to what could be a lift shaft and stairs. It's dark, so it's difficult to make out too many details. There's a layer of untouched dust on the floor. It doesn't look like anyone's been here for a long time."

"You and Rowan, scout ahead. Keep in comms contact."

"Yes, sir," Prason said, disappearing into the building. Rowan followed.

Yorvin waited while the marines did their work.

Finally, Prason's voice came through the comms.

"Sir, we've descended about twenty metres to a reception area and a small complex of rooms. It's been abandoned, probably for centuries. There's no sign of any recent activity."

"Any idea what type of facility it is, Sergeant?" Yorvin asked.

"Negative, sir. The stairs do go down further. We're preparing to investigate."

"Understood. Go careful, Prason."

"That doesn't make sense, sir," Cobannis said. "Twenty metres isn't deep enough to make a base safe from planetary bombardment. If you're only going that far, why not build on the surface?"

"I don't know. Perhaps the builders wanted to keep the place a secret, or there's something at that depth that was of interest. Some rare minerals, perhaps?"

"Secrecy seems more likely. This upper level wasn't designed for transporting minerals, unless it was very small quantities."

Yorvin now faced another equally difficult wait. Rare minerals or metals would be of little use in their efforts to get home. He hoped

Cobannis was right, that this building with its own defence array held something of worth that would need to be kept secret. But what?

"Sir," Prason's voice came through the comms link, "you'd better get down here."

"What is it, Prason?"

"I'm not sure. A force field by the looks of it. I've never seen anything like it before."

"Is the area secure?"

"Affirmative."

"On my way." Yorvin rose to his feet. "We have the all-clear. Let's go and see what's got Prason so excited."

Yorvin made his way across the clearing, sticking to the safe route he had already used. Dornis followed close behind, his spear hefted in readiness, with Cobannis, Tobin, Adran and Sharna taking up the rear.

At the doorway, Yorvin could see the corridor Prason had described over the comms link. A smooth passage, made of a silvery metal, led into the complex and ended in what appeared to be the entrance to a lift with a stairway to its left. It was bathed in a low light from a strip near the ceiling running the length of both walls. The only other features that struck him, were the layer of, now disturbed, dust on the floor and an opened door a few metres in on the right.

Despite the assurances of the marines, Yorvin advanced slowly with laser rifle readied. Weapon first, he investigated the doorway. Footprints indicated Prason and Rowan had been here – no doubt in far more professional a manner. The room looked like a guardroom, with a small console and some screens, most likely to display views of the clearing and forest. Somewhere, there should be controls for the defence system. That would need to be investigated to make the exterior safe; it would wait.

Towards the end of the corridor, Dornis was peering down the stairway. Yorvin walked over to join him.

A flight of stairs disappeared down and around the lift shaft. Bathed in the same glow of light that lit the corridor, they were wide enough to take two men. Following the footprints in the dust, they began to descend the stairs.

Before long, they reached an open landing with several passageways leading off from it, probably the reception area Prason had mentioned. They continued round and down the stairs at the far side of the lift. After two more flights, they came to a short passage and a heavy door. It was standing ajar. Beyond it, the passage had doors to left and right. And then it opened out into a chamber.

Yorvin could make out a brighter glow from a strong light out of sight, away to one side of the chamber. As he and Dornis approached, Yorvin saw the marines standing, transfixed.

A wall of shimmering light overwhelmed the far side of the otherwise empty chamber. As they watched, random patterns of brightness interweaved with one another, pulling them into a hypnotic state.

18.

It took a force of will for Yorvin to pull himself back into the moment. The shimmering wall of light was clearly a form of force field, though very different from the shields the Searcher could generate. It was about eight metres wide and some three or four metres in height and, now he was studying it rather than gaping at it, Yorvin could see small clusters of metal bars at each edge. Those must be generating the field.

He walked closer towards one of the corners. It was more than a single wall. It had a depth of less than half a metre, but with another force field wall at its back. It was a rectangular box framed by the same metal bars.

Although it was fascinating, it didn't tell him a great deal. He turned, looking for the others. Dornis and the other Corini were gazing, mouths agape. Cobannis was close by, scanner in hand, moving towards him with it held up to the wall of light, staring intently at the screen in her hand.

"Sorry," she mumbled, bumping into him. "I mean... Sorry, sir."

Yorvin smiled. "What do you make of it?"

"It's a high energy force field, sir."

"I'd got that far without the aid of a scanner, Cobannis."

She grimaced. "It's an effective one. The only readings I'm getting are of the field itself. I'm not reading a thing from whatever's inside it."

"Couldn't it just be empty?"

"It could, but I think it's the field blocking the scans. If it was simply empty then part of the readings would be from the field on the far side. I'm not getting even the slightest variation when I change the angle of my scans."

"So you're saying we have no idea what, if anything, is inside this?"

"I'm afraid so, sir. There is one interesting thing, though, to do with the generating rods." She walked over to the nearest cluster of poles.

"If you look at the shape of them, they're arranged so one generates the fields that form the two sides of the rectangular box coming from this edge. The other two rods are placed so they generate a much smaller field that cuts off the corner and protects the first rod."

"Meaning?"

"Meaning that the designers have gone to a lot of trouble to protect the generating rods from whatever might be inside."

"Which means it could be extremely dangerous?"

"It would appear so, sir."

"Terrific. Not exactly what we were hoping for." Yorvin stared up at the vast wall of light. "How easy is it to generate a force field impervious to scanners?"

"Difficult, sir. It's beyond anything we can do."

"And it'll prevent anything from going through it?"

"Almost certainly."

Yorvin looked back to the rest of the group who were still gazing at the field. Prason and Rowan had relaxed and were talking with each other, while the Corini seemed overawed at the sight. He walked over towards them, Cobannis following.

"Chieftain," he said, "would you throw your spear at the light, please?"

"You wish me to attack it?"

"No," Yorvin said. "We want to see whether objects can pass through it and I'd rather nobody was touching the first one that we try."

"You are sure this is safe, Bandrell?"

"Not entirely. That's why we're being so cautious."

Dornis took up position fifteen metres from the force field, drew back his arm, stepped forward and let fly with his spear. It travelled hard and fast, hitting near the centre of the wall before bouncing and falling to the floor. A sudden burst of brightness propagated away from the impact point and quickly died.

"Energy levels rose briefly, sir, by a small amount. It looks like it adapts its strength to what's needed."

He looked over to the marines. "Prason, it's your turn."

She took aim with her laser rifle and sent a pulse of energy into the field. It flared more brightly this time, absorbing the energy from the weapon. He turned to Cobannis. The young engineer was still examining the readout.

"A larger increase in the energy levels but still not much of one. It didn't get through, sir, and there's still no indication what's behind the field."

A high technology force field had been the last thing Yorvin had expected to find. Just as the laser array on the building above indicated something of importance within, this pinnacle of pre-Fall technology surely meant there was something significant behind it.

He was a hair's breadth away from finding out what was worth all this security. "All right, Cobannis," he said, "we're not getting anywhere here. There must be some controls in the other rooms on this level. Go find them."

A door off the passageway to the chamber led to a room containing three control consoles. Leaving the others in the chamber, Yorvin followed Cobannis into the room. She approached one and set to work, soon powering up the console. After a short while, she brought up several different screens of information and moved from one console to the other.

Yorvin looked around the room. There were no real clues here. It looked like something he would have found on Sattoria, but the state of the world outside the complex suggested it had been here some time.

"Lieutenant," Cobannis said.

Yorvin looked over her shoulder. "You got something?"

"It's simple enough, sir. Dual controls for the field with a third console for redundancy."

"Good work, Cobannis. Are there any records to say what this place is?"

"No, sir. The logs say all records were wiped a little over three hundred years ago."

"Three hundred years? About the time of the Great Conflict. They must have a heck of a power source to keep the place running all this time."

"I don't know the details of it," she said, "but the readout says it's still got plenty of juice in it."

Yorvin paused. "So, we still don't have any clues as to what's behind that force field?"

"I'm afraid not, sir."

"What are your instincts telling you?"

"Well," she said, "we know the field is effectively impervious to physical objects and anything we can scan for. That suggests it's there as a protection, either for us on the outside or for whatever's inside. I'd guess it is something very sensitive to harm or something giving off a dangerous radiation."

"Could you lower it for a fraction of a second and then raise it again?"

"It wouldn't be a problem, sir, but we don't know what might happen as a result."

He called the marines over. "Prason, I want you to scan and record what happens in the chamber while we lower the force field. Just set up the equipment on the floor and stay out of sight yourself. Let me know when you're ready."

"Yes, sir." She left the room, returning soon after with Dornis and the Corini before her.

Yorvin nodded to Cobannis. "Do it."

She pressed a button on one of the consoles, then pressed it again. "It's back?"

"Yes, sir, readings are all as they were before."

"Then let's take a look at the scanner."

Yorvin left the room with Cobannis and the others close behind. He handed her the scanner, watching as she played back the recording. The light of the force field had disappeared to leave a large swathe of darkness.

"What the heck is that?" Yorvin said.

Cobannis shook her head. "I've no idea. I've not seen anything like it before." She examined the scanner. "It's not giving off any unusual radiation though, sir."

"So it would be safe to take the field down and have a proper look at it."

"I don't see why not," Cobannis said. "Though somebody should be by the controls all the time in case we need to raise the field again."

"All right," Yorvin said. "Show Rowan how to restart the force field. Then let's see what we've got here."

Cobannis took Rowan to the control room, returning a minute or so later.

Yorvin activated his comms link. "Okay, Rowan, drop the field."

The light disappeared. It took a moment for Yorvin's eyes to adjust, even though the light from the walls was still shining. Soon he was able to make out the area of blackness where the light had been.

This was no ordinary darkness. It was impossible to make out any detail or texture at all. It was complete, an absence of anything but pure black. The edges were jagged, uneven and immobile.

"Cobannis?"

She was staring at the scanner, making frequent adjustments as she cycled between the different functions.

"Cobannis?" he said again. "What is that?"

She glanced at him and then returned to the scanner. "It's not reading as anything, sir. It's as if it isn't there. There's no visible light – obviously – but there's no other electro-magnetic frequencies either. I can't detect radiation of any sort. Like I said, it's as if it's not there."

Yorvin walked towards it, moving towards one of its sides. It was roughly the same size as the force field had been, so the field had probably been designed around it. It was like a huge tear in the air itself. Yorvin reached its edge and, for a second, as he passed from front to back, it disappeared from sight. The rear looked exactly like the front. It had no depth at all.

"Do you have anything, Cobannis?"

She shook her head. "No, sir. No readings from it whatsoever."

"So what's your best guess?"

"Without some experimentation, it would be a blind one."

Bandrell looked over towards Dornis. He and the other Corini were keeping their distance and Yorvin could fully understand their wariness. The complete absence of light and texture was unnatural.

"Chieftain, may I borrow your spear?"

Still staring at the black wall, Dornis handed it over.

Yorvin looked to Cobannis. "Are you recording this?"

She nodded.

Yorvin approached to a metre distance from the blackness. He could feel nothing from it. But this close, the nothingness dominated him. If it hadn't been for the spear visible in his hands, he would have thought he had his eyes shut.

Bracing his feet for an impact, he pushed the tip of the spear towards the black. His mouth went dry. When the spear touched, there was no resistance, no impact. The tip of the spear disappeared.

Yorvin pushed until about half a metre had gone in. Still no resistance.

Prason walked to the side and looked around the back. "Sir… there's no sign of it on the other side."

As Yorvin withdrew it, the spear came out as easily as it had gone in.

Cobannis scanned it. "Nothing abnormal, sir."

"Can we get a camera into it?"

"Not a problem, sir. If we tie a scanner to the spear, it can record as well as transmit by radio. Either way, we should be able to get an idea of what's inside this… if 'inside' is the right word."

Cobannis attached a second scanner to the spear and Yorvin pushed it into the darkness. As it disappeared, she said, "It's stopped transmitting."

Yorvin jerked the scanner back out.

"And now it's transmitting again." She went over the device on the spear and read the display.

"According to this it was transmitting all along, sir. Maybe this wall shields against radio comms?" She examined the recorded data. "No unusual readings. There's a dark, irregular chamber a little smaller than this one. Atmosphere and temperature are the same as here. No life signs."

The next step was obvious. Yorvin pushed the tip of his right index finger a fraction into the dark wall.

"Sir!" Cobannis gasped.

He felt no different. Pulling his hand back, he examined his hand. Nothing.

Best get this over with.

He prodded the spear downwards through the wall and felt the reassuring resistance of something solid. He heard no sound. He stepped forward, aiming his foot at the spot where he had grounded the spear.

He felt nothing unusual at all. It was almost a disappointment. One moment, he was in the brightness of the chamber and, the next, he was surrounded by darkness.

He reached for the scanner, still attached to the spear, and switched on its torch. The beam hardly penetrated the darkness, but he could see the red rock walls of a cavern – very different from the chamber he'd just left. A cavern that shouldn't be here.

Part 7. Amber

19.

Amber smoothed her jacket, trying to remove a stubborn wrinkle. She didn't normally pay much attention to her dress, other than make sure it was appropriate to the culture she was studying. She had considered wearing one of the outfits Bayl's sister had helped her buy, one that would show her as a lady of station in Enodia. But she decided it was best to be who she really was – an academic from a scientifically advanced world – and hope this would give the air of authority she needed.

She smoothed her jacket again, folded her arms. Why was she so nervous? She'd had audiences with rulers many times before, some more grand than King Zandis. But this was potentially far more serious than any of her previous encounters. She was convinced something significant was happening, that an ancient ruler, this self-styled King Arthur, was sending a message across hundreds of years. Given the company he kept, it could be something of genuine importance.

Why was Bayl taking so long? He had been more nervous about this audience than her. Of course, he had good reason. He was about to ask his monarch for permission to exhume the remains of the first – and most illustrious – King of Enodia. Hardly a request to win immediate favour, particularly since their case was built on circumstantial evidence.

She paced the ornate antechamber, still trying to smooth out her jacket. Then she saw Bayl striding down the corridor towards her.

"I had to call in a few favours," he said, "but the King has granted us a ten-minute audience before he leaves on a hunting trip."

Amber rolled her eyes. "A hunting trip? Doesn't he realise how important this could be?"

"Of course he doesn't," Bayl said, "which makes it all the more remarkable he's agreed to see you at all at such short notice."

They walked back up the corridor towards the audience chamber.

"Now, do you remember the protocols for meeting the King?" Bayl said.

"Yes," she said. "Don't fuss about it. I'm not going to deliberately antagonise him, am I? And I'm sure I'll be granted some leeway since I'm a stranger."

Two courtiers were guarding the carved wooden doors leading to the King's rooms. As Bayl and Amber approached, they stood aside and opened them.

Amber paused to take in the scene. A polished wooden floor stretched before them with a broad red carpet leading up its centre to a raised dais. Life-size statues of past kings lined each side of the room, interspersed by wide purple drapes reaching from the high ceiling all the way to the floor. It was clearly designed to impress and, Amber admitted, it did a very effective job.

At the far end of the room, on the dais, two golden thrones were flanked by armed guards in ceremonial uniforms. King Zandis sat, wearing embroidered riding leathers, reading a paper. As they approached, he looked up and handed the paper to a richly dressed man by his side. Bayl stopped short of the dais and performed a well-practised bow. Amber followed with a clumsy attempt at a curtsey she knew looked ridiculous with her wearing trousers.

"Miss Stefans," the King said, "it is a pleasure to meet you at last."

"Thank you, Your Majesty."

The King gestured to the man by his side. "This is Duke Edrik. He has been intrigued by your work and requested to join us."

Amber nodded towards the man. "Your Grace."

He responded with a thin smile.

"Groms has been keeping us informed of your progress," King Zandis continued. "Some of what we've heard has been quite unexpected. We had not seen much importance in the nature of your study, but we have already learnt surprising things about our past. You are convinced that our nation was founded with the help of men from this world called Sattoria?"

"Yes, Your Majesty. There is no absolute proof of it, as yet, but it's too much of a coincidence for it not to be the case. The arrival of a spaceship would have been of great significance seven hundred years ago. Given that kingdom was founded by King Arthur during the same time period, I can't see how the two events are unrelated."

"And you have found something important? What is so serious that you ask an audience of us at such short notice?"

"Your Majesty," Amber said, "we have uncovered evidence that the prophecy of the eclipse may be genuine and that Enodia may be in danger."

"Danger, you say? We must admit having been unnerved by the events of Founder's Day. But that was over a month ago and there has been nothing since that would suggest that the rest of the prophecy is coming true."

"I understand, Your Majesty, but the Sattorians could have predicted the date of the eclipse. Consequently, I believe something more is going on. Last night, a member of the Guardians was caught trying to break into King Arthur's tomb. Again, this can be no coincidence."

"The Guardians are moving openly?" Zandis said. "How can that be? There has been no reliable evidence of them for centuries. Is this true, Groms?"

"Yes, Majesty," Bayl said. "Without a doubt. Professor Stefans and I interrogated the man ourselves."

"This is the reason for your requesting an audience?"

"It is, Your Majesty," Amber said. "In our interrogation, we learned they too had a prophecy related to the recent eclipse. It appears they do not have the full detail of what is to happen next but, for seven hundred years, they have been waiting to find the answer. And that answer, I believe, lies within the tomb of King Arthur."

"You give us pause for thought, Miss Stefans. Are you asking us for permission to open the tomb of Enodia's first monarch? Groms, what do you have to say?"

"Sire, I know the request we are making seems shocking to you. If I had not witnessed the events of the past few days with my own eyes, I would share your indignation.

"But I have stood within a fallen skyship from this distant world, a ship that Sattorian records show comes from the days of King Arthur himself. I have seen instruments in Professor Stefans's possession that can predict the movement of the stars and planets centuries in advance. The Sattorians would most certainly have been known to Arthur and they could have given the information needed to make an accurate prophecy.

"Although I do not know what, something is about to happen that will put Enodia in great danger from a threat we know nothing about. The prophecy that has been known to us down through the centuries gives us only vague information. We need to know more in order to defend ourselves.

"Your Majesty, we have to open the tomb in order to defend our world."

The king looked down, then stared at the ceiling. He shook his head. "What do you expect to find?"

"We don't know, Your Majesty," Bayl said. "We do know it will be what Arthur feels we need to deal with the impending crisis."

"What you ask, Miss Stefans," the king said, "is no small thing." He stared at her, then turned to the duke. "Edrik?"

"Your Majesty, we seem to have the choice between definite sacrilege and a possible destruction of the Kingdom."

"We could have worked that out for ourselves, Edrik," the King replied. "We asked for your advice, not a statement of the obvious."

"Of course, your Majesty," Edrik said, bowing, "but sometimes an open stating of a problem can clarify the choices. While the proposal is repugnant, it is the prudent course."

"History," the king sighed, "will not judge us kindly if we make the wrong decision today. There is a possibility of the destruction of our kingdom from a threat that has been known about for hundreds of years. We must not allow that to happen. You may open the tomb, Miss Stefans. But it must be done with all possible discretion."

"Your Majesty," Duke Edrik said. "Might I suggest this task be performed by those whose loyalty to you is beyond question and not entrusted to an Off Worlder. I would consider it an honour to supervise it myself – "

"Miss Stefans has shown great diligence in bringing this matter to our attention, Edrik. We would have been unaware of it were it not for her efforts. We may need her knowledge to comprehend whatever is found within the tomb. We accept we need a closer representative involved, however. You may assist her. You will ensure she can perform her task. You have our authority in this."

"As you will, Your Majesty," the duke said, bowing.

"You," the king said to Bayl and Amber, "have your request."

"Thank you, Your Majesty," Amber said.

"You shall make every possible effort not to damage the tomb. We want it to look exactly as it did once you have finished. We expect a detailed report the minute it is opened."

"Of course," Bayl said.

"Oh, and Groms… You had better be right about this. If history judges us to be a tomb robber, you can guarantee that your own judgment will be more immediate."

"I understand, Majesty."

The king turned to Duke Edrik. "We may be living in dark times. Have this Guardian interrogated. We want to know who these people are and what they intend to do. Go and do what must be done."

"Your Majesty," Edrik said, bowing. "Groms, we will meet at the Mausoleum at noon."

20.

For the second time that day, Amber approached the Mausoleum in Founder's Square. This time, the extra guards and commotion at the gates were attracting attention. A small crowd had gathered in the square. A murmur broke out as she and Bayl were spotted. Although this would not prevent speculation about her connection with the prophecy, there was nothing she could do about it.

The crowd unnerved her. Although it was only natural for rumours to fly and people to come to see for themselves, Guardians on the scene changed everything. What had started out as a treasure trail for Bayl and Amber had now drawn a different set of hunters, ones whose motivations were unclear. It was reasonable to assume they were trying to avert the impending crisis – as she and Bayl were – but how would they react to being denied access to the tomb, especially with one of their number in custody?

Amber scanned the crowd, looking for hostile faces. It was a pointless exercise. If there were a Guardian in the crowd, he wouldn't show himself. He would watch from a safe distance. Anyway, there were too many faces. They would just have to wait for their next move.

As they neared the gates, a two-horsed carriage rolled up and pulled to a stop. A uniformed footman opened the door and Duke Edrik stepped out.

He nodded to them, before leading them towards the gates.

At the sight of the duke, the guards immediately stepped aside and they passed through.

"Professor Stefans," Duke Edrik said, "do you have a guess as to what we'll find?"

"The most literal interpretation of Arthur rising," she said, "would mean his cryogenically frozen body, which we would unfreeze and revive."

"You're not serious!" Bayl said, stopping dead in his tracks. "Can such a thing be done?"

"Yes, it could be done," Amber said, "but no, I'm not serious. That was only ever an experimental technology, even before the Fall. We don't have the capability now and I would seriously doubt the Sattorians from the Searcher would have either. No, what I'm hoping for is an explanation of the prophecy, what the threat is and what we can do about it."

They continued walking.

After a pause, Bayl said, "we are working on the assumption we are piecing together a puzzle Arthur left for us. That he planned a set of events that would be necessary to achieve success. From what we've seen, the Guardians might be part of those events, with their own instructions to guide them. Perhaps they were meant to open the tomb? What if we have pushed events on to a different course?"

"There is no way to know for sure, Mr Groms," Duke Edrik said. "What's done is done. If the tomb must be opened, then we are now the ones to do it."

"And in any case," Amber said, "we have a member of the Guardians in custody. We have a chance of finding out more through him."

They reached the central chamber from which the tombs radiated. The gate to the room containing Arthur and his queen remained open. As they neared it, Amber could see several craftsmen were completing a wooden hoist that would be used to raise the stone lid of the coffin. Two other men were slowly circling it, carefully tapping at the cement that sealed the lid to the coffin, trying to cause as little damage as possible. Other than the sounds of the tools, the work was being carried on in silence.

After a few minutes, the craftsmen finished their work. Thick leather straps that would form a cradle were looped underneath the protruding edges at either end of the lid. Using the hoist with three men on each of the four ropes at the corners, one end and then the other was raised so other straps could be secured safely under the lid. It took only a few minutes and then all was ready. The craftsmen stood back and waited in silence.

Amber reached out and touched Bayl on the arm. He was staring at the lid, deep in thought, but, at her touch, he turned towards her. He nodded and then turned to the men.

"Get ready to lift," he said. "What we do is necessary for the safety of Enodia. It is what Arthur himself knew would happen, what he arranged to happen. Do not harbour doubts about the rights of it. Let us treat his tomb with all the reverence we can. When I give the order, lift slowly and steadily from all four corners." He took a few deep breaths and then called, "Lift!"

As the twelve men took the strain, they pulled with all their strength and the lid slowly began to rise, Bayl organising them, making each group hold or pull so the lid stayed level.

Soon it had raised almost half a metre.

Bayl called a halt and looked inside the coffin. Edrik and Amber moved closer. A second, plain stone coffin was within.

The lid was lifted a full metre above the outer coffin and tied off. Two of the straps were threaded underneath and reattached to the hoist to get to the inner coffin. Getting the straps secured under the inner lid took more effort due to the cramped conditions. The lid was much lighter than its more ornate companion, though, and it was accomplished without fuss. Again, a silence descended upon the men and then Bayl ordered them to lift. The lid was raised at a steady pace.

As Bayl had to concentrate on keeping the lid level, it was Amber and Edrik who got the first proper sight of the coffin's contents.

Both gasped at what they saw. If there had been any doubt in Amber's mind about the Sattorian influence upon Arthur it was now totally dispelled.

"Then it is all true," Edrik said.

A figure lay within, dressed in battle armour. Amber knew research would show it to be that worn by the Sattorian Navy seven hundred years ago.

The inner lid was raised until it hung just below the outer, then it was tied in place allowing all present to get a better view.

Moving in again, Amber could see the skull of the king within the opened helmet of the battle armour. A laser rifle lay cradled in his hands across his chest. Several objects rested at his side: a hand-computer, some power cells and a small storage box. There was also a stone tablet with engravings on it and a smoothed, palm-sized pebble made of a lustrous silvery metal.

"I think your career is safe, Bayl."

He didn't reply. He was reaching out to touch something up by the helmet of the armour.

"Bayl?"

He reached within the helmet, pulled out a metal disk and chain and examined it.

"There's something written here," he said. "I think it's a name."

Amber took a step towards him and read:

Lieutenant Yorvin Bandrell
Sattorian Navy

The Enodia Enigma

Part 8. Yorvin

21.

As Yorvin stepped backwards, the darkness gave way to the light of the chamber. The wall of absolute blackness was, once again, in front of him.

"How do you feel, sir?" Cobannis said.

Yorvin looked at his hands and body. "Absolutely fine. As if nothing happened at all."

Cobannis scanned him and confirmed he was right.

"Let's take a proper look, shall we?" he said.

He stepped forward again into the darkness, lit only by his torch and those of his companions. Turning, he saw the same sheet of black behind him. It had to be a transportation device, but to where? And why wasn't this side protected by the same kind of force field?

Due to the low light, it was difficult to make out the features of the new chamber. It improved as Prason and Rowan distributed glow-pebbles, small but effective diffuse light sources that could last for a month or more. The cavern was formed from natural rock, about half the size of the chamber they had left. Yorvin did a visual sweep of the place. There was no way out.

"Do you have any more idea what's going on than I do?" he asked Cobannis.

"I doubt it, sir. I don't need the scanner to work out that this must be a doorway between two locations. I didn't know this was possible. There've been no reports of any technology or natural phenomenon that could do this, even pre-Fall. Nothing that could effectively teleport matter. And yet it's happened."

"Any idea where we are, then?"

Cobannis shook her head. "None whatsoever, sir. We're probably not close to the other end. The rock formations are very different here and there's enough rock to block the scanner's radio signal. We could be ten kilometres away or even a thousand, and we wouldn't know any differently."

"Do you have anything at all for me?"

"A couple of things," she said. "First, this cavern isn't natural, despite its appearance. It's been blasted and cleared. Also, there's an exit over there." Cobannis pointed to a part of the wall covered in rubble. "It's a collapsed tunnel. Difficult to say whether it's deliberate or a natural fall but, if there's a way out, that's it."

"Looks like we have some work ahead of us," he said. "Good thing we have the marines."

* * * * *

Yorvin had claimed it wasn't magic. But Sharna had stepped through a black curtain into a cavern she knew was not there. It wasn't natural. Either this was magic, or the word Yorvin had used meant the same thing.

Dornis was sitting cross-legged near the curtain watching the strangers as they investigated a portion of the wall covered with rubble.

"Perhaps you were right to heal the young woman after all," he smiled. "The sorcerers have great power. Since I was a boy, I have wanted to know what lies within this building. Now I am here inside it because of them."

"I am sorry that I went against your word, Dornis."

"I'm sure you are," he said, "but I wonder if you understand the effects of what you did."

"Cobannis was dying. I had to act or it would have been too late."

"That's true," Dornis said, "but remember, I will not remain Chieftain long if I am seen as weak. If I am challenged and overcome because I allowed a woman to defy me, you can be sure the new

Chieftain will not be as tolerant. If it had been anyone else, I would have had no choice but to punish them."

"I'm sorry, Chieftain," she whispered, bowing her head. "I will remember." She looked him straight in the eye. "Of course, Dornis, it will be much easier if you – "

"Make the right decisions," the Chieftain said. "Yes, I know. I'll try to bear that in mind." He smiled. "Now, to other matters. What has happened to us?"

"Yorvin uses another word for it," she said. "Technology. But we know it as the Old Magic, the same that made your robes and the Aydoc. The black curtain has taken us to another place. I have no idea where we are and, from the looks of it, neither do Yorvin and the other sorcerers."

"Yorvin?"

"Yes, he said his friends use that name for him. It seems wasteful to have three names when one is enough."

"Be careful, Sharna. We know little of these people. They seem to be our friends but we do not know for sure. None of the other sorcerers address him by that name, so he is giving you a high honour in a short time. He may have other intentions."

"He has a wife and children of his own. He would hardly have told me about them if he looked upon me in that way."

Dornis ran a hand through his beard. "As I said, we know little of these people. We cannot know their intentions."

She watched Yorvin working away at the rubble. Dornis was wrong.

* * * * *

Yorvin had to admit battle armour was a wonderful thing. If they had tried to clear the roof fall by human strength alone, it would have taken weeks. The enhanced strength Prason and Rowan gained from

153

the power-assisted armour, however, gave them superhuman abilities. He watched as they lifted a boulder more than the size of a man and carried it a few metres to where a new pile of rubble was accumulating.

It was still going to take a few hours, though. Cobannis reckoned the passageway was blocked for about five metres. With the risk of further falls from the ceiling, the extra care needed would slow the process.

After a while, all but Sharna had joined in the task under Cobannis's direction. The roof held and, after about three hours, the passageway was clear enough for them to walk through. Beyond, the corridor continued, straight and rising steadily.

Yorvin instructed the two marines to take the lead, with the rest ten paces behind. The walls had the same smoothness as in the first chamber, meaning this tunnel was man made. They had been walking for two minutes when the walls became irregular and the passage widened out into a natural cavern.

Cobannis indicated to the left.

"We're not far from the exit."

It wasn't long before they saw a soft glow of light from a thousand stars in the night sky.

"It should be late afternoon, sir. We must have travelled some distance."

Hurrying to the entrance, Yorvin gasped. The cave entrance was on a hillside with more hills stretching away over a vast plain and into the distance. Halfway across to the horizon, a grid of lights shone over what looked like a town. They did not flicker. It took Yorvin only a few seconds to see they were streetlamps. This settlement was far more advanced than the Corini – they might be able to help repair the Searcher.

"Cobannis," he said. "I'd like an idea of where we are. And as quickly as you can."

"Yes, sir," she said, setting to work with her scanner.

"Prason, do a sweep of the area. We need to make sure there are no surprises."

With a nod from the sergeant, the marines disappeared off into the night.

Sitting at the mouth of the cave, Yorvin gazed down at the town.

Dornis sat next to him. "What manner of magic is this, Bandrell? How can it be night?"

"The black wall must have transported us a large distance, Chieftain. Different parts of your planet have day and night at different times. We might be on the opposite side of the world."

"The *opposite side* of the world?"

For a moment, Yorvin was at a loss. Could a people forget so much knowledge in the space of a few centuries?

"It is complex, Chieftain. We don't understand this all ourselves, yet. It means we're a long way from the village."

Cobannis drew near. "Sir, may I have a word in private?"

Yorvin pulled himself up and walked a few paces with her. "What is it?" he said.

"We're not on Enodia anymore."

"What?"

"There's no point on the surface of Enodia that would have this pattern of stars. We can no longer be on the planet."

Yorvin ran a hand through his hair. "That means we must have travelled light years in a split second. Is that possible?"

"The facts are there, sir."

"Do you know where we are?"

Cobannis shook her head. "Not yet. I'll need to do the same analysis for every star system we want to check for. Obviously, I'll start with nearby systems and work outwards, but it'll take an average of a minute for each one. There are a hundred billion or so stars in the galaxy, so it would take around two centuries to do a complete scan. If we're in a nearby system, we'll know soon but, if we've travelled more than a few hundred light years, we might never be sure."

"And there's no guarantee we're even in the same galaxy," Yorvin said. "If we've definitely travelled light years, who's to say what limits there are?"

"I'll start the calculations running straight away, sir."

"Run them for systems near to Sattoria as well. You never know, we may have got lucky."

Prason and Rowan returned to the camp, reporting only small wildlife.

Yorvin set Prason to observe the settlement. She soon saw land vehicles on the town's roads. She reported later that she had even seen airborne craft in the skies – but she could get no more detail because of the distance.

A lot would depend on what sort of men inhabited this world. Yorvin's journey on the Searcher had taught him that goodwill was not always to be found in difficult times. The more people had, the more aggressively they defended it. As this civilisation clearly had a great deal, it would be tough going.

The only way to find out was to approach them – and that was best done in daylight. After ordering a rest period for everyone, he settled down at the cave entrance, gazing at their hope for a way home.

22.

This land felt wrong.

Adran watched as the dawning Sun brought light to the hills and the plain. The trees and other vegetation were types he had never seen before. The few animals he had observed were unfamiliar – small nervous creatures with loping gaits. It all added weight to Bandrell's claims that they were on the other side of the world, far from the village.

Though the daylight was growing, the lights of the village ahead still shone out as brightly as the stars. This village was far larger than any he had seen before, possibly as great as all the Corini villages put together. From the conversations between the sorcerers, this place was home to those who understood their magic. What wonders would such a great village possess?

Tobin sat close by, also looking down towards the plain.

"Well, we made it here," Adran said, "but I wasn't expecting anything like this."

"I thought there would be a hoard of gold or gems," Tobin said. "Still, this could turn out to be more interesting."

"I don't like this place," Adran said. "Everyone seems to have forgotten that the black wall was sealed up. This could be a dangerous place."

"You see danger everywhere," Tobin said. "Even when there isn't any."

"That's what you said before you were hit by the blue fire last autumn."

"Not fair! I saw the danger. I just wasn't as scared of it as you."

"Well, maybe you should be. If the people who made that fire sealed off the black wall, they must have been scared by something."

Chieftain Dornis, Sharna and the sorcerers had started to move now. As the sun drew clear of the horizon, shedding its full light across the plain, they began to pick their way down the hillside towards the village.

Bandrell ordered his two warriors to walk ahead of the main group, to left and right, and they soon descended to level ground. It was a barren place compared to the grasslands of his home. Isolated trees and sickly bushes were the only major vegetation.

About an hour later, Bandrell signalled for the group to halt. Adran could hear Rowan's voice coming from Bandrell's arm. The warrior must have seen something. Adran edged closer.

"Investigate," Bandrell was saying, "but do not make contact."

"Rowan, you heard the Lieutenant," Prason said. "Engage camouflage and take the right."

"Understood."

Looking ahead, Adran could see the two warriors- in their outlandish armour.

They moved forward and left towards some bushes and then, as he watched, they disappeared. He strained his eyes to see what had happened. Then he noticed disturbances in the air.

Now he saw them, they were easy to track. Adran realised that he had stopped breathing and let out a breath. Was there nothing that was beyond these men?

"Have they found something, Bandrell?" Chieftain Dornis said.

"They think they may have detected somebody, but they're not sure. We should know soon."

They waited.

"Sir, you're not going to believe this," Prason said in far from her usual monotone. "I've got visual on the target. It's not human."

"Does it look dangerous?" Bandrell said.

"No, sir, you don't understand. It's not an animal, but it's definitely not human either."

"Are you saying we've discovered aliens, Sergeant?"

"Affirmative, sir," Prason replied, "though I can't believe I'm saying it."

Yorvin took a moment to steady himself. It couldn't be true. It was more than ten thousand years since Man had reached beyond Earth and explored the systems close to Sol.

Like all on Sattoria, he had grown up learning the histories of that ancient expansion. How the first explorers had expected to find aliens scattered across the galaxy. They had found alien life in abundance – vegetation, simple animal life – but nothing that could be remotely termed 'alien' in the sense that the explorers had expected. Nothing that had developed a civilisation or made scientific advancement. For several thousand years, Man had accepted he was alone in the universe.

"Sir?" Prason said. "What are your orders?"

"I need to get a look at this, Sergeant," he replied. "Guide me in."

Yorvin started walking to the bushes into which the marines had disappeared, taking guidance from Prason, adjusting his direction.

He neared the cover of the bushes.

"Careful, sir," Prason said. "As little noise as possible from here."

He slowed down even more and stooped to a crouch. He moved as quietly as he could, hearing every sound he was making. There was a loud thumping. The sound of his own heartbeat.

"Three more paces, sir," Prason said, "and then stop. You're now ten paces in front of me."

He had forgotten how completely effective the stealth capabilities of the marines' battle armour was when the wearer was still. Something had caught his eye, nothing more than a minor disturbance in the colouring of one of the bushes. Prason informed him this was her, waving to attract his attention.

He crept towards the bush.

"Stop," she said. "Now look to your right."

Yorvin turned his head.

It was a large area of clear terrain through the branches. And a humanoid figure about a hundred metres away.

It was crouching, interested in something on the ground. It had larger, more powerful legs than any man had and a smaller body, arms and head. It stood and stretched.

Yorvin stifled a gasp. He was looking at an alien.

Its grey skin contrasted with blue and red on the torso and legs, which looked like clothing. But it was the alien's face that caught his attention. A reptilian set of features. Hairless. A protruding, rounded mouth.

"Sir, what's the plan?" Prason said.

"All right," he whispered, "I'm going to walk out and make contact with it. I'll leave a broadcast channel open. I want you and Rowan to monitor it. Keep me covered at all times. Don't intervene unless you absolutely have to. If I move off with it, then follow me and get the others to do likewise at a safe distance and out of sight."

"Understood, sir."

Yorvin shouldered his rifle, readied himself.

Prason raised her own rifle to the firing position.

He made his way through the last of the bushes. Pulling himself to his feet, Yorvin walked slowly and deliberately towards the alien.

It was still crouched, staring at something on the ground. When he got to about fifty metres, it still hadn't noticed him. He would have to attract its attention.

"Hello," he called, trying not to scare it.

Facing away from Yorvin, the alien's head lifted, sniffing at the air. It searched around and soon saw him. Keeping its slitted eyes fixed on him, it rose to its feet. It was the same height as Yorvin.

"Krishak!"

Yorvin held out his hands, palms showing, hoping it would be interpreted as peaceful.

"Hello," he called, pointing to himself. "I am Yorvin."

"Krishak! Oshha dez pirrin!"

Movement to the right caught his eye.

A second alien, similar to the first except for orange and white clothing, was running towards them faster than a man at a full sprint. "Gorva rees jaak," it called.

"Sir?" Prason's voice said from his comms link.

"Hold, sergeant," he whispered. "Last resort."

The second alien caught sight of Yorvin and, still some distance away, slowed to a walk. Like the first, it inspected him.

Then both approached to just a few paces away from him.

Yorvin pointed to himself again. "Yorvin."

The orange clothed alien looked to the first. They exchanged a few guttural sounding words.

Then the alien pointed to itself. "Krishak."

Yorvin smiled and nodded. The first alien had called for his friend. It had a name. He pointed towards the alien and repeated, "Krishak." The aliens exchanged some words, in a mixture of guttural sounds and high-pitched whistling.

The first alien stepped forward, pointing at itself. "Gorva."

Yorvin repeated the alien's name. Again, they whistled and chattered.

So far, so good.

Krishak had been the boldest, introducing himself first. Perhaps he held a higher station than Gorva. Turning to face Krishak, Yorvin tapped his own chest, then swept his arm outwards to point in the direction of the settlement.

"Krishak," he said, "I must go to your town."

Krishak and Gorva chattered back and forth, leaving Yorvin hopeful he had made himself understood. Then Krishak moved towards the settlement, beckoning him on.

"Yorvin, reesk," it said – and walked slowly away, still watching him.

The word he had used, 'reesk', must mean something like walk or come. Yorvin repeated it. "Reesk." Then he started to follow.

Krishak and Gorva stopped and stared at him. The now familiar whistling sound followed and they both began to talk to him at the same time.

He held up his hands. "Reesk," he said. "That's all I've got."

The two aliens settled down and they continued their journey. As they walked, Krishak and Gorva pointed at various objects and spoke a word. Yorvin repeated each as they said them, but he couldn't retain more than a few. It was encouraging, though, as it suggested the aliens were open to newcomers – and that meant they might be willing to help.

After half an hour, the settlement came into view. It was a jumble of rounded, clay-coloured structures. Aside from an architecture which favoured curves over edges, the buildings had the properties of a medium-sized town on Sattoria. There were smaller buildings at the edges, probably residential, and a core of taller buildings in the centre.

Krishak was leading the way – but rather than head for the centre, he was veering off to the left, aiming for the lower buildings.

It wasn't much longer before it became clear they were headed for one building in particular. It was an unremarkable single-storey structure, right on the edge of the settlement. This didn't feel right. Why was he being brought here?

Ten metres from it, Krishak halted and Gorva stood beside Yorvin. Krishak went ahead. As he got closer to it, Yorvin saw how big the building was. Now that Krishak was standing by the door, he saw the alien was only a little over half its size.

Yorvin deduced why at the exact moment events made it obvious. Krishak came back leading another alien by the hand. This one was more than eight feet tall. Krishak and Gorva were children and Yorvin was the stray animal they had found and brought home.

What followed came as no surprise. Yorvin pictured what he or Jan – or any other human parent – would have done. He watched in despair as it played out before him.

On catching sight of him, the larger alien emitted a high-pitched screech.   "Rok   Gorva!"

23.

Gorva shifted on his feet looking from his parent to Yorvin and back again.

"Akkan dez pirrin."

Yorvin could only guess at what the words meant but it sounded like a disagreement that a child was unlikely to win. Then other aliens emerged from nearby buildings. A small audience was going to develop. Things were spiralling out of control.

"Rok Gorva bak! Pak koora dez ash!"

Gorva looked at Yorvin and backed away.

"Rok!" the shout came again, but now from Krishak.

Time to leave. Yorvin held his arms up, hands at shoulder height, showing his palms. One of the gathering group came closer, pointing at him with what was probably a weapon.

Yorvin continued to back away, now focused on this new threat.

"No need for any trouble, I'm leaving," he said, although he knew it wouldn't be understood.

The crowd was stirring up, the words 'pak koora' repeated on the lips of many of the aliens.

Then there was a loud clap.

Suddenly, he was on his back, looking up at the sky, a sharp pain in his stomach. He raised his head to look at his abdomen and was relieved to see that, while his Civ Armour was marked, it hadn't been breached. It had saved his life.

The alien with the weapon approached and took careful aim at his head. Yorvin touched his comms link. "Now would be good, Prason."

"Already on it, sir," Prason said through the communicator. Two bolts of blue energy struck the alien's torso and it slumped to the ground. "We decided you were running out of diplomatic options."

The crowd backed away. As Yorvin got to his feet, two human shapes disturbed the air, moved past him and stopped. Switching out of stealth mode, they materialised into the two marines.

The crowd broke and ran in all directions. Krishak and his parent disappeared into the building, closely followed by Gorva, who stopped at the door, looked back at Yorvin, and then was gone.

"Recommend we get out of here, sir," Prason said, weapon still readied and trained on the fleeing aliens.

"Agreed. We should get back to the portal."

Opening a line on his comms link, he contacted the rest of the group. "Cobannis, things have gone badly here. Get back to the cave and wait for us there. I'm sending Rowan over to escort you."

"Understood, sir."

"I'll get them back safe, sir," Rowan said. He turned, making off at a sprint he could maintain all day with the assistance of his armour.

"I could do with one of those suits myself, Prason," Yorvin said.

"The first few attempts to run in armour are not pretty to watch, sir," she smiled. "Amusing, but not pretty."

"We'd best get going," he said, setting off at a steady jog. "Those things can run faster than me. And they'll probably have vehicles as well. We're going to need some luck."

"If our luck runs out, we've still got some firepower."

"I hope it doesn't come to that," he said. "We've probably lost any chance of aid here already. A fire-fight would remove any remaining hopes."

* * * * *

"We have to get back to the cave right away," Cobannis said.

"What has happened?" Sharna said. "Is Yorvin all right?"

"The Lieutenant didn't mention any casualties. He said we need to go back."

Sharna wanted to race towards the settlement to make sure he was unharmed. The strength of her feelings surprised her. Yorvin was kind and gentle in a way that she had not seen in any Corini man, and yet he was not weak – his people followed him without question. But he had a woman and daughters. She must put such thoughts aside.

Sharna hurried after Dornis and the others, breaking into a run to keep up with them. They all seemed to be coping with it well enough, but she doubted that she would make it all the way to the cave without resting.

They had been running for a short while when one of Yorvin's warriors – Rowan, judging from his height – caught up with them. He was sprinting and Sharna marvelled at the man's stamina, that he could have run at such a speed for any length of time. He slowed and joined the group.

As they passed through the dry, dusty terrain, the hills ahead drew closer.

Sharna was struggling with the continued exertion, her lungs burning from the effort of breathing, her legs growing weak. Even though she concentrated on the ground ahead of her, trying to put one foot in front of the other, she could barely keep up.

Adran dropped back to run beside her

"Thank you," she spluttered.

A distant rumble was growing behind them.

She glanced back but saw nothing.

It continued to grow until it became a wall of enveloping noise. A dark shape screamed overhead and sped away.

Cobannis pulled one of her devices from her belt and tracked it.

"Move to the bushes!" Rowan shouted, veering to the left, making for one of the larger clumps of vegetation. Sharna and the others followed, hiding as best they could.

"Lieutenant Bandrell says to wait here until they reach us," Rowan called out.

The noise from the dark flying shape faded until it was nothing more than a faint hum.

"What was that?" Dornis said. "A ship like your own?"

"No," Cobannis said, "it's an atmospheric flyer, not able to leave this world. It's designed for air combat, but it will have been sent to locate us."

"Can it harm us?"

"Very easily," Cobannis nodded. "It'll have weaponry meant for other flyers or ground vehicles, but it's very effective against personnel too."

The noise began to grow again.

"This could be an attack run," Rowan said. "Everybody stay where you are. I'll draw his attention."

Getting to his feet, he ran into the open, looking up at the approaching flyer. Dropping to a crouch, he watched and waited as the roar of the plane grew louder. As it neared its peak, Sharna heard a new sound; a thudding noise quickly repeating itself and merging into one. A split second later, Rowan was airborne, springing upwards and sideways, twisting in mid-air to land ten paces to the side and facing in the opposite direction.

As he landed, two rows of small explosions of dirt raced through where he had been. The flyer screamed overhead once again. Rowan aimed his weapon and fired a dozen firebolts upwards one after another, chasing after it. Sharna couldn't see whether the fire had hit its target. But, because Rowan moved back to his previous position and crouched again, she assumed it had not.

The sound of the flyer faded once more.

Sharna saw Yorvin and Prason over at the next clump of bushes taking up firing positions, adjusting their weapons and waiting.

The low rumble returned, again growing in intensity. This time, Rowan reacted earlier, aiming upwards and firing his weapon. However, instead of several bolts of fire, the weapon shot out a continuous stream of intense light – as it had done at the clearing.

Yorvin and Prason also fired streams of light and, looking upwards, Sharna saw they had crossed each other in front of the flyer. An instant later, it passed through the fire with a shower of sparks, debris falling from the flyer as it sped past them with a loud roar.

Yorvin was already on his feet. "We have to get out of here, now. Everybody to the cave!"

A loud explosion erupted from where the flyer had gone. A large ball of fire rose in the distance.

They started to run. The encounter had given her energy and she ran with renewed vigour. They reached the base of the hills. Soon they were climbing steadily. Sharna knew she was holding the group up and cursed the weakness of her frame, but she gained comfort from seeing Cobannis struggle as much as her.

A few hundred paces from the cave, Prason shouted, "Sir, we have two more incoming targets – airborne."

Sharna's heart sank. Apart from the cave, there was nowhere to hide. She pushed herself harder.

Ahead of her, Yorvin halted, brought a twin-barreled device up to cover his eyes and stood a moment. As she was passing him, he turned and started running again.

"They're moving a lot slower," he called out, "and they're still a way off. They're probably troop carriers. It's no reason to slow down."

Sharna saw two dark objects in the air, still small in the distance. By the time she reached the cave entrance, they were closer. They would soon land.

Prason and Rowan stopped at the entrance.

Yorvin halted next to them. "Get back through the portal, Cobannis. I want that force-field activated the second we're all safely through."

"Sir, you should go as well," Prason said. "Rowan and I will be all right, but if they have anything resembling heavy weaponry, your armour will be useless."

"All right, Sergeant," he said. "Buy us two minutes if you can and then get out of here."

"You've got it, sir. Just have that force-field ready."

Then Yorvin was racing into the cave with the rest of them. To avoid falling, they had to go more carefully in the natural part. But once in the smooth walled tunnel, they could run once more. Behind them, Sharna heard the now familiar sound of Prason and Rowan's weapons as well as the rapid thumping sounds of the creatures' own in response. As they neared the cavern, she heard, from far behind, an enormous explosion.

Once again, the black curtain stood before them. This time, and without their earlier caution, they raced straight through it.

Back in the chamber on the other side, Sharna continued for another twenty paces before she, Dornis and the boys – breathing heavily – dropped to the ground.

As the noise of the weapons stopped, Yorvin and Cobannis carried on into the side room where they had discovered how to make the wall of light disappear.

Then the two warriors came running through the curtain, Rowan shouting, "Grenade!"

In an instant, a shimmering wall of light hid the black curtain. A moment later, a huge section of it flared brightly, then dimmed.

They were safe.

Part 9. Amber

24.

As the Duke's carriage drew to a halt, Doctor Fryer climbed quickly in.

Edrik's satisfied smile told him immediately that the trip to the Mausoleum had been successful. The smile faded as the duke looked over Fryer's clothing. "You could have made more of an effort to blend in."

"Your Grace," Fryer said. "This is the oldest and most worn clothing I possess. In any case, look at me. I would never pass as a labourer to any but the most casual of inspections. I couldn't affect the roughness of manner."

"Then you'll need to stay in the background. I don't want the King or that Stefans woman to know you've examined the artefacts from the tomb."

"Would it not be simpler to reveal our mission to the King? I have no doubts he would assist our cause."

Edrik rubbed his brow. "Fryer, you have to accept my judgement in this. We have the necessary resources and these artefacts will give us the location of the portal. We have no need of Zandis. By doing this on our own, we will emphasise his weakness, and circumstances will be ripe for us to assume power. Only then can Enodia progress in the way we must, the way Arthur intended."

The carriage rolled through the streets of Denford and was waved through into the Palace grounds. Fryer had sat back, upright, ensuring he would be no more than a shadow if the guardsman saw him. He didn't like the idea of such subterfuge, but His Grace was insistent. The Duke was risking much with his strategy but Fryer had to admit he may be right. Although events had conspired against them, in another hour the plan would be on track once more.

The Duke's men were already unloading the artefacts from a cart and taking them into one of the outer wings of the palace. As Edrik left the carriage, he waved him to join the labourers.

Fryer reached the back of the cart and looked for something to carry. He recognised the case containing the storage device, the one that would reveal the portal and the labour for which he had been preparing himself all these years. He took it into his arms and carried it into the palace building. A door on the left led to a workshop which the Duke had commandeered for the safe keeping of the items. Fryer placed the box on a table in the centre of the room and surveyed the items already there. There was a second storage device, like the one he expected to find in the box, and a handful of grey, dull, rectangular objects, with three metallic strips at one edge. A sparsely engraved stone tablet completed the set. Two of the Duke's men came into the room, one carrying the palm-sized object resembling a pebble, the other holding the musket that had been placed across Arthur's body.

The Duke stood beside Fryer. "Well?"

"It's the box that is of interest to us, Your Grace."

The clasp resisted his first efforts to open it. Very gently, he increased the pressure until it gave way. He lifted the lid. The box was filled to the brim with small, thumb-sized pieces of a soft material – which was as the ancient documents had promised. He pushed the top layers to one side and found the object he sought. It was identical to the other already on the table – a rectangular box the size of his hand. Mostly smooth, one of the two larger sides had some buttons at one edge.

"This is what you expected?" the Duke said.

"Exactly, Your Grace."

Fryer placed a finger on two of the buttons. The area above the buttons sprang to life with a glow of light which coalesced into the writing and images illustrated in the documents. He touched the portion of the screen containing an image.

Fryer held the storage device flat while they waited the few seconds for it to perform its task. Then the lit portion became a large black arrow on a white background. which rotated like an ordinary compass would.

"And there we have it," Fryer said. "That is the direction to the portal."

"How far?"

"We are not told. That would have tempted us to seek it out too early. We know it is a few tens of kilometres."

"Then we must hasten our efforts. Fryer, you must take this device and complete the preparations for the expedition. You must leave now, before the Off Worlder and Groms arrive. Without this, they will not be able to follow?"

"No, Your Grace. This is the means to locate the portal."

"Then it is fortunate indeed that the device worked so well after such a length of time."

Fryer pressed another button on the device causing the light to dim and fade completely. He reached to put it back into the box.

"No, Fryer. Stefans has already seen the box. That has to stay. Take just the device."

Fryer slipped the artefact into his jacket pocket.

"The protective material should be disposed of too, Your Grace. It would seem odd to have a box prepared for valuable contents with nothing inside."

"True enough," Edrik said. "I shall see it is attended to. Now, go. There should be a second carriage ready for you by now."

Fryer inclined his head and left. The carriage was waiting for him, which he directed to take him to the Duke's estate. There was still much work to do, of course, but he knew he could deliver.

25.

Bayl helped Amber from the carriage and made his way across the courtyard to the wing of the palace which now stored the artefacts.

He watched her striding in front of him, hardly believing what they were about to do.

Events had turned his world on its head. Here he was, about to examine objects found inside the tomb of King Arthur himself – Arthur, a man from another world, who had taken control of Enodia to warn of impending trouble. Ever since that first spaceship had landed near Denford a year ago, the knocks to Bayl's most basic beliefs had been unrelenting. And things had only accelerated after Amber's arrival and the eclipse. Amber had put a more human face to it, and so, here he was, accepting it all without question.

They found the Duke in a workshop close by the entrance.

"Your Grace."

"Miss Stefans, Groms," Edrik smiled. "I can see you are eager to make a start. As am I."

The objects from the tomb were spread out on a large table. Amber took her scanner from its pouch on her belt and examined each object in turn.

Bayl was drawn to the silver coloured box. "Would it be all right for me to open this."

"As long as you're careful and don't use any force on it."

A single clasp held it shut and Bayl lifted it. Duke Edrik and Amber moved closer as Bayl raised the lid. It was empty.

"Why would they place an empty box in the tomb?"

"You'd be surprised what gets chosen to accompany a burial," Amber said.

"Could the box have any intrinsic value of its own?" Edrik said, pulling back.

"It's possible, but it seems ordinary enough. It's metal, probably aluminium."

As Bayl surveyed the other objects, Amber resumed her own examinations. It was obvious what the armour and weapon were for, even if they were of unfamiliar design. It was common for the kings of old to be buried with them. Amongst the other finds were a collection of small, smooth, rectangular objects.

Bayl picked one up. "What are these?"

"Power cells," Amber said, "used in electrical devices. I've got some myself. I'll check their levels in a moment but they're most likely drained after all this time."

That left four other objects.

The first was similar to a device Amber often carried, an information storage device and analysis tool she called "a computer". She tried to switch it on, but it didn't respond. Turning the device over, she opened a panel on the reverse side, taking a power cell out. She fitted one of her own, pulled from a pocket, and replaced the panel. Still, the computer didn't respond.

"Oh," she sighed.

"Can it be repaired?" Duke Edrik said.

"I'm not an expert on this. I'll have to consult my database back at the inn to even know where to start."

The other three objects were a mystery: a stone tablet with a wavy line and two crosses carved into it; a hand-sized pebble made of a silvery metal with no discernible features; and a cylinder with a small display panel and several buttons.

"I've scanned and recorded images of everything," she said, "but there's little more I can do here. I need to continue back at the inn. I'd like to take the computer with me, Your Grace, if that is acceptable?"

"Is that really necessary? I am reluctant to allow these artefacts to be split up. They are our heritage after all."

"I understand," Amber said, "but I will take great care of it and, since it is apparently broken, there's little harm I can do to it."

"I suppose you are right, but I'd like a report of any news as soon as you have it."

"Of course, Your Grace."

* * * * *

It was after midnight.

As Bayl watched, Amber worked at the recovered computer with a thin dagger-like instrument. After a few minutes, she pulled back and slapped the tool down.

"It's no use. I can't do this. I was stupid to think I might be able to." She held the computer in her hands, turning it over as she spoke. "Just think what information could be on this thing. It might have explained everything to us in a moment." She put it down and wiped her brow.

"Perhaps we should start again in the morning," Bayl said. He wasn't really ready to give up, but Amber needed some rest.

"We can at least try to identify those other two objects before we stop," she said, turning to her computer, pulling up their images, keying in commands. "It'll look for anything in the database that matches them. It should only take a few minutes."

Before long, a dozen or so pictures resembling the pebble-shaped object came up. After quickly discarding the majority, they were soon left with one image and some text below it.

Bayl read the first line. "An AutoDoc. A healing device?"

"So it seems," Amber said, scanning down the rest of the text. "That's odd… This is hundreds of years older than the Sattorians. What would it be doing here?"

"What about the cylinder?"

Again, the initial matches were quickly whittled down to one, which was given the prominent position on the display.

Bayl read the beginning of the accompanying text.

"What is it Amber? What's a nuclear warhead? Some kind of weapon?"

She nodded, her face white.

"One of the most devastating known. That cylinder is amongst the smallest but it could destroy a large portion of the city if it exploded. You'd need to be over two kilometres away to be safe."

"Is it dangerous to us?"

Amber read the text.

"No, it would have to be activated. And that would need a code. That's if it's even functional at all. It's a strange thing to leave in a tomb, though."

"It might be better if we don't mention this to anybody," Bayl said. "There are some in the government who would regard such a weapon as very desirable."

"Sadly, that's always been the case. These weapons have been banned from use on planets for most of history, but there are still worlds that have been made unfit to live on because of them."

"It seems we have reached an impasse, Amber. Perhaps we should get some sleep and try again in the morning?"

Amber nodded, switching off her computer.

* * * * *

After rising late, Amber breakfasted and settled at her desk. As she tried one more time to repair the broken terminal, heavy footsteps thumped on the stairs, followed by loud bashing at her door.

"Who is it?"

"Amber," Bayl called, "I think I have the answer."

She opened the door.

"It's the stone tablet," he gasped.

"The tablet?" she said. "Bayl, you look terrible."

He looked down at himself. "I do rather, don't I?" He smiled. "I didn't sleep a wink last night, trying to work it out." He came into the room. "It has to be the tablet. It's the failsafe. If the computer or the other devices couldn't tell us, it's the one thing that was guaranteed to reach us totally intact."

Amber enlarged its image on her computer. "A meandering line and two crosses. I understand your reasoning, but are you sure? It's not much to go on."

"I believe it is a very crude map. Bring up the globe on your computer. I think the line might match the coastline not far from here."

She fired up the holographic view of Enodia. "Coastlines change. So slowly that it takes decades to notice. But over seven hundred years, they could change out of all recognition."

"Let's try it, anyway. You've said yourself they were intelligent and advanced. They had time to think about this. Perhaps they've taken that into account?"

She focused the viewer on the city at a scale which showed the nearest coast some sixty kilometres away at the same size as the markings on the stone. Although the coastline was similar to the curved line, it was not a close match.

"I think you may have been right, Bayl," she said. "That was the coast, but it was the coast of seven hundred years ago. Do you have maps from that time period?"

"We have very little written records from that time and certainly no maps." He slumped into a chair and rubbed his eyes. "I was sure that was the answer."

"What else could the line be, other than a coastline?" she said.

"A cliff face, perhaps? There's nothing of note anywhere near here. Perhaps there's a match somewhere else on the planet."

"It's a possibility," Amber replied. "I'll set the computer to do a search for all major cliffs away from a coast." After she had done that, she sat back and thought again. "A river or political border would be way too fluid. How about a line joining a range of mountain peaks?"

Bayl nodded. "It could be. That's something else to search for."

After a few minutes the cliff search was completed and eight significant possibilities were highlighted in red. They checked each in turn but none was even a remote match.

"Maybe we're coming at it from the wrong angle" she said. "We're only worrying about the line. What do the crosses represent?"

Bayl sat forward. "If it is a map, one must be the place we're supposed to find."

"Agreed," Amber said. "The other would most likely be a frame of reference. It would have to be something that existed back then and could be assumed to last until now."

"Arthur's tomb?"

"But you said the Mausoleum was only recently rebuilt. Is the original site still known?"

"Yes, the same site was used. It was rebuilt so it would be fit to hold the remains of our kings."

"There's a lot of 'ifs' here," she said, processing the new information, "but if the Mausoleum is one of the crosses and the line is a representation of the coastline, then we might be able to get a rough idea of the location of the other cross."

Amber superimposed the tablet's image on to the viewer, positioning one of the crosses on the location of the Mausoleum. When it was obvious the coastline was completely wrong, she placed the other cross on to the Mausoleum. The coastline was now aligned more closely to the carved line. Adjusting the scale up and down, the first cross moved in a line on the viewer's map of Enodia.

"If we're on the right track, then the place we're after is somewhere on that line," she said. "However, even if we assume the coast hasn't moved more than a few kilometres, that's still a lot of places to search. After all, we don't even know what we're looking for."

She stared at the screen for a minute or two.

"When I was choosing the sites for our dig, I looked at metal concentrations and there were a couple of other sites. If I remember correctly, one was somewhere around this area."

She brought up the metal density scans. A high concentration area, deep within a hill, appeared close to the position of the second cross. She adjusted the scale of the viewer. The cross moved directly over the hill.

"Got it," she said, beaming at Bayl.

26.

"Edrik certainly doesn't live in squalor."

Amber surveyed the duke's estate from the window as the carriage rolled through the grounds. To the left, horses grazed in pasture, trees behind, while carefully tended lawns and flower beds stretched to the right. Ahead, a spacious two-storey brick building greeted them, imposingly large windows providing views of the grounds.

"He is a wealthy man," Bayl sighed. "His family has been close to power throughout our history, and wealth follows power closely enough."

"You disapprove?"

"Am I so transparent? I was born to a good family but nothing approaching this. I have to work hard for all I achieve but, for the Duke and his ilk, position and wealth are expected from birth and they flow freely."

"Is that a hint of revolution, Bayl? I never thought you'd be the type."

"Frustration rather than revolution" he said. "I can have no real complaints, given the lot of so many. At least for me, hard work can bring significant reward."

"It's good he's taking an interest in our work, though. A man with access to such resources could prove useful and it'll certainly make things easier than having to go to the King on a regular basis."

"Indeed," Bayl said. "But that doesn't mean I can't dislike the man."

The carriage slowed to a halt outside the house as a smartly dressed footman approached and opened the carriage door.

Amber and then Bayl stepped out.

A more ornately dressed second servant approached them. "His Grace awaits you in the drawing room. If you would follow me."

The entrance was built from cut stone, standing out impressively from the brick of the rest of the building. Above the double doors was a coat of arms carved into the stone and painted, six golden stars on a dark blue background, no doubt a local constellation.

Amber and Bayl followed the servant through the doorway into a large hallway, the floor tiled in black and white. Above, portraits of a dozen of the Duke's ancestors looked down upon them. Ahead, a spacious staircase, carpeted in rich green, ascended before dividing into two at the far wall. It all gave the impression of long-established power, as it was undoubtedly supposed to, designed to inspire awe and induce subservience in those who visited the duke.

They were ushered through a door to the left into a library where Duke Edrik sat behind a large desk, attending to some papers.

"Professor Stefans, Mr Groms."

Edrik rose and gestured to a couch to one side of the desk, seating himself on an identical one opposite. As they sat, he nodded to a servant who arrived with a tray containing three glasses of a dark red liquid.

"Will you join me in a glass of wine?"

Amber took a glass from the tray, Bayl following suit. A rich aroma accompanied the smooth, woody taste of the wine as she took a sip.

"It's produced from our own vineyards," the duke said, savouring his own glass. "It really ought to accompany a meal to bring out its flavour fully, but it seems a shame to restrict oneself. Now, you said you had some news concerning the objects in the tomb?"

"Yes, Your Grace," Amber said. "I believe we've found the location of the site which Arthur marked out."

Edrik stopped mid-sip before putting his glass on a table by the couch. "You've found it? But how? The objects seemed so unhelpful."

"I've been studying images I took of them. I felt there had to be some meaning in them and it turned out in the case of the carved stone there was. It was a very crude map."

"That is astounding news. Is it far from Denford?"

"About fifty kilometres, to the north west. Do you have a map?"

Edrik rose and moved to his desk, searching through some papers. He pulled one out from underneath and spread it out on top.

Amber took in the detail of the map. It was hand-drawn, without contours, focusing on habitation and major landmarks, which made it difficult to pinpoint the location accurately.

She pulled the hand terminal from her pocket, fired it up and selected the map image from the menu, comparing the holographic projection to the paper one. She pointed to a spot on the physical map. "Here. There's a small hill and it's my belief that what we're searching for lies within it."

As Amber waited for the duke to respond, he stared, mouth open, at the terminal. "How," he stuttered, "can you be sure that is the intended location?"

"Well, I can't absolutely. The location does fit with the map on the stone and matches with a high underground metal deposit at the same location. I'm fairly sure this is it."

Edrik fell back into his chair, still staring at the terminal. "That is quite remarkable. Well, obviously we must go to this place and find out what is there. Fortunately, I own significant holdings in that area and I am confident this site falls within them. We shall not have to be concerned with difficult landowners."

"I can contact His Majesty to arrange for men and equipment," Bayl said. "We should be able to leave in a few days."

"Nonsense, Groms. I can have what's needed ready in less time than that. I shall have a carriage pick you up first thing the day after tomorrow and then we shall get to the bottom of this matter."

* * * * *

As Bayl sat in Amber's now comfortable and familiar room at the Beacon, she gathered a last few belongings for the coming dig. He smiled at the memory of his first visit, the unease and the wide-eyed wonder of seeing the holo-recorder in action. Discovering the Off Worlders' technology had been one of his goals and he had certainly accomplished that. Although the intricacies of it eluded him, he had started to see how such items could become, rather than some semi-magical wonder, another tool to help achieve a task. His desire was far from satiated, however. Denford, even all of Enodia, seemed so much smaller now.

"Do you think one day I might visit Vindor or even Sattoria?"

"There's no reason why not, Bayl," Amber said. "Interstellar travel isn't common. For most people, it's something that only happens a handful of times in their lives. But Enodia will need to make its presence felt in the League eventually – assuming the king doesn't choose an isolationist path – and that will lead to opportunities."

"Is that common? Isolationism, I mean."

"A few worlds choose it, maybe twenty per cent or so. Depending on how the culture has developed, it can be too much of a shock for some to realise what's out there. Or sometimes a ruler feels threatened by a wider galaxy and has the power to impose it. It's hard to see how it can ever truly work, though. They can only pretend they're still alone. And there are independent traders who ignore such restrictions and visit anyway."

There was a knock at the door.

"My pardon, Professor Amber, but your carriage is here."

"Thank you, Mr Travis. Tell them we'll be down in a few moments."

The innkeeper's footsteps receded down the corridor.

"Professor Amber?" Bayl smiled.

"I've been trying to get him to call me by my first name for weeks. We're making progress."

Having been assured by Duke Edrik that all the physical necessities of a dig were in hand, they only had a few bags of personal essentials to load. Fifty kilometres was a full day's journey by carriage, even by road, and it passed slowly.

"Edrik seems committed to the investigation," Amber said when they stopped for lunch. "Has he shown much interest in such things before?"

"Well, we've never had anything remotely like this occur before now, so it's hard to say," Bayl said. "He is one of the main benefactors of the university and I believe he does take an active interest in some research there. So I suppose that his direct involvement here is in character. I must admit I was a little surprised at his readiness to back us in the audience with the king. What we asked was controversial, to say the least, and his backing was a factor in His Majesty's decision."

"Despite your reservations about the man himself."

"Indeed, but I am ready to admit that those are simple prejudice. He does seem to accept the seriousness of what is happening."

"And we are fortunate that he does."

The carriage rolled on through the gentle countryside, passing well-tended fields and the occasional village. The sun was low in the sky when they reached their destination. From the window, Bayl could see an already substantial camp with over a dozen tents and scores of men visible. The duke had even seen the wisdom of an armed guard with muskets watching the road.

As they pulled to a halt, one of the guards approached. "Mr Groms, Professor Stefans. If you would follow me, his Grace is expecting you."

They followed through the bustle of the camp toward a larger tent. To the right, Bayl could see what must be the hill Amber had identified. Already, there were signs of a tunnel being dug into the slope.

"Edrik should have waited for us," Amber said. "I could have helped pinpoint the best place to dig to minimise the work needed."

"They have got off to a good start, to accomplish so much in so little time," Bayl said. He looked back to the camp, now noticing the worn grass and mud at the entrances of the tents. They must have been here at least a couple of days, even with so many men using them.

He turned to Amber but, before he could say anything, she placed a finger to her lips. Pulling something from her pocket, she put it in his hand and mouthed, "Hide this."

It was cold and metallic, like a pistol – but smaller and more compact. A weapon? Amber carried a weapon?

"Hide it," she whispered.

Bayl placed it in an inner jacket pocket. He couldn't be sure, but nobody showed any sign of seeing what they had done.

The tent was guarded by armed men, one on each side of the entrance. They followed Amber and Bayl in.

Edrik was seated on a couch, rising as they entered. "Welcome. As you can see, we've made a start on the work."

"I could have assisted in your choice of where to begin," Amber said.

Bayl looked at a table next to the duke, where papers were laid out. A hexagon was drawn around the hill on one of the maps.

"I'm sure you could, Professor. However, your assistance is not required. In fact, your involvement has been intrusive and unwelcome almost since your arrival here. It will now come to a halt."

Bayl heard the click of pistols being cocked. The two armed men held their weapons pointed at Amber and him. He didn't try reaching inside his jacket for her weapon. She had given it him to keep it hidden. And, anyway, he would be killed even before he had a chance to try to deduce how it worked.

"You realise," he said, "that I am an official in His Majesty's service. It is treason if any harm comes to myself or Professor Stefans."

Edrik smiled. "I think you overestimate your importance to the kingdom, Mr Groms. In any case, no harm will come to you unless you force my hand."

"Then what is your purpose here? Why hold us at all?"

"Simply put, you are in the way. The events of the coming months have been planned for centuries. By blundering around as you have, you risk drawing Zandis's attention and taking control away from where it needs to be."

"By which you mean, you yourself will lose control."

"Yes, I do," Edrik said, "but this is not some personal vanity. The safety of this world is at risk and the solution cannot be put in jeopardy."

"What is this all about?" Amber said. "Why do any of this?"

"I may perhaps enlighten you with that information at some point," he said. "But now is not that time." He stepped towards Amber. "You will give me the device you presented at our last meeting, and any other such – *technology* – you have."

Amber pulled her hand terminal from one pocket and a scanner and the holo-recorder from another. She handed them over.

"There is nothing else?"

Amber removed her jacket and offered it to him. "Check for yourself. There's nothing."

"There will be no need for that, Professor." He placed the devices on the table. "Now, if you would accompany my men, they will make sure you are comfortable."

Christopher J Wright

Part 10. Yorvin

27.

Breathing heavily, Yorvin slumped to the ground in the control room.

They were safe. But that wasn't good enough. Yet again, hope had been dangled before him only to be snatched away by hostility from strangers. Why would they have reacted in such an extreme way?

The force field protecting the portal suggested there had been previous contact. The aliens might view humans as ancient enemies or bogeymen. So fear was the likely answer and, with a flyer downed, they had no reason to change their views. Whatever the cause, the result was the same. Another door had been slammed in their faces. Yorvin couldn't see where the next source of hope to get home would come from.

A hand touched his shoulder. He looked up. Sharna was staring down at him. He looked away.

"There is still hope," she said.

"No, Sharna. I think that might have been the last real chance. We'll keep looking, of course, but from now on, it will be a fading hope."

"You must not give up. But perhaps you need to find purpose here with us as well. You and your people have knowledge that could be of great benefit to the village."

To start integrating themselves into the life of the village would be admitting they might not be going home. It would, though, be a relief from the constant stream of setbacks they had endured. "You're right. You have been very kind to us and we have done little but take from you so far. I'm sure Cobannis and I can offer ideas that will help with your farming and smithing, while Prason and Rowan could aid your warriors."

Sharna smiled. "You are a most resilient man, Yorvin. I thought it would take much more than that to lift your mood."

"They'd have made a mistake choosing me for this mission if I gave up on things too easily," he said, "but thank you." He pulled himself to his feet. "Cobannis, tell me there's no danger of that shield going down any time soon."

She looked at her display. "There's no fear of that, sir. There's enough juice in there to power the force-field for several hundred years. They knew how to make things in the old days."

"That's a relief," he said. "At least we don't have to worry about a horde of angry lizards rampaging through the portal. Make sure everything is secure here and then join the rest of us on the upper level."

"Yes, sir."

Searching the rest of the complex uncovered a few signs of pre-Fall technology, but nothing of any real use. The complex had been virtually emptied when it was abandoned long ago. Yorvin had Cobannis reset the access codes to the entrance so they could easily gain entry. They left the defence system off, though, as neither the Corini nor, more importantly, the Utani could open the door. He didn't want to be the cause of any unnecessary deaths.

When they returned to the village, he called a meeting of his three remaining crew members.

"It's been almost a month since we reached Minerva," he said, "and we've had to endure a series of terrible setbacks since then. The loss of the captain, Gildoman, Garcia and Richards. The damaging of the ship beyond anything we could repair ourselves. The destruction of the Astracomm so we can't even call for help. And now we have the failure of our efforts to find help to repair either the ship or the comms system. It's a hell of a lot for anyone to deal with, and all three of you have performed exceptionally.

"On the other hand, we have been treated with kindness and dignity by the people of this village. We could well have died but for their help and I think it's time we repaid that kindness. We can help them with our knowledge. We might be able to make their lives easier and their village safer."

"May I speak freely, sir?" Prason said.

"Of course. That goes for all of you."

"Are you saying that we should give up on going home, sir? I'm not sure I'm ready to do that yet. There's still a huge amount of this planet we haven't seen, not to mention the planet we've just been to."

"I understand, Prason," he said. "I'm not saying we give up. I have family back home and I want to see them again as much as you do. What I am saying is that getting home is not going to be easy and it may well be impossible. So, we have to start considering where we fit into this world in the meantime. There is a lot of this planet left to explore but without a flyer, searching further than a couple of hundred kilometres from here will be extremely slow. I want Cobannis working on cobbling something together so we can get into the air. But that's going to take time.

"As for the planet we've just been to, they may be relatively low technology, but we've already seen what their heavier weapons can do. They'll be watching that portal non-stop now and they'll consider us to be enemies. I don't think that returning there is an option. Even if it were, there would be a very small chance of finding anything useful."

"We may have to wait for a while to try the portal again, sir," Prason said, "but with the battle armour's stealth, we could probably get through. I'd like to try."

"All right, but we wait at least a month for things to quieten down. I don't want to start a war. And once we get a flyer in the air, we start serious exploration of this world." Yorvin looked at the young engineer. "That's your focus."

Cobannis nodded. "Yes, sir."

"One other thing. Cobannis, can you get a radio transmitter up that can send a message home?"

"I'm sure I could, sir. I'd need to rig something up to make the power strong enough for the signal to be detected, but it wouldn't take long. Any message would take sixty standard years to reach home, though."

"I know," he said. "All the more reason to get it done sooner rather than later. It's my hope that we'll all be able to meet up in sixty years and reminisce about our short time here. We can listen to the messages when they finally reach Sattoria. But, in the worst case, this is the only way we can report what's happened and get messages to our families. So, get that set up as your first priority."

"Sir." She nodded.

"Lieutenant?" Rowan said. "What sort of help did you have in mind for us to give the Corini?"

"Anything that will give them a boost. Maybe some simple agricultural techniques. I'm sure Cobannis could help with some smithing improvements. You could help them with your medical knowledge, when they're not using the AutoDoc, that is. And Prason and you should be able to add to their military training and tactics.

"I'm not saying that we transform their ways with technology they can't maintain. But we have an encyclopaedia of knowledge on the computers that will contain a lot that can help them."

"Aren't you worried about what sort of effect this might have on the politics here, sir?" Rowan asked.

"I know what you mean," Yorvin replied. "The Corini will gain an advantage over the Utani and any other nearby tribes. That will fundamentally change the balance of power. However, their reaction to our arrival showed they're far from bloodthirsty. I don't think we'll be creating a monster. They've been attacked once already because of our presence. We have an obligation to help them meet any future threats. And if we do end up spending some time here, then I'd rather be helping make a difference."

* * * * *

Yorvin stayed up late into the night, walking outside the village, thinking and gazing upwards at the star around which his home world circled. He imagined Jan doing the same back on Sattoria.

But then he remembered she wouldn't yet even be aware that there was a problem. For another month, she would receive messages containing nothing more than trivia and minor details of how the mission had been going. But he knew that, in a month's time, the news of the encounter at Minerva and the impending crash landing would arrive. Then the messages would stop. For that month, she would keep on sending her own news: how her work was going, how she longed for him to return, the girls' progress at school – things he would now never hear or see.

But that month's delay was as nothing compared to the message he was about to send. By the time it reached Sattoria, Jan would be in her declining years, his daughters middle-aged and he, without the anti-aging drugs he'd always taken for granted, dead.

He'd spoken to the others of the continuing efforts to find a way home, but he knew it wasn't going to happen. The best chance now was that Sattoria would send out a ship for them, but that was too unlikely to be a realistic hope. Interstellar ships were too rare and valuable to send this far out when all they might find was a wreck with no survivors. They hadn't sent one when contact was lost with the Explorer.

No, the message he was about to send was goodbye to the woman he had loved for more than fifteen years. It was goodbye also to the daughters he had adored since he had first seen them as tiny bundles of life only a few short years ago. What could he possibly say to them? For a time, he wondered if it would be better to say nothing at all. Why open up old wounds for them decades after they had finished mourning his death, found what peace they could and moved on? But in time, as he walked, he realised he couldn't do that. To send no personal message with his report would be hurtful in a wholly different way. It would be like abandoning them, saying he could move on and forget them in only a short time.

In the morning, Yorvin felt weary and haggard. He could see none of the others had slept well, either.

After Cobannis had finished her work on the transmitter, it was time to send the messages. She had put it in their hut so each could have privacy. Yorvin decided to send his status report to the Naval Authorities first, followed by each of the crew's individual messages, his own being last. Cobannis set the frequency and broadcast identification codes before leaving the hut.

The factual nature of the report was a temporary relief. He reported the events that had occurred, starting with the crash and the deaths of the rest of the crew. He detailed their efforts to find parts for the ship, the discovery of the portal and sentient alien life. That last part would cause a stir in the upper echelons of government.

When he was done, he left the hut and Rowan took over. He stayed in for five minutes or so and emerged looking even more drawn than before.

Prason was next. She was inside for barely two minutes before emerging with her face as impassive as ever. She turned and headed, alone, towards the edge of the village.

Cobannis stayed in for ten minutes and emerged crying. Rowan put his arms around her and comforted her.

Yorvin could delay it no longer. He went into the hut, stood before the transmitter and took some deep breaths.

"This is Lieutenant Yorvin Bandrell with a personal message for my wife, Jan Bandrell. In the event that she is no longer alive, it should be delivered to any surviving family."

"Jan, I know this message might well come as a huge shock to you. It is my fervent hope I'm sitting beside you right now and we've had a long and happy life together. It's my fear that I won't have made it back home and, if that's the case, I'm so very sorry for the hurt this will cause you.

"I have loved you since the day we met all those years ago. I will love you each and every day for the years this message takes to reach you. Know that I have been trying, and will keep on trying, to get back to you. I will always hold a hope we will see each other again.

"Sixty years is a long time, and I know you will have assumed I was dead. If you moved on and married again, I understand and I'm glad if you found happiness.

"I hope your life has been full and that the girls have made you proud as they have grown. I'll leave it to you to decide whether or not to tell them about this but, if you do, tell them I love them dearly.

"I can just make out our Sun from this world. I'll look at it often, every evening, and think of you all. Goodbye my love."

Yorvin reached down and switched the transmitter off. He stood for a moment, numb. Like Prason, he left the hut and walked out beyond the edge of the village.

* * * * *

Bursting into the hut, Adran startled Sharna. "Mother, something's going on with the strangers."

"At least you've stopped calling them sorcerers," she said. "Now they're only strangers, are they?"

"What?"

She shook her head. "What's happened?"

197

"I don't know, but the warrior woman has walked out of the village alone and Sarah – I mean, Cobannis – came out of their hut crying. I think something awful must have happened."

"You seem quite concerned for the girl," Sharna said. "Be careful, Adran. They might leave us as suddenly as they came, and we still don't know much about them."

"I'm going to see how Cobannis is," he said, blushing. "I thought you'd want to know what was happening."

With that, he left the hut.

A few minutes later, Sharna went to the hut the strangers shared. Rowan was alone.

"Where's Yorvin?"

"Gone walking."

When she reached the outskirts of the village, she saw him sitting against an isolated tree a couple of hundred paces beyond.

"Something has happened," she said.

"In a manner of speaking. We've sent messages back to our home, to our families."

"Then you should be happy. Your wife will know you are alive."

Yorvin shook his head. "Eventually. Our way of sending messages quickly was destroyed when our ship crashed. We have a slower way, but it will take sixty years to reach her."

"But that is longer than most people live. Will she hear your message?"

"Probably. On my world, we can live beyond a hundred years. But she will be very old when she hears it."

While it was Sharna's role to ease the pain of others and there was always something to be done for physical wounds, the wounds of the mind were often beyond the help of anything but time.

"Do you wish me to go?"

He shook his head.

Sharna sat down next to him. "Tell me of your world."

The Enodia Enigma

28.

Adran hefted the wooden shield on his left arm. It was heavy and awkward but he already knew enough to appreciate its worth.

As a tradition, the Corini and the surrounding tribes had avoided the use of shields in combat, most warriors feeling that the limited protection they offered did not justify the loss of speed and agility. A true warrior used his skills to protect him.

But now, the female warrior from another world had turned things upside down by proposing a shield that was bigger and heavier than any that had ever been used. And she had shown how it could protect a man completely from arrows.

Prason was saying archery, too, was of far greater importance than the Corini believed. This made perfect sense to Adran. Ever since he could remember, he knew the bow was a formidable weapon. It could kill a man long before he could use his sword or axe. But, because the skill was difficult to learn, only a few warriors spent the countless hours needed to make an archer more dangerous to his enemies than his friends. Now, she was saying all men of a fighting age should have a bow and should practice every day.

There had been resistance, of course.

The warriors of the village didn't like being told how to fight. They especially didn't like being told by a stranger or a woman. And while she was impressively athletic, she was clearly no physical match for any of them except the youngest of the men.

But when Hiram challenged Prason, to show just how weak she was, the mood changed.

She threw him to the ground, with her boot on his neck before he could move. When he got to his feet, Prason goaded him into trying again. This time, Hiram was more cautious. But, again, the woman pulled him off-balance and, once more, he was thrown to the ground, her boot on his neck, his arm in a painful lock.

Prason then challenged him to a test of raw strength. They arm-wrestled. Hiram won. They lifted weights. Hiram won again.

His fellow warriors applauded him.

"You're right," Prason called out. "Hiram has greater strength than I do. But if we had met in battle Hiram would have died."

She turned to face Hiram.

"What I am teaching you will allow you to defeat an enemy who is larger and stronger than you. And you'll more easily beat one who is weaker. Hiram, you have shown you're stronger than me. Would you like to show I was lucky the first two times?"

Hiram thought a moment, glancing towards the other warriors Then shook his head and stepped back.

With that battle won, the warriors were more willing to listen. She showed them how devastating a group of archers could be when protected by a row of men armed with the new large shields.

Now, Adran waited with his shield and a wooden practice sword in the middle of a row of ten other younger warriors. She was showing them another use for the shields. Twenty metres ahead eleven of the older men waited, armed only with practise swords.

Prason signalled to the older men to charge. Shouting, they ran forward. Several in the shield line took a step back and Adran had to force himself to hold the line.

"Back in line!" Prason ordered. "Hold your shields up and close to the next man's. Swords between the gaps."

The younger men moved back in line, her words reminding them this was practice. They adopted the position they had been taught, and then the attackers were upon them. The older men were forced to slow to avoid the bristle of wooden swords.

Luran, one of the older warriors, came at Adran, his sword high, trying to stab at him over the shield. Lowering his body and raising his shield, Adran prodded to the left with his sword around the shield. It struck home. Luran grunted and moved away-and out of the conflict, as Prason had instructed those who were hit should do.

Then Nerac hit a blow against Adran's exposed left side.

"Sorry, lad," he said, moving into the gap Adran left as he dropped back, aiming another blow which Tobin blocked.

By the time Adran was safely back, Tobin was fending off Nerac and Hiram with other older warriors looking on. Tobin put up a desperate defence, but the two experienced warriors were more skilful. They moved to opposite sides, despite his trying to stop them, where they found the gap in his guard. Nerac dealt the blow that ended the contest.

"Good!" Prason called, walking inwards. "Experience won out over the new tactics this time, but the youngsters did well."

Adran looked over to the seven older warriors who had been hit. In a straight fight, the number would have been half that or even less. The thoughtful looks on the faces of those fallen men showed they saw the significance of the training.

Prason had them try the tactics out twice more. In the first, the older men won again but Nerac had to finish the last two defenders himself. In the second, Adran and Tobin faced Hiram, the last attacker – and with no shield to defend himself – they easily landed the needed blow.

Nerac hurried off to the Chieftain's hut to tell him of the events.

The next day, Dornis attended Prason's teaching.

* * * * *

As the afternoon turned to evening, Yorvin was walking outside the village. It had become his custom over the past month to find time for himself at this time of day. He enjoyed watching the first stars as they began to shine in the darkening sky. One of the first to show was close to Sattoria, which was only visible on the clearest of nights. He would gaze up at it from time to time, feeling a small connection with home. By now, his family would have received the last of the Astracomm messages and know that they had crash landed.

Hearing movement, he turned and saw Cobannis coming from the village.

"Lieutenant."

"You want to talk with me?"

"Yes, sir. I suppose I was wondering where you were going with all this training and teaching."

"There's no real goal. I'm trying to help people who have shown themselves to be friends."

"You care what happens to these people, don't you?"

"Yes I do," he said. "They went out of their way to help us, and they're about the only ones we've met on our journey who have. We have a way of helping them in return, so I see no reason not to. Besides, don't think I haven't noticed that you've taken a bit of a shine to one of them yourself."

"Adran is so keen to learn about our 'magic'," she said, "it's hard not to care about him. In a way, it's a shame he's so old. Technology will never be second nature to him despite his quick mind."

"Still, in other ways, his age isn't such a problem. Or is he a little young on that score?"

"Sir!" she said, reddening.

"Sorry, Cobannis. I shouldn't tease you, but it's good that you're forging links in the village. Was there anything else?"

"Yes, sir. Something that struck me last night. The force field that covers the portal to the alien world has about seven hundred years of power left."

"I'd forgotten the figure, but I remember you saying it would last a long while. It's just as well since we don't have the means to power it ourselves."

"That's just it, sir. In seven hundred years, the field will go down and there will be free access between the two worlds."

"Is that really our problem?" Yorvin asked. "We'll be long gone. We've mentioned it in our report to Sattoria, so whoever's in control should know about it by then. It would be a simple matter to provide another power source. We could have done it ourselves if we'd still had the ship. And that's if the aliens still remain a threat. We've got far more immediate things to worry about."

"You may be right, sir, but I'm not so sure. Civilisation has been going downhill for more than three centuries. How can we be sure it will have recovered in seven hundred more years? If we get home or are rescued, then we can make sure that the existence of the portal is recorded. But if we don't… There may not be anybody listening for radio messages on Sattoria in sixty years. Even if they are, then they may have more immediate things to worry about."

"A fair point, Cobannis. I think you win the prize for forward thinking. We can't rely on the rest of humanity helping out with this problem. But I'm not sure there's much we can do about it, either. I'm still not convinced it will be a problem even when it does go down."

"I've been thinking about that as well, sir."

"I thought you might have done. Go on."

"The portal must have protected this world since the Fall. Which means it's been at least three centuries since the aliens saw a human. Yet the ones in the settlement recognised you as an enemy immediately.

"What we did to escape killed at least two more and shot down an atmospheric flyer. That will confirm to them we're dangerous. They're going to watch their end like hawks for years and they're going to believe they can never completely relax their guard, even after hundreds of years. Over the centuries, their technology will probably advance and they may even be capable of interstellar travel by the time the force field fails."

"So," he said, "you're saying that seven hundred years from now, an advanced race of aliens who view humanity as the ancient enemy could emerge from that portal. They could be in a position not only to take over Enodia but also to use it as a base. Then they would expand outwards and combat a stagnant or, at best, re-emerging human race."

"There are a lot of 'ifs' in there, sir," she said, "but it's a scenario we can't dismiss. The question is what can we do about it?"

Christopher J Wright

Part 11. Amber

29.

Amber tried to make herself comfortable. The wooden bench she was sitting on was the only piece of furniture in the small shack. Bayl was pacing the room, looking through the windows. The hut was about a kilometre from the camp, and had only two guards – all of which made it easier to escape.

He sat beside her.

"You have a weapon. I had not expected that."

"It wasn't my idea. I'm against them as a rule, but the Captain who brought me here insisted I have it. I've had it with me whenever we've left Denford."

"Well, it's good you did. How does it work?"

As the shadow of one of the guards passed across a window, she waited for the sound of his footsteps to recede. "I don't want anybody to die, Bayl. Edrik has said he won't harm us."

"Forgive me if I do not take all he says at face value anymore. There are no guarantees. Either you take it back or you show me how to use it."

"You're right," she said.

Keeping an eye on the windows, Bayl pulled the weapon from his pocket.

"There's a catch on the left side," she said. "If you slide it sideways, a green light comes on. Pull the trigger to fire it."

As he tested the catch, Amber went to a window to see where the guards were. "Somebody's coming."

Bayl pushed the laser pistol back into his pocket and smoothed his jacket.

The door opened. A guard came in, his hand on his holstered pistol, suspicious eyes scanning the room. He stepped to one side, still watching, as another came in.

This man was an altogether different sort – taller, thinner than the guard, with an angular face. His clothing showed him to be a man of some means, even though they were not well tended. He was holding Amber's scanner.

"Professor Stefans," he said, holding out a hand, "it is a pleasure to meet you at last."

Amber pulled away. "I would believe that if you didn't have an armed man behind you and we were not prisoners."

"Quite," he said, looking over his shoulder. "These are not the circumstances I would have chosen, or if I am honest, the timing. I would that we had met much sooner. I am Karl Fryer, Doctor of Science at the University. I seek your assistance with this device." He held up the scanner.

"You need my help?"

"Need is a stronger term than I would have chosen. We will achieve our task with or without it, but yes, I would request your aid.

"His Grace told me what you said about assisting with the dig site and an underground metal deposit. I looked at your items and this appears to be a detector of some sort, but I am unable to make proper use of it. Would you be willing to show me?"

"Edrik said that you already had details of where to begin," she said. "Does the scanner really matter?"

"That's true, we have the direction and distance from the peak of the hill for where to dig. But I am not so foolish as to believe that seven-hundred-year-old instructions will be absolutely precise. If I could confirm that we are making good progress, then my mind would rest easier."

"That device could help you, but I'd have to show you how to set it to detect the right materials."

Fryer handed it over.

She fired it into life, moving slowly through the menu system. "Now will you be searching for stone, metal – ?"

"The upper reaches are mostly stone," he said, "although there is a lower chamber built into the bedrock which will contain significant metal."

"So it sounds like it would be best to detect the upper stone area, which you can do by setting it like this. Then you need to scan using this button and walk around the hill directing the front towards the centre. The scanner will track your movement and orientation. That will let it build up a three-dimensional image of the stone below. With any luck, your target will be obvious."

Fryer focused on the scanner as he processed what Amber had shown him. "My thanks, Professor Stefans. You have been very helpful when I know you did not have to."

"If there is a danger, then of course I want to help, Doctor Fryer. I have seen enough to believe that's quite probable."

Fryer took the scanner and left the hut.

"Was that wise?" Bayl asked when they were alone again.

"I think so. He seemed uneasy at our imprisonment and might even be a potential ally. More importantly, we now know they're looking for a buried stone building with an underground installation below it. Not much, I know, but a step nearer to working out what is happening."

* * * * *

The looks the labourers kept giving him made him feel ridiculous. Fryer had been circling and crossing the hillock for some thirty minutes now, always pointing the scanner towards its centre. He didn't know if he had to hold it away from his body to avoid contaminating the process. Or how long he should take readings. He

210

should have asked Stefans, but it would feel foolish to return. Fryer decided to cross the hillock one last time.

A few minutes later and breathless from his prolonged exertions, he stopped, examined the device and instructed the scanner to display its findings. Still amazed at something that could provide data without the need to move tonnes of earth, he watched as the screen showed a sloping bedrock with a prominent hexagonal protrusion. He rotated the image on the screen. When he moved up the hill, the hexagon moved towards the centre of the screen.

After experimenting with location and the numeric readings, he discovered the passage being dug was a few degrees off target and did not need to incline as steeply. This knowledge would save several hours. It also confirmed the task was on target.

There was no more to do but wait. The digging continued for the rest of that day and into the next.

Mid-morning, Fryer stood with the duke observing the final stages.

"And you say we will reach the gatehouse imminently?" the duke said. "I see nothing but soil and mud."

"Stefans's scanner can probe into the earth, Your Grace. It is no more than a metre or two beyond what we can see."

"Yes, Fryer, I heard you had been in discussion with the Off Worlder. Be careful she does not cause you to lose your focus."

"Of course. It's still my belief that she is a resource which can be of use to us."

Duke Edrik turned to him. "Or have you already lost your focus?"

"No, Your Grace," Fryer said, looking away.

He was rescued by the sound of metal clanging against stone. Then another clang. As the labourer pulled earth away with his hands, he uncovered a patch of smooth, cut stonework.

"By the gods, Fryer," Edrik said, "you were right."

Fryer made his way up the hillock, to the excavation trench.

The labourers had uncovered a recessed area, one wall of which was metallic – probably a door. Although there was more waiting, of course, progress could now be monitored.

By late afternoon, they could see the door. A metal rod was wedged in to prevent it shutting – which gave enough leverage for two of the labourers to slide it open.

Duke Edrik had the men light three torches and one was handed to Fryer.

Before them, a short corridor ended at a doorway, a downward stairwell by its side.

Accompanied by four guards, they followed the stairs into the depths of the earth. Just as Fryer was beginning to think they had gone too far, the stairs opened out into a large room. Several passageways led from it.

But it wasn't the room or the passageways that mattered. A soft glow of light was shining from the next flight of stairs.

"Ready your muskets," the duke ordered the guards. "We're going down."

In single file, the duke leading, they descended, all the time the light drawing them on. Step by step, footfall by footfall, down they went – first, one stairway and then, the light growing stronger, a second stairway. And finally, a passageway.

As Duke Edrik strode on, Fryer and the guards following, darkness fled from the shimmering light.

The duke stopped, held up his hand, bringing the group to a halt.

Then, he and Fryer took three steps forward into a huge chamber and gaped at a curtain of mesmerising brilliance.

30.

For three days Bayl and Amber were incarcerated in the shack, frustrated that events were progressing at the dig and they knew nothing of it. Surely with the weapon that Bayl now held, he should be acting to inform His Majesty. Yet he found himself unwilling to do so because of Amber's request. He'd come to the realisation that he trusted her implicitly, that he was concerned about more than just the task that had been assigned to him

"What will happen after you complete your studies here?" he asked during one of the long evenings.

"It'll be back to the university on Vindor," she said, "to pay my academic penance for this visit."

"Do you spend much time there?"

"More than I'd like. Probably about the same that I spend on new worlds."

"Can it be so bad?" Bayl said. "There are many who would grasp at a chance to live on a world like yours, I assure you."

Amber smiled, gesturing around the shack. "And miss all this? You're right, of course. I'm lucky to have been born on a world at the centre of humanity. I wouldn't have been able to choose my vocation on many planets."

"Then why do you rail against it so?"

"It's the control, Bayl. For all the advantages, life is mapped out for people back home. There are always expectations – conform for your parents, for your school, for your job, for the nation." She looked up at him. "I know that doesn't sound much different to Enodia. But it's the level of control. On Vindor, your business is never just your own. You have to act a certain way. You even have to think a certain way."

Bayl scratched his chin. "And you chose anthropology – the study of people and culture – to see if there might be another way?"

Amber met his gaze with a wry smile. "Are you analysing me, Mr. Groms?" She hesitated a moment. "I do sometimes wonder if my motives are that obvious. A researcher using her studies to make sense of her own world, of her own problems. It's occurred to me, and maybe there's some truth in it." She paused. "Not enough to sustain a career, though. I think it's more that I enjoy the freedoms that being a stranger affords me."

Bayl nodded. "You're automatically outside the usual expectations in my world. In fact, we expect you to break the rules."

"I think you have me summed up," she said with a grin.

"And would it work the other way? Would I be allowed to break the rules on Vindor?"

"Yes, though only so much. There's an arrogance there, an assumption that we're the pinnacle of humanity, so we must have it right. It was like that before the Fall, too. We learnt some humility as we struggled to survive but human nature is what it is, and the arrogance returned all too soon."

"That I can recognise," Bayl said. "There is arrogance among the nobility of Enodia as well. I've shown myself capable, of use to them, and so I gain some status. But they are sure they know how things should be and expect the rest of us to follow. It seems people are the same whether they can leave their world or not."

Finally, on the fourth morning after their arrival, they were summoned by Duke Edrik and led back to the camp. In stark contrast to a few days earlier, there was a lack of activity – men playing dice, talking, even sleeping.

They were led on towards the hill and the trench leading into it. Here, there were signs of purpose. Carpenters worked at constructing a wooden frame to secure its sides.

At the far end was a doorway in a smooth stone wall. As they drew close, Bayl could see that the wall was weathered, though still intact. It was old, but well-constructed.

They were led down into a chamber where Duke Edrik and Professor Fryer awaited them. A huge curtain of light, of differing intensities and swirling in constant movement, dominated the room, demanding attention.

"So," Amber said, "this is the reason for all that has happened these past months. A force field?"

"That is the term that our texts from Arthur's time use," Fryer said. "The word means little, but it is a protective device for our world."

"Protection from what?" Bayl said.

"From a portal to another world."

"Then you have found what you have been expecting," Bayl said. "I don't understand why you are now showing it to us. His Grace has made it abundantly clear that we are not to be involved in this."

"That has become less absolute," Edrik said, shooting a bristling glance at Fryer, "or at least so I am reliably informed."

"It will be clearer," Fryer said, avoiding the duke's gaze, "if you see for yourself."

He led them back into the corridor and then into a room containing three desks with panels on them – different from those Amber used but, Bayl suspected, similar in function.

Fryer pressed a button on the nearest of the three. The panel began to glow, forming a picture of a grey rectangle on a circular blue background. Bayl could just make out a thin vertical red line on the left edge of the rectangle.

Above were the words "Power Reserves".

Underneath were two numbers. On the left 0.0056%. On the right, 2,591,896.

As they watched, the righthand number began to decrease at the rate of one digit per second. It was clear the electricity powering the wall of light was limited.

Fryer looked at Amber.

"About thirty days?" she said.

Raising his hand to rub his face, Fryer nodded. "In thirty days, the force field, as you call it, will lose its power."

"But this is what you prepared for," Bayl said. "You can implement your plans?"

"That figure should be over nine million. We have allowed some leeway of course, but it will take at least sixty days to build a generator the size we need."

"So," Bayl said, "you intend to continue powering this wall of light. Why? What does it do which is so vital?"

"It is a barrier impervious to all things," Duke Edrik said. "Behind it is a portal or gateway of some kind leading to a far-off land. In that place is a race of intelligent creatures which are not human. They intend harm to us and the wall of light is the only thing protecting us."

"You're speaking of sentient, alien life," Amber said. "In over ten thousand years of exploration, there has been no confirmed record of intelligent aliens. If this is true, then it is an incredible opportunity, Your Grace. We should go through and try to make contact."

"Arthur tried this," Edrik said, "and confirmed that they were implacably hostile to men. Worse still, they had weapons we cannot match. The gods alone know what they might now possess."

Amber shook her head. "But that was seven hundred years ago. So much could have changed by now. Anything that happened then would have been long forgotten."

"That attitude is why we have worked in secret," Edrik said. "In a few minutes, you think you know better than Arthur, who saw those events and spent a lifetime preparing for this moment. This is a danger to our world. The aliens have not forgotten."

"I'm sure," Bayl said, "that whatever the rights and wrongs of making contact, the immediate need is to continue powering the force field. Surely none of us would advocate allowing it to fail without a means of restoring it?"

Edrik, Fryer and Amber nodded.

"I have spent all night going over the plans," Fryer said. "The lack of time means we will need the help of the government, Mr Groms."

"I will approach His Majesty," Edrik said, his voice solemn, even defeated. "Your verification of our plight will be useful in helping the king focus on the problem rather than see it as a betrayal."

"King Zandis will not be pleased," Bayl said.

"I am well aware of that. I will accept the consequences when it is all done, but this task must be accomplished."

"I have no doubt you shall have all the resources that you need from the king." Bayl turned to Fryer. "Do you know why the time is so much less than you expected?"

"I don't," Fryer said. "It concerns me greatly, and not only because we have to complete the work in four weeks when we planned for ten with six to spare."

"Twelve weeks' error in seven hundred years is not a large one," Amber said. "There could easily have been some fluctuations in power use. We should really be grateful the error was not greater."

"That may be the case," Fryer said, "but we are left with an enormous logistical problem."

"Can it be done in time?" Bayl said.

"I don't honestly know. I will have to reschedule the transport and assembly of the generator. I will be counting on massive resources from you, Mr Groms. Your help would be much appreciated too, Professor Stefans."

"But I am not a physical scientist." Amber said. "My help will be very limited."

"I understand that you have access to a wealth of knowledge through your equipment. That may help us find ways to adjust our designs and reduce the time we need."

Amber nodded.

"Doctor Fryer," Bayl said, "you must provide us with a list of equipment and how many men you will need. Then Duke Edrik and I will seek an audience with the king to inform him of this situation and request his aid. We must return to Denford with all haste."

* * * * *

Amber hurried back to The Beacon and activated her Astracomm. She sent a detailed summary of the events so far on the League's emergency channel, warning of the possibility of hostile alien life on the other side of an unseen wormhole. When she switched off the Astracomm and played back her report, she was shocked at its starkness. She hoped the officials who received it would treat it seriously.

It would be three weeks before the message arrived anywhere likely to have a ship available. Even if one were sent immediately to Enodia, any help would arrive more than two weeks after the force field's power had run down. Either they were going to have to get the generator working in time or hope this new alien race was no longer a threat.

Two hours later, Bayl arrived from the Palace.

"I'm sorry you were excluded, Amber," he said as he fell into his now customary chair. "Edrik is a proud man and did not want anyone to see his downfall."

"What happened?"

"He successfully argued that his role as leader of the Guardians meant he was best placed to continue leading the efforts to power the force field. His knowledge and the instructions handed down give him a unique qualification to do so. Once this is over, he will be finished at court and he knows it."

"But King Zandis agreed to help?"

"Yes, fifty labourers, a blacksmith and two other experts in electrical power are preparing to leave in the morning, along with all the equipment Fryer has requested. He also would like to borrow a computer along with instruction in its use to research historical and scientific matters."

"He shall have it." She took a deep breath. "I have a confession to make. I've requested assistance from home. I'm not subscribing to Edrik and Fryer's doomsday theory. But, if a warship is in orbit here, it will only help."

"His Majesty will not be pleased at the lack of consultation, but I understand why you did it. Will they be able to help with the powering of the force field."

"I'm sure they could and in a way you could rely upon. But they will not be here until two weeks after the power fails. We will have to find our own answer."

"Two weeks? That's insignificant compared to the centuries that have passed."

"If there is a genuine danger, it is a very long time. If I had known about this at the time of the eclipse, something could have been done. Edrik and his secretive ways have a lot to answer for."

"They do," he said, "and he shall. For now, we will assist him and his every action will be watched and reported."

* * * * *

Once Amber had shown Doctor Fryer the computer terminal and how to access research materials, there was little she or Bayl could do. They remained in Denford and investigated the items from Arthur's tomb.

The laser rifle that had been placed on the king's chest was damaged beyond use. The armour was still serviceable, if only to a degree. Its powered systems were damaged far beyond repair. So now it was just a bulky but effective suit of armour.

Amber returned to her original task of analysing Enodia's culture, which now felt a hollow exercise.

The people of Denford knew something was afoot. Rumours of the movement of wagons, troops and labourers were spreading throughout the city, hindering her work.

It was a relief when Edrik and Fryer returned to the city to attend an audience with King Zandis. It was late afternoon by the time they were taken to the palace.

This time, the king had chosen a far more informal location, a room with comfortable seating and personal effects. Inside, Edrik and Fryer stood waiting, nodding at Amber and Bayl in acknowledgement.

The king, flanked by two guards, arrived almost immediately and took a seat before them.

"Duke Edrik. What is it that demands such urgent attention? Good news I trust?"

"I'm afraid not, Your Majesty. To put it bluntly, we're not going to be ready in time."

"How can that be?" Zandis said, "If you need more men or resources, you shall have them. We shall provide enough men for you to work through the night."

Edrik rubbed his forehead.

"We're working nightshifts already, Your Majesty. More men will make only a small difference. There are only so many things that can be done separately at the same time. Some parts must be done in sequence and I can see no way to avoid our being late by about five days."

"Why did you contact us now?" Amber said. "What has tipped the balance away from us?"

"Our initial plan," Fryer said, "was to build the generator above ground and to run cables down to power the force field. Unfortunately, the portal is much deeper below ground than I anticipated and the power loss along the cables is too great for the generator to sustain the force field. The only way round it is to move the generator and the force field closer together. That means building it in the complex."

"I appreciate that is more awkward," Bayl said, "but surely it can still be done?"

"If it were just the building of it, then you might be right. However, a steam-powered generator is one the noisiest and messiest machines known. It has to have adequate ventilation. Putting one in an enclosed space twenty metres under the ground is a recipe for disaster."

"What needs to be done?" Bayl said.

"We have two choices," Fryer said. "We can construct a pipe to take the excess steam out of the complex via the stairs. But I believe the better solution is to dig a tunnel down through the hillside to the engine."

"And there isn't any way this could be done in time?" Amber said.

"No. That's why I called you here. The digging of the tunnel and the adjustments needed to the design of the generator make it impossible, I'm afraid. I've begun the work already, but we have to decide what we are going to do."

"It may not be an issue," Amber said. "As I said before, there is no reason for us to assume the aliens still mean us harm. Who is to say they're even there anymore?"

"They will be there," Edrik said, rolling his eyes, "and they will be hostile. I am certain of it."

"You are *certain* of it only because you've built your life around an assumption for which you have no current evidence."

"The evidence may be old," Edrik said, "but it *is* reliable. We cannot take risks with the whole future of Enodia because of your –"

"Enough," King Zandis said. "You all forget yourselves. Fryer, you have just told us, if I am not mistaken, that the force field will power down before the generator is ready to sustain it?"

"Your Majesty," Fryer nodded.

"Then it seems to us that we should lower the force field on our terms and see if there is any actual danger. It will be folly to allow ourselves to become defenceless when that is unknown. That will take place tomorrow. Edrik, Groms, we will trust you to make the arrangements and report back to us at the earliest opportunity."

Part 12. Yorvin

31.

Prason's voice came through Yorvin's comms badge. "We're in position now, sir."

"Any sign that you've been spotted?"

"Negative. Their attention is all forward."

"What's your status, Rowan?"

"We'll be ready in thirty seconds, sir," he said. "No sign we've been spotted either."

Yorvin surveyed the scene. After five long years of trying to avoid a large-scale pitched battle, it had come to this. The entire military might of the Corini tribe stood there, arrayed across the slope he had chosen for their defensive positions. Nine hundred infantry, most armed with spears, swords and large shields, together with four hundred bowmen, were standing in well-arranged ranks. On either flank, sixty cavalry and a Sattorian marine in battle armour waited in forward positions, ready to move in against the enemy archers on Yorvin's signal.

On any other day, he would have been confident of an easy victory, but this was the sternest test the Corini had faced or were ever likely to. Three hundred metres away, the combined forces of three other tribes lay waiting.

The Utani were less numerous now, but they had convinced two other tribes, the Ascani and the Judini, to join them. Their total strength was almost three times the Corini forces.

Yorvin felt an old and familiar frustration. Hundreds were likely to die today and there was no need for it. Under the changes and improvements that he and Cobannis had introduced, the Corini lived more stable, comfortable lives. Prason and Rowan had ensured that they had the strength to defend their newfound wealth.

But, of course, the Utani had seen this aid from the "Sorcerers" as a direct threat and the raids against the Corini had escalated. Yorvin had extended the new military training to the other villages within the tribe, always on the understanding it be used for defence and not aggression. He had tried to set up trade links with the Utani and the other nearby tribes, to allow a trickle of the benefits to reach them and promote peace. It had worked for a time, but eventually, the Utani had declared war.

The Chieftains of the Corini now looked to Yorvin for guidance and he had ended up as general in command of the conflict. He had fought a defensive war, repelling each attack, hoping the Utani would see sense and talk once again.

In desperation, the Utani had sought aid from other fearful and jealous tribes, and Yorvin realised he would have to strike a final blow. Events had spiralled into conflict despite his best efforts. It had been so with the Minervans, the aliens beyond the portal and now the Utani.

The enemy lines were beginning to advance, a strange mix of traditional warriors in furs and groups of Utani who had copied some of the new tactics, wielding their own spears and large shields.

Prason's insistence that she teach tactics in small steps rather than a huge jump had proved to be wise in the conflict Yorvin had chosen to fight. As the Utani reacted to each new tactic, Prason had been ready with the next development from ancient Earth warfare. She was now employing the tactics of Philip of Macedonia, who made use of cavalry to harry the enemy's rear. It would be all the more devastating due to the rarity of horses on this world. Prason assured him there were plenty more tactics to come, but Yorvin hoped this was the last that would be needed.

He spoke into his communicator. "Prepare the defensive line. Archers, get ready to fire."

Acknowledgements returned from the chieftains of each unit. Yorvin recognised Dornis among them, leading one of the three elite units that were held in reserve.

The enemy broke into a charge, their archers following a distance behind. Yorvin let the leading ranks enter bow range and waited a moment before moving his forces into action.

"Archers, fire! Cavalry, charge!"

A volley of arrows rose into the air and rained down on the charging enemy. Many fell, wounded or dying.

At the same time, two groups of cavalry broke from their hiding places, a forest to the left, a hillock to the right. They charged headlong at the enemy archers, who had only a few infantry for protection.

Yorvin watched the blue pulse of laser rifles from the right – and then the left – aiming at the archer's leaders. The Utani and their allies returned fire at the oncoming cavalry, not the Corini's main line. Several horsemen dropped.

A blue bolt of energy shot from within the enemy ranks. Another Corini rider fell. Immediately, two bolts struck from the Corini flanks. An explosion in the Utani camp told Yorvin that the marines had silenced the enemy's laser weapon.

Another volley of Corini arrows sailed over the enemy line. More stumbled and fell under the rain of death. But two parts of the enemy charging line were doing better than the others. The Utani had concentrated their shield-bearing warriors there.

"Archers," Yorvin barked into his communicator, "concentrate your fire on the two shielded groups."

Although he heard the order relayed, not all the archers reacted in time. A third volley of arrows showered over them. Two walls of shields came up and it was too late for another volley.

"Reserves," he ordered, "left and right units move to reinforce behind the oncoming shielded groups."

Arrows fizzed over Tobin's head as the archers behind loosed their bows. Sailing beyond the Corini defensive lines, the arrows rained down upon the advancing Utani. Tobin's mouth was dry, and he shifted from foot to foot, eager for the waiting to be done.

He stood in a group of forty warriors formed into two rows. Nerac stood to his left. Dornis to his right. His father focused on the distance as he listened to his earpiece.

"Understood, Bandrell," Dornis said. He turned to the men and called, "We are needed. Forward."

As one, the warriors raised their shields and advanced toward the forward line. The Corini warriors ahead still held the line. Why was there any need for reserves?

Five metres short of the line, Dornis signalled a halt.

"Fill any gaps in the wall," he shouted over the clash of steel and wood ahead.

Movement caught Tobin's eye. A small, round ball rose over the Corini shield wall, coming from the Utani lines. Glancing to the left he saw another a few metres to the left and others beyond. The nearest landed in the grass between the line and the reserves, glistening in the light of the Sun.

Nerac edged forward towards it, sword stretched out, preparing to test the ball.

"What sorcery…?" Tobin wondered. His eyes widened. "Sorcery!" he shouted. "Take cover!"

Tobin planted his shield on the ground. As he did, Nerac turned to him, their eyes meeting for a moment as Tobin dropped to a crouch behind his shield.

The air was filled with fire and thunder. A blow beyond any man's strength slammed into Tobin's shield, bowling him backwards into the warriors behind. He lay sprawled on the ground. Around him, men shouted but he could hear nothing.

227

Climbing to his feet, Tobin looked forward. Smoke hid the Corini line. Nerac lay on the ground, unmoving, his face scorched and blackened. His eyes were open, but sightless.

To Tobin's side, Dornis coughed and began pushing himself up. Around them, most of the other warriors were struggling to their feet.

The smoke cleared. Shadowy figures emerged, looming over the crumpled bodies of men. One raised a sword, slamming it downwards into a prone figure which arched upwards before falling limply back to the ground.

"Shield wall," Tobin shouted, but he could barely hear his own voice.

Countless hours of training kicked in. As the number of Utani emerging through the smoke grew, so did the wall of Corini shields waiting for them. Dornis's shield came into place. Tobin looked to his right. His father was grim-faced, blood oozing from a dozen cuts, mouthing soundless words.

The shield wall took a step forward, ragged at first. Then a second, and a third. Now they stepped as one and the Utani crashed against a solid wall of wood.

Tobin braced himself against the onslaught, holding his ground. He thrust his sword between the shields. It was blocked. He pushed harder. It slid forward into unseen flesh.

A spear thrust came over the top of his shield. Tobin ducked, feeling the tip strike a glancing blow on his helmet. Again, he thrust his sword, this time feeling the tip strike wood.

Blows hammered against his shield, but the line held.

Yorvin watched, ashen faced. The reserves plugged the holes in the Corini lines caused by the grenades. The shield walls of his elite troops caught the Utani wedges seeking to break through. But how many had just died?

"Defensive line, wheel to engage the enemy," he ordered. "Central reserves, make sure nothing gets through to our rear."

The Corini line split in the centre, moving to the sides of the two wedges, each man focused on his next opponent, on his own battle to stay alive.

"Cavalry, we need you to attack the rear of the wedges."

"The archers have broken, sir," Prason shouted, "but if we ease up on them now, they might reform."

"It has to be done," Yorvin said. "Charge the wedges. Send in some laser fire."

"Yes, sir."

At the far end of the field, the cavalry, reduced to two thirds of its original numbers, wheeled round and charged. The marines ran by the side of the horses, not quite able to keep up. Then they stopped, blue laser pulses streaming from their weapons in rapid fire.

Taking his own rifle from his shoulder, Yorvin fired into the central mass of one of the wedges.

As the cavalry grew close to engaging, it became too much for many at the Utani rear. They scattered, fleeing the field. Then the horses were upon the remainder.

Seconds later, the enemy chieftains blew horns to sound the retreat.

Yorvin watched the broken ranks of the three tribes scatter as they ran.

He raised his communicator. "Sharna, it's safe now. Do what you can for the wounded."

Hundreds of bodies were strewn across the ground. Sharna heard the intakes of breath and the exclamations of the healers from the other villages. They had dealt with the effects of sword and arrow on men's flesh before. But none had seen anything like this.

The first warrior Sharna reached was lying on his front. Rolling him over, she found his face and arms severely burnt. He was impaled in the stomach by the tip of a spear. He groaned. He was barely conscious. She held the Aydoc over him and brought it to life. Adjusting the settings to concentrate on bleeding, she made the mist descend. She pulled on the broken spear. It withdrew from his body, with only a little extra blood as the technology worked within him. The mist rose. She looked at the man's burns. As they did not threaten his life, she moved on.

The second warrior was dead, part of his face burned away. She moved on.

The third warrior was dead, the fourth also. Each time, she moved on.

Circling outwards, finding a warrior still alive, she put the Aydoc into action to reattach a near-severed arm.

So it went on, moving from man to man, doing what she could for each, then moving on.

A battle-armoured marine came close, removed their helmet. It was Prason. Rowan would be using his own medical skills somewhere.

"Is there anything I can do to help?" she said.

"I think," Sharna snapped, "you and the rest of the warriors have done enough already."

"I only offered help. A simple no would have done."

"I'm sorry," Sharna said. "That was unfair. If you could move ahead and see which men are alive and dead, that would be of help."

"Of course."

With Prason's help, she worked more quickly, eventually reaching the last of the wounded who could be helped by the Aydoc. More needed to be done on burns and smaller wounds, but that could wait.

* * * * *

"Yorvin," Dornis called. He looked weary, his face covered in grime and blood.

"Chieftain," Yorvin said. "You fought well. All the Corini did."

Dornis nodded. "They did. But we were glad of your training and knowledge."

"Advantages which caused the conflict in the first place, my friend. I'm sorry that my wish to help has brought this trouble upon you."

"There are one or two of the chieftains who might agree with that, but even they have to recognise how much we have gained. No-one in our villages has died from lack of food since you arrived. Disease is rare. The life you gave to the Aydoc has prevented many more deaths. And that is why I have come to speak with you. I believe the chieftains are now ready, with the victory in this battle, to proclaim you king."

Although it was the goal he had been working towards for five years, it still came as a shock that the moment had arrived.

Dornis, having seen the threat the aliens represented for himself, had worked throughout to prepare the ground. Yorvin's transfer of knowledge had been effective. The Corini were stronger than ever before, which had given Dornis the tools to win the Chieftains over.

"That's excellent news," Yorvin said. "I'll do my best to make sure the Corini prosper now, as well as in the future."

"I know you will," Dornis said. "That's why I have worked for this moment."

Dornis went off to tend to the more sobering matter of discovering which of his warriors had died. By the latest estimates, there were fewer than one hundred dead, a significant proportion from the two blasts.

231

Prason had informed him, given the signature and effects of the explosions, they were most likely grenades hoarded for more than three hundred years. They must have been stored properly, or they would have been inert or gone off in the hands of their owners. That and the enemy laser-rifle showed this was not just a re-enactment of ancient Earth warfare.

Looking out across the field once more Yorvin saw Sharna. She was gaunt and ashen, spatters of blood covering the front of her dress. She was desperately trying to hold back tears, losing the struggle.

He watched, as she came close, unsure what to say. He gathered her into his arms. Guilt flooded through him – stronger than usual. There was the familiar feeling of betrayal that had come from his marrying Sharna. He knew Jan was probably still alive on Sattoria, waiting for his return. It had been more than a year now and still the feeling had not dimmed. But Sharna understood, tolerated his evening walks, his gazing towards his homeworld. She was a good and gentle woman. And now he had put her through hell on a battlefield while he watched from a safe, insulated distance.

"Sharna, I'm so sorry. I should not have asked you to do that."

The floodgates of her grief opened. She sobbed against his shoulder, her frame juddering. He knew no way of taking her pain away, so he held her close, stroked her hair, whispered hopelessly inadequate platitudes.

"It had to be done," she whispered back eventually, "and I had to be one of the healers. Just tell me it will never be like that again."

"It won't. The Ascani and the Judini will not want to fight us. The Utani will not find new allies easy to come by."

He drew her away from the field where the Corini dead and wounded were being loaded on to wagons. She did not have to see any more.

32.

From the edge of the village, Adran looked towards the horizon.

"I feel so useless, Sarah!" he said, kicking a loose stone. "I should be out there helping, not sitting on my backside here."

"You know the reasons why you should stay back, Adran," his wife said, showing signs she bore his child. "They will return safely. The lieutenant will see to that."

It was one thing to understand that those who had spent years learning the new technologies were too important to risk in battle. It was quite another to feel comfortable with it when your friends, even your mother, were risking their lives.

"Come on," she said. "Let's get those calculations completed before they return."

Adran accompanied her to the two-storey wooden building towering over the rest of the village. The university, as Cobannis called it, was the centre for the new knowledge. The brightest young Corini men and women from all the villages came here to learn. Most then returned to their villages after a few months, with knowledge to boost the agriculture, metal working and other crafts of their villages, making the tribe prosper more than ever before.

A small number, who showed a quick understanding of technology, were invited to stay and learn more advanced knowledge: how to read and write, how to use the technological devices Yorvin and Sarah had brought with them to this world, and even about the stars and planets. It opened up a whole new understanding. It still amazed Adran that a significant number of the stars he could see in the night sky had worlds orbiting them with men and women living on them. It was both tantalising and frustrating to know this, for the next lesson was that the Fall had made it impossible to see these things for himself.

They were working on calculating the precise dates and locations of solar eclipses using the computer, after Sarah had suggested these might be a way of warning when the force field was about to fail. Adran didn't fully understand how such a thing could be predicted so long in advance. He'd been forced to abandon his disbelief when Sarah had told him the date of such an eclipse over a month before it happened.

It was his job to check the first set of figures by re-entering the numbers that represented the positions of the sun and the moon into the computer for a new calculation. He did so, set the program running once more, then brought up some pages of a text on astronomy he was studying.

Adran found it difficult to concentrate, knowing news of the battle would reach them soon. But he forced himself to read on. It wasn't long before he gave up, barely remembering anything he had read. He went to the window to gaze once more at the horizon that hid his mother and friends.

A horseman galloping at full pace came into view.

"There's a messenger coming," Adran called.

They raced downstairs and out to meet him.

It was Tobin. He looked weary, blackened, a bandage around his right arm, but there was a smile on his face. "Adran, we were victorious."

"Is everybody safe?" Sarah said.

"Most are," he said. "Yorvin, Sharna and my father are. Prason and Rowan are all right too, but I'm not sure anything could harm them."

"Thank the gods," Adran said.

Tobin paused. "Nerac is dead. There were more than a hundred who perished. There could be others from our village, but I left before it was known."

"Nerac," Adran repeated. He thought back to the time when the older warrior had encouraged a naïve young boy. A boy who missed a throw on his first hunt. "He was a good man."

Tobin nodded. "He was. Many good men have died today."

"What now?" Sarah asked.

"Everybody is on their way here," Tobin said, "including all the chieftains. I need to talk to my mother so preparations can be made. I'll speak to you properly when I've done that."

With that, he raced off.

The village was a bustle of preparations until the chieftains returned. The two hundred warriors escorting them made for an impressive sight – and this cheered the villagers who had congregated to welcome the victors.

Adran caught sight of his mother and Yorvin near the front. In a stark contrast to those smiling around her, she was subdued and pale, making him wonder if she had been wounded after all.

Dornis led the chieftains to the university building. Its lower floor contained the largest room in the village and could easily house all twenty-six of them in comfort. His mother and Yorvin made their way upstairs, clearly not required for whatever discussion was taking place. As Yorvin had been in the middle of everything for more than four years, his exclusion meant something was afoot.

Adran followed them up, Cobannis close behind.

"Mother," he said, "are you hurt?"

She shook her head and smiled. "I'm fine, Adran. I've just had a troubling day."

"But we won the battle, didn't we? And easily, from what Tobin was saying."

235

"Yes, we won well," Yorvin said. "There were six hundred or more bodies at the end of the battle and twice as many wounded. Your mother spent hours seeing suffering that nobody should. Relatively few were Corini, thankfully, but it was not something I or your mother want to see again. Enough of that. How has your work been going?"

"Adran's run the confirmatory calculation, sir," Sarah said. "It backed up my earlier one. We have a solar eclipse marked for this region about six months before the force field powers down."

"Excellent news, Cobannis. Can we be absolutely sure of the date?"

"We're ninety-five per cent sure at the minute," she said. "I'll need to monitor the times of dawn and dusk to check my estimate of the variation of planetary spin is correct. I'll also watch the field's power reserves drop to make sure the rate of loss stays constant. It'll be ten years or so before we can be absolutely sure but it's looking good."

"Then everything is coming together at last," Yorvin said. "The Chieftains are discussing whether to make me king. If they do, then we have a chance of keeping this world safe."

* * * * *

Yorvin gazed at Sharna. She smiled back. She wore a lustrous red dress that accentuated her mature beauty. Perhaps it was because he knew her and loved her so greatly, perhaps it was simply an inner nobility, but she already had the air of the queen she was about to become.

"Are you ready?"

"No," she said, extending her arm. "Are you?"

He shook his head. Taking her outstretched hand, he led her out of their hut.

236

The crowd erupted, the first wave of cheers forcing them back a step because of its intensity. Many of the faces were familiar, inhabitants of the village he had come to know. More still were unfamiliar. Some from all the Corini villages had made the journey.

He and Sharna turned towards the university building, where the coronation was to take place. They took up a slow but steady pace so they could acknowledge as many as possible. Sharna's grip on his hand tightened. He loosened his hand. He tried to relax.

Prason and Rowan, who had been standing on either side of the doorway, fell into step behind them, their full battle armour and laser rifles complementing his own Civ Armour.

So, it had finally come to it. He had planned for over three years to have himself installed as king of these tribesmen. Of course, it was for the people's good, both now and in the long term. How many despots through history have claimed that? And how many had meant it sincerely when they began their rule? It had been necessary. It had to be done.

No ships had come from Sattoria. None would. They would have too many problems of their own to send a valuable ship on the faint possibility they might still be alive.

Cobannis had cobbled together a drone that had lasted long enough to scout about five hundred kilometres in all directions. The sad truth was that what little technology and civilisation that existed was centred on the old starport. The Corini were at the pinnacle of this world's development – and all the more so now he had been guiding its progress for the past few years. That meant there was no way to get off the planet without outside help.

The only other possibility was the alien planet on the other side of the portal. At Prason's request, the marines had tried a covert expedition through it about a year after the first contact. But the aliens were vigilant and preparing defences. The marines had been forced to flee. They had managed to place a radio beacon on the alien world but there was no way of knowing whether any human would ever hear it.

All possibilities were exhausted. All he could do now was prepare this world as best he could. With luck, its technology and infrastructure would be ready to power the force field when its own power failed. It was not going to be easy. There was so much advancement to be made. But he and the other Sattorians could push them far in the right direction in their lifetimes and leave written knowledge to keep the momentum going after their deaths.

Would there really be a threat in seven hundred years? The alien society could collapse; their hostility towards humans might subside; they might forget about the portal. But if they grew, if they remembered, then this world would be helpless and mankind as a whole might not be able to resist them. Having seen the danger, Yorvin knew he could not just let events run their course, even though they would not do so until he was centuries dead.

They reached the university, the crowd showing no signs of settling down. At its front stood two elaborately carved wooden chairs. The Chieftains stood behind, arrayed in the splendour of their furs, Dornis prominent in the centre.

And so he would become king because he must.

It would be a role he would play for the people. To those he knew well, he would still be Yorvin, or Bandrell, or the Lieutenant. He had realised immediately he could not face being known as King Yorvin. It would never sit comfortably. If he was to play a role, then he would do it under an assumed name so he could keep it separate from who he truly was. And none but his comrades from Sattoria would understand the significant irony of his choice.

At Dornis's bidding, he and Sharna sat on the rudimentary thrones with the marines taking guarding positions behind.

Dornis stepped into the area before them.

"People of the Corini," he bellowed, fighting against the clamour of the crowds.

Their cheers and shouts subsided slowly, a few stragglers trying to make themselves heard.

"People of the Corini," he said, now in nothing more than a raised voice. "Five years ago, we gave help to men who fell from the sky in a metal bird. We believed them to be sorcerers and, in a way, it was true. Although we learned it was not magic they brought but knowledge, the effects on our people have been like magic. We have food in plenty, our craftsmen have learned new ways that have transformed all our lives. Other tribes have grown envious and sought to take this from us. Our warriors swept them aside."

The crowd cheered, Dornis allowing a few moments before quieting them with a motion of his hands.

"It has all come about because of this man and those he leads. Your chieftains have decided it is now time to acknowledge him and what he has done for us. Will you have him as your king?"

The crowd erupted once again and took far longer to quiet.

Dornis was handed two golden circlets. He placed the first, the smaller one, upon Sharna's head.

He held the larger one above Yorvin's head and slowly lowered it.

He turned to the crowd. "Give praise to your King! Give praise to Arthur of the Corini!"

Christopher J Wright

Part 13. Amber

33.

The blackness was complete and unyielding. Although Amber scanned it every way she knew how, it revealed nothing. Duke Edrik and Doctor Fryer maintained this was a portal to another, hostile, world but the Guardians' records gave no more information than that.

The lowering of the force field had been a strain on them all. They had risked it for a few seconds after halting the work to build the steam engine and emptying the chamber of people – time they could ill afford to lose.

This thin, jagged curtain of black was not what Amber had expected. But then "portal" conjured up thoughts of a doorway with a frame and that was unlikely. Nothing had happened on the first lowering of the force field so they had risked a minute the next time. When nothing happened that time either, they prepared to investigate beyond the blackness.

Edrik insisted he was the best placed to lead the expedition due to a lifetime's awareness of this other world. He chose twenty trusted men from his personal company of soldiers to accompany Bayl, Fryer and Amber through the portal.

At Edrik's command, ten of the men took up position five metres in front of the force field, their muskets at the ready. The other soldiers stood in two groups, one at either side, ready to move at his signal.

Amber pushed the edge of her scanner against the blackness, making sure she herself did not touch it. When it met with no resistance, she held it steady and read the display. It showed a large room on the other side with breathable atmosphere.

"There's nothing that indicates danger," she said.

Edrik gestured at the lead soldier on either side to advance. They stepped into the portal and were gone. After a few seconds, they emerged back through the curtain.

"What did you see?" Edrik said.

"An empty room, Your Grace," one of the soldiers said. "There is some sort of metallic object by the left side of the portal but it didn't react to us being there."

"Front ten men through and secure the room," Edrik ordered.

The men moved forward and disappeared. After a couple of minutes, one strode back through.

"The room is secure, Your Grace."

Fryer was through before the man had finished.

Amber stepped forward. Darkness gave way to a stark, empty, dimly lit room. For a few seconds, she was overcome with dizziness. When she recovered, she saw a wide passageway, the only exit from the room. Bayl and Edrik stood close by.

The only feature within the room, other than the portal itself, was the metal object the soldier had mentioned.

It was a circular vertical pole about half a metre in diameter and made of gleaming metal. A smaller horizontal pole was attached to it, about two metres off the ground, running parallel to the portal. The entire structure was bolted to the floor.

"Do you have any idea what this might be, Professor Stefans?" Fryer said. "It seems very deliberately placed but I see no purpose for it."

"There's nothing to suggest it's a protective system," she said. "And it's too large and bulky to be a sensor." She took a step closer. "On the other hand, a sensor doesn't need to do anything."

"Duke Edrik has decided to explore a little way up the corridor," Bayl said, joining them. "We have the room to ourselves. There are no signs of any life."

"This place may be empty," Amber said, "but it doesn't look abandoned to me. It's too clean for one thing, and somebody must have left the lights on."

"I know," said Bayl. "We will have to go carefully. Have you and Doctor Fryer worked out what this might be?"

"No," Amber said. "It might be a sensor but it doesn't seem like one."

Fryer was on his knees examining it.

"I think I've found something," he said, pointing to a very fine line making a rectangle.

"It could be an access panel," Amber said. "Try pushing gently around its inner edges."

As he pressed the top of the area, the panel came forward into his hands.

"That looks like it might be a motor," Amber said, pointing at a case attached to a central circular bar. "And that next to it could be a control device."

Fryer leaned in to examine it.

Then, a soft hum rose from it and the central bar rotated.

"I didn't touch anything," Fryer exclaimed. "I didn't do that. I can't have done."

The horizontal arm began to move, swinging in an arc, its tip disappearing into the black of the portal for almost half a metre of its length.

After a few seconds, the motor switched into reverse and the horizontal arm swung back out of the portal to its original position. The hum died and silence was restored.

For another few seconds, Amber and Bayl, not moving, stared at each other.

"They'll know the force field isn't there now," she said. "If anyone is monitoring it, they'll know."

"Duke Edrik," Bayl called, "The object has just moved. We may be getting some visitors soon."

"Understood," Edrik said. He barked an order to two of his men who then hurried up the corridor, taking position at a bend fifteen metres down its length. Another man was sent back through the portal to ensure that the force field could be re-established.

Five minutes later, the two soldiers came back from the corridor.

"There's a creature coming down the passageway," one of the soldiers stammered, sweating and shaking.

"It looks like an animal," the other spluttered. "But it's walking like a man."

"Everybody take positions out of sight," Edrik ordered "Was it armed?"

"I don't think so, Your Grace. It was carrying a bag, I think, but no weapon."

"Let it get into the room before I challenge it," Edrik said.

Amber rested against one of the walls and took out her laser-pistol.

The reptile strode on long legs, taking two paces into the room and then froze. Well over two metres in height, it towered above the humans.

They, too, were rooted to the spot.

But Amber, experienced in dealing with the unknown and the unexpected, stepped forward, making a show of pointing her laser away from the alien.

"Hello," she said. "We mean you no harm." She knew the words themselves were unimportant. It was the calmness of her voice that mattered.

Edrik raised his pistol to take aim, the twenty muskets of his men following suit.

The alien dropped its bag and bolted for the corridor. One of the soldiers let fly with his musket, hitting the wall above the head of another of the soldiers.

"After it!" Edrik shouted.

The men closest to the corridor gave chase. By the time Amber reached the opening, the alien, moving extremely quickly – faster than a man could run – had reached the first turn.

"Don't let it get away," Edrik shouted.

The alien disappeared around the corner. A few seconds later, the first two of the soldiers reached the turn, slowed to a halt, took aim, fired up the corridor and then ran again.

The next man to reach the turn slowed. "We got it, Your Grace."

Amber sighed.

34.

The creature was still alive, although wounded and in no condition to communicate.

Bayl could scarcely believe what he was looking at. It looked like an animal, yet it was wearing grey-green clothing and it had been carrying a bag.

Duke Edrik crouched beside it, examining the wound. "We need to get a stretcher and take this creature to a doctor back at the camp." A soldier headed back towards the portal.

"We should place guards further up the corridor," Bayl said. "We need to know if more of these creatures come to investigate."

Edrik nodded towards two of his men who then made their way forward.

Bayl joined Amber and Fryer back in the room. They were looking through the bag the creature had dropped.

"What was it carrying?" he said.

"Tools," Fryer said. "It looks as if they thought the arm had malfunctioned and had come to check it."

"They tell us more than that," Amber said. "The tools are well made from a high technology society. The question is how advanced?"

"What can we do?" Bayl said.

"Either," she said, "we retreat immediately and make what preparations we can, or we try to find out more about this civilisation."

"As we are here, we should try to find out more," Edrik said, now standing beside Bayl. "The more information we have, the better our chances. I'll leave the bulk of the men to guard the portal and take the creature through. The rest can come with us."

Edrik turned to the leader of his troops. "Sergeant, you are to hold the portal against any more of these creatures. Only open fire if you're under direct threat. If you're forced back through the portal while we are away, switch the force field on immediately. Then, lower it for one minute on the hour for the next six hours."

"If you haven't returned by then, Your Grace?"

"Then you are to assume the worst," Edrik said, "and get news of this to His Majesty."

"Understood, Your Grace."

The corridor in which the creature had been wounded stretched more than a hundred metres. This meant that it provided a good defensive position from either direction.

With two soldiers at the front and a further two at the rear, the group made their way along. The corner revealed another stretch of passageway, as long as the previous one, but with a door about thirty metres along on the right.

Edrik opened it. Beyond, a flight of stairs led upward.

The stairs were difficult to manage, too large for comfortable climbing. They had been designed for longer and more powerful legs than a human's.

After several flights, they came to another door. And beyond that was another corridor, this time with many doors on either side. They tried the nearest two – both were locked.

"Locked doors suggest something of worth behind them," Fryer said.

"Yes, indeed, Doctor," Bayl said. "Perhaps one of the men should do the honours?"

At Edrik's nod, a soldier forced his shoulder against the door. Although it shuddered at the blow, it remained in place. At the second attempt, the door burst inwards. Beyond was a small office.

Amber went to a desk with a screen upon it. She examined it for a moment, then pressed a button. The screen sprang to life, displaying some writing which made no sense to Bayl. Even the letters that made it up were unrecognisable.

"Does that mean anything to you?" he said.

"Not a thing. It's no surprise, though. This is a language and writing system that has arisen independently of humankind. It's bound to be very different."

Bayl looked around the room, his attention drawn to two bookshelves. At least, they appeared to be bookshelves, but the rectangular contents were too thin to be books and were made of a harder, more lustrous substance of varying colours. They all exhibited the same style of writing on their edges. Bayl pulled a red "book" from one of the shelves and examined it. One of the sides contained a series of buttons along one edge in the style of the alien lettering.

"What is this?"

Amber joined him. "Information storage, I would say."

She touched one of the buttons. A panel of dim white light appeared next to the buttons with alien lettering on it.

"See," Amber smiled.

Edrik stepped into the office for a closer look. "Will you be able to learn anything from these books or this device?"

"Nothing specific," Amber said. "It would take months with the help of one of the aliens or years without. But it does tell us something. This comes from an advanced society and there is no sign of any input device for the computer which means it will be voice controlled."

"You can be sure of this?"

"Not sure, no. At least not from just one room and what we saw downstairs. Let's move on to the next door."

The soldiers applied themselves to a door along the passage on the opposite side. It opened at the first attempt. The room was similar in layout, with bookshelves and a desk with viewing screen, but this wasn't what caught Bayl's attention. The far wall was covered with a long, closed blind.

Pulling the blind aside, he gasped.

The room was high up on a hillside and provided a panoramic view of a city stretching away on a plain below. But this was a city unlike any Bayl had seen before. In terms of its size alone, Denford was nothing more than a hamlet in comparison. It was night outside, which surprised Bayl, as it had been morning when they passed through the portal. The lights of the city disappeared into the distance as far as he could see. Buildings towered like gem-encrusted arms stretching upwards towards the sky. Little fireflies of light moved slowly among them.

Amber was standing close beside him.

"No," she breathed.

"What are those lights moving amongst the buildings?" he said.

"They're vehicles, Bayl, and that means they are technologically very advanced. This rivals Vindor, where I was born, and that is the capital of the League."

"You mean," he said, still transfixed by the majestic display, "that there are worlds where men live like this?"

"Yes," she said. "'Though not that many. In one sense, this is as bad as things could be. If the aliens are hostile, then Enodia is in great danger. Shooting the one alien we've met so far is not going to help relations."

"It is as Arthur warned," Edrik said, coming forward. "We must return home and prepare as best we can."

"But we don't know," Bayl said, "that this has to end in conflict. If we can show them we mean no harm, then perhaps we can make peace."

"Do not be naïve," Edrik said. "Can't you see what is going to happen?"

Bayl stared at Amber, willing her to agree with him. Edrik and Fryer also looked to her, challenging her to disagree with the duke. She was gazing at the city below them.

"I think," she said, bowing her head, "I must agree with Duke Edrik."

"Amber – ?" Bayl whispered.

"Events are too far along a course," she said. "They can't realistically be turned back now. We've seen their language. There's no way we will be able to communicate with them well enough to negotiate. If this was the first ever contact between us, then there might be hope. But we know that Arthur's dealings with them ended in conflict. What's more, the technology needed to construct the force field is so advanced, it must be from before the Fall. That means there was previous contact between mankind and the aliens and that went badly. If we're lucky, they might not be sufficiently interested in us to investigate. But, given what we've seen, I think we have to assume the worst."

"I'm glad you finally see the reality of our situation," Edrik said. "It gives me no pleasure to be right, but Arthur had seen them for himself. He knew this was a highly probable outcome."

"In that case," Bayl said, "we should take whatever we can for study and return home before they react to our presence."

"Agreed." Amber set about taking a handful of books.

Bayl grabbed some from the other bookshelf and then took a final look at the alien city. "Amber," he said. "I look forward to visiting Vindor and properly seeing a city such as this."

She looked out at the city. "It's not the perfection that a view like this might make it seem."

"That's hard to believe looking at this." He watched one of the flying vehicles, larger and brighter than the others. It took him a few moments to realise it was because it was drawing closer to the hillside.

"There's a vehicle approaching us," he said, pointing.

"It's close," she said, following the line of his arm, "and it's big enough to be a troop carrier. We have to get back to the portal now."

"Everybody grab what you can and go," Edrik ordered.

He gathered some books into his arms.

Amber had put hers down on to the desk and was scrutinising the back of the display panel.

"What are you doing, Amber? We don't have time."

"The computer might be built into the display. This could be valuable." She pulled some wires from the screen and lifted it up. "Let's go."

They hurried from the office and retraced their path along the corridor and down the flights of stairs. As they neared the bottom, Bayl heard musket fire and another, unfamiliar, sound like the screeching of a wounded bird.

At the bottom of the stairs, Edrik opened the door and glanced out into the corridor. He signalled for everybody to follow and then ran out.

Bayl was near the rear. When he got out into the corridor, he looked to the sound of the muskets. Three soldiers were standing at the next corner beyond the stairs. Two were reloading, the third crouched at the corner taking aim. As Bayl watched, a glow of white light slammed into the wall behind the man taking chunks of masonry out of it.

While all the others fled towards the portal room, Edrik ran towards his men.

As Bayl neared the corner, he heard a scream. One of the soldiers was lying on the ground. Edrik was pulling him away from the corner. He checked the man for a pulse, shaking his head.

"Run!" he shouted, seeing Bayl. "They'll be on us soon."

Edrik and the two other soldiers with him sprinted back towards Bayl.

Bayl ran on, past another group of three soldiers guarding the next corner and then he could see the portal, the sight of safety spurring him on. Four more men, taking up firing positions, guarded the chamber. He ran past them and through the portal to the familiar sight of the partially built steam engine. He made for the control room, dumping the books on the floor.

"Get ready to restore the force field on my order," he shouted.

He waited in a silence that was shattered by a glowing bolt of white light, streaking through the portal and striking the far wall.

Four soldiers emerged, running at a crouch and scattering to either side, two bolts of light following them

Edrik was next. He dived through the portal and landed in a heap on the floor. Smoke rose from his body and he lay where he had fallen.

Three men were still unaccounted for, but they could wait no longer.

"Now," Bayl shouted.

It took a second for the force field to spring into life, but Bayl watched, horrified. One of the reptiles had stepped through the portal before the field had formed, its face and body hidden behind a suit of armour.

It looked back at the shimmering light of the force field, then turned towards the remaining soldiers as it raised its own weapon.

A volley of musket fire rang out.

The alien staggered backwards under the onslaught. It steadied itself then stepped forward, unharmed. Aiming at one of the soldiers, it felled him with a bolt of laser fire. Some of the soldiers ran forwards, bayonets held ready. Others fled. The alien took aim again. One of the charging soldiers dropped.

Before they reached the alien, another soldier fell to the ground. Only two remained.

They stabbed forward, but their blades were even less effective than their musket balls, sliding harmlessly off the battle armour. The alien struck out at one with a powerful leg, sending the man sliding across the floor like a fallen skittle. The other turned to run, his courage spent, but a swipe of an armoured hand knocked him senseless to the ground.

As the alien took careful aim at the fallen man, Amber raised her laser-pistol and shot the creature in the back.

It staggered, crying out, and turned towards her, raising its weapon.

She fired again, and again, not counting how many shots she fired, not knowing how many hit the alien. But when she finally dared to stop, it lay on the ground lifeless.

She looked around, taking in the shocked, silent scene.

Only six of the soldiers were standing. Their comrades lay scattered about the room, dead or wounded. Duke Edrik among them.

In eight days, the power would fail and they would be defenceless.

The situation could not be worse.

The force field flared.

The aliens were probing it, awaiting their chance.

35.

Relieved he was still alive, Bayl got up and approached the alien's body. As he drew close, he slowed, watching for any sign of life. Amber's pistol had punched half a dozen black-edged holes in the creature's armour. It lay unmoving.

Bayl picked up the alien's musket. He needed to be sure there would be no more deaths. Looking around, six men lay dead or wounded on the ground. Some of them were moving, thank the gods.

"Get a doctor down here," he called to one of the soldiers. Dazed, the man didn't hear him. Bayl went to him and placed a hand on his shoulder. "We need a doctor, here."

"Yes, Sir," he said, running off towards the stairs.

"The rest of you, check the wounded and do what you can till the doctor gets here."

Then Bayl recognised that Duke Edrik was among the fallen and rushed to his side.

Edrik was face down. A large wound on his back had burned through his clothing, destroying flesh and bone beneath. Bayl rolled him over, checked for a pulse. He could find none and the duke's open eyes were lifeless.

"He turned towards his men rather than the portal when we were fleeing," Amber said, now standing beside Bayl. "I wouldn't have expected that of him."

"I was surprised he insisted on coming with us. I wonder if he was looking for an honourable death."

Amber nodded. "He was an arrogant, ambitious man, but I think he was doing what he thought was right. The past few days must have been humiliating."

Bayl stood. "Thank you for saving our lives," he said. "You showed great courage to face that – that monster."

"I was weak, Bayl," she said, blushing. "I could have shot the alien sooner, but I froze. Some of those men died because of me."

Bayl rose and put his arm around her. "No, Amber. If you were a trained soldier, I could accept that, but you're a scholar. I doubt you've been forced to kill before?"

She shook her head and turned away.

"That you could do it at all is proof of your courage and strength. That thing was terrifying."

Amber forced a weak smile, wiped her eyes with the back of her hand. "I need to be away from this place. I need to be outside."

Bayl squeezed her arm. "I'll follow you up soon."

As Amber walked towards the stairway, Bayl went over to Doctor Fryer. He was examining the steam engine.

"Is it damaged?"

"Largely superficial," Fryer said, squinting at a partially melted area on the main boiler. "A couple of areas will need reinforcing but there doesn't seem to be any critical damage."

"Good. We need to get the men back to work as quickly as possible."

"Is there any point?" Fryer said. "Duke Edrik is dead and we're not going to finish in time. Perhaps we should think about preparing for the worst."

"I'm not ready to give up yet, Doctor," Bayl said. "We still have eight days and there might be something we can do. Having the generator as near complete as possible can only help."

Fryer shrugged. "I wondered whether – "

"Have you thought of something?"

"No," he said, shaking his head, "I was wondering how best to assign the men. I'll get them back to work."

* * * * *

On their return to Denford, Bayl went straight to the palace for an immediate audience with King Zandis and to prepare for invasion. Amber's task was to call Vindor's military might here as soon as possible.

The transfer of her holo-recordings to her main computer were complete. She prepared the Astracomm for transmission and activated the camera.

"This is Professor Amber Stefans of the Department of Anthropology, Central University of Vindor. Broadcasting from Denford, capital city of Enodia. Broadcast date: 319-047.

"This message is of vital importance to the security of the Vindoran League and should be forwarded to the nearest officials of the League or its allies. If you can reach us within seven days, please come to our assistance. The rest of this message will be encoded with Vindoran Public Key Beta-3."

Amber tapped a key on the computer, beginning the encryption. She didn't want to cause a panic and this information would shake humanity to its innermost core. A Beta-3 encryption would allow the governments of all allies to see the message. That was crucial. Anything higher would mean the message would have to travel too far before anybody could hear it and react.

"I am including recordings that I personally have made of a portal to another world which was discovered on this planet. This new world is home to an alien civilisation which is the equal of the most advanced of those in the League. The aliens are reptilian in nature and have shown extreme hostility. Historical records here suggest that at least two previous contacts have been made, both of which ended in conflict. The portal is protected by an advanced pre-Fall force field. The energy source is due to fail in seven days. Efforts to power it with local technology have been unsuccessful.

"It is my belief that we will be invaded soon after the field powers down. This world is unable to mount a defence against the laser weapons and battle armour the aliens possess. A military response should be mounted with all urgency and to the maximum extent possible. I am including recordings of their world and a defeated alien soldier, together with a full report of events that will confirm that this is a genuine threat to Vindor and the League.

"This is not a hoax. The threat cannot be overestimated. Please help us."

Amber terminated the recording, attached the promised files and set the Astracomm to wide broadcast. The message would stream towards the hub of the League at the rate of a light year a day. Here, on the edge of civilisation, she was twenty light years from the nearest military base and more than fifty from any of the core systems of the League.

She had no doubt there would be a response of some sort. With any luck, there would already be a ship on the way due to her previous message.

The most she could hope was her message would be taken seriously. And that they'd get here while there was something still here worth rescuing.

* * * * *

Fryer watched the men work at a feverish pace.

Those who had seen the armoured creature burst through the portal, scattering death like monsters of their worst nightmares, understood the true importance of their work. Their frightened tales to those above ground brought it home to them as well. So now they worked without the murmurs and grumbling of the previous three weeks.

In the past few hours, he had gone over the schedules time and again. They were going to miss their deadline by less than six days. It might as well be six months for all the difference it would make.

What he didn't understand was how it had come to this.

The Guardians' plans, laid for seven hundred years, had progressed on schedule. They had guided events to the right degree, pushed scientific effort in the right areas, amassed enough wealth to carry everything through.

When Edrik chose him to lead their preparations to construct the generator, it had been the greatest honour imaginable. The predicted eclipse would come under his stewardship. He had seen to every detail, believing he had covered every possibility.

And, because of three lost months, everything had unravelled.

But now, Fryer understood the reason.

Every time the alien creatures probed the force field, it flared and power was used. Admittedly, it was only a tiny amount for each probe – but, over the centuries, that would have added up. And, at some point after Arthur did his calculations, the creatures must have increased their probing.

And there was no way to grab the lost time back.

He looked at the force field, drawn once again to its beautiful patterns, trying to think of how to turn things round. He could think of nothing.

Almost an hour since the last probe, the force field's brightness flared up. A machine relentlessly following its orders, each probe knocking a second or two from the power reserves.

Fryer noted the time and called an assistant over. They waited. Eventually, the patterns of the force field brightened and shifted at a new probing. He pulled his pocket watch from his waistcoat.

"Confirm the time," he called to his assistant.

"Fifty-two minutes, eighteen seconds."

Again, they waited.

"Confirm the time," he called at the next flaring.

"Fifty-two minutes, eighteen seconds."

For a third time, they waited. Fryer watched the hands of his watch crawl around. Finally, the force field flared once more.

"Confirm the time."

"Fifty-two minutes, eighteen seconds."

Fryer ran from the room, leaping up steps, along corridors, men jumping out of the way as he rushed towards the stables. A saddle was thrown across a horse when he got there, the bridle strapped securely. He mounted, kicked the beast into a gallop before he had left the camp, pushing as hard as he dared.

There was a way. They would succeed after all.

36.

Amber looked at yet another page of, to her, meaningless symbols in one of the alien books. Her head spinning, she wondered why she had subjected herself to this ordeal.

Frustration. That had been the reason. Scanning information into her computer from the recovered viewers ceased to be interesting after thirty screens and became outright tedious after a hundred.

Each viewer could hold thousands of screens worth of writing, so the stack that had been recovered might run into the hundreds of thousands, even millions, of pages. When she could face no more, she let the computer analyse the two hundred she had scanned.

It would be easier to try to communicate with the captured alien. It had been brought to Denford now and was being tended to by King Zandis's personal surgeon. There was no telling how long it might be before it was well enough to speak.

The problem was the lack of time. With the day drawing to its end, there were only five more left. It was futile to try to achieve understanding of this language in such a short time. Perhaps she should just gather a few things and travel as far away as she could – or maybe in a couple more days when all hope had gone.

Amber looked up. Somebody was running up the stairs to her room. They knocked on the door and, without a pause, Bayl stepped in.

"Quickly, Amber. We're needed at the palace."

"What's happened? The aliens haven't got through, have they?"

"Nothing like that. Karl Fryer has requested an audience with King Zandis and we've been instructed to attend."

The light was fading, the pleasant warmth of a late summer evening providing a stark contrast with the seriousness of their fate.

As she climbed into the carriage Bayl had brought, she was struck by the normality of things. People were walking the streets, on their way home, some taking the evening air. They had no idea their world was about to be turned upside down.

When Bayl and Amber arrived at the Palace, they were ushered past the sentries to the king's personal rooms.

There was now a large desk in the room. Neat piles of papers were covered with an unruly layer of others, hastily discarded. Doctor Fryer was sitting in one of six armchairs arranged for those privileged enough to meet with the King.

As they went in, Fryer stood.

"What's happened, Doctor?" Bayl said.

"I should wait for His Majesty before saying anything," he said. "It wouldn't do to start without him, but it could be a way out."

Amber's frustration at Fryer's words did not last long. King Zandis emerged from an adjoining room with a sharp-faced official at his side. Bayl and Fryer bowed, Amber performing another woeful attempt at a curtsey.

Zandis looked tired, his smile equally weary. "Please sit down." He turned to Fryer. "We understand you have a matter of import that requires our immediate attention."

"Yes, Your Majesty," Fryer said. "The aliens are continuing to probe the force field, which is no great surprise. But they must be doing it in an automated fashion. Each probe causes a flaring of the shield which we can detect. My observations have determined this is happening every fifty-two minutes, eighteen seconds."

He looked at the king, then Amber, Bayl and the frowning official.

"You're not suggesting what I think you're suggesting, are you?" Amber said.

"Professor Stefans, I suspect I am. We can switch the force field off between each probing to conserve enough power to allow us to complete the generator."

The official's face went bright red, his cheeks puffed out.

King Zandis held up his hand. "That sounds like a huge risk. More a plan of desperation."

"It is, Your Majesty," Fryer said. "I make no bones about it. We know for certain we will fail in a little under five days. This offers the possibility of success."

"And also the possibility of failure in less than five days," Zandis retorted. "The creatures could break through and catch us before we use our time to the full."

"Yes, Sire, they could," Fryer said. "That is why I have requested this audience with you and asked that the Off Worlder, Miss Stefans, be present. This is too great a decision for me to take, although I believe it is our only hope."

"Professor Stefans," King Zandis said, "it seems Doctor Fryer values your opinion, perhaps because you are the one person on Enodia who might understand the technology of these creatures and how they might use it. What is your opinion?"

"I really don't know what to say, Your Majesty," she said, her mouth going dry. "This sort of decision is so far outside of my expertise."

"We realise that," Zandis said. "But we were unaware of the existence of humans beyond our own world a few short months ago, let alone other intelligent creatures that might see us as enemies. What do your instincts tell you?"

Amber looked down, gathering her thoughts.

"Societies can sometimes over-rely on technology and become lazy. They might well rely on the automated probing as they have obviously been doing for a long time. However, our expedition to their world will have, unfortunately, brought us to the attention of their leaders. They might increase the rate of probing. They might set up a random pattern. Or even do it manually. The one positive thing is, they have no reason to suspect that the force field is about to give out."

The King raised an eyebrow.

"That isn't an answer. Do you think it can work?"

"Yes, Your Majesty," Amber said. "It could work. But it is an enormous risk. It would take just one act of individualism to destroy our hopes. I don't know enough about the aliens' society to have any clear idea how likely that is."

Zandis looked to his official. "Your opinion?"

"I think it unwise to trust a member of a subversive organisation," he said, holding Fryer's eye, "and Miss Stefans admits she can't estimate the risk. We have requested aid from the Vindoran League and we are assured it will come. My advice is to use the five days we have wisely. We should prepare our city's defences and wait for that aid."

Zandis nodded, then turned to Bayl.

"Groms, what is your advice?"

"Your Majesty, I don't think that is an option. We cannot defend Denford. I also suspect that only those who have seen these creatures can fully appreciate the danger we are in. Fortunately, Professor Stefans is in a position to give you a better understanding. Amber, show his Majesty the holo-recorder."

Amber took the recorder from her belt and placed it at the front of the desk. The king's and his official's eyes widened as the holographic menu system sprang into life. They gasped when she selected a file and pulled up the image of the fallen alien soldier.

"The creature," Bayl continued, "was hit by more than ten musket balls and struck by two blades but was unharmed. His armour rendered our weapons useless. It was only Amber's laser-pistol that prevented it from slaughtering our entire group." Bayl rubbed his forehead. "I'm not even sure a cannon would stop these creatures. But for a real understanding, you must see the creature's own world."

Amber returned to the menu, selected the recording of the alien city and displayed it in all its resplendent glory.

As King Zandis and his advisor watched in absolute shock, a silence descended on the room. Bayl allowed the recording to play for a short while longer.

"As you can see," he said at last, "their world is so far ahead of ours that we cannot hope to defeat them. We must evacuate the city or try Doctor Fryer's plan. My advice would be to choose the latter and pray that fortune is with us."

King Zandis lowered his chin into his hands. "It seems that one of the most difficult and weighty decisions in our history has fallen to us. How long would the force field have to be switched off to provide you with enough time to complete your work, Doctor Fryer?"

"Just over half of the time, Your Majesty. I've calculated that it would be sufficient to keep the field running for ten minutes before and after each probe."

"Your Majesty," Amber said, "if I may make a suggestion?"

The King nodded.

"The most likely change the aliens might make is to double the rate of probing. If we reduced the time to five minutes either side of the probe, then this could be covered as well."

Zandis looked to Fryer.

"It would be a sensible precaution, Sire. Five minutes should be enough leeway to cover the expected probes."

"Then our decision is made. We will begin preparations for evacuation of the city. But we will also do as Fryer suggests."

* * * * *

"Switch the force field off!" the foreman shouted.

The shifting wall of light disappeared, leaving the jagged black tear that was the portal.

Fryer nodded.

They had already extended the life of the force field by more than a day. At least his plan had caused no harm. The risk had been justified. When the force field was first switched off, the work suffered as the men stared at the blackness from time to time, knowing nothing could protect them from the alien creatures. But they went on and, as the probes of the field continued to occur at precisely the expected times, they got on with the work without worry.

Despite a sense of optimism, he was not so foolish as to assume all would be well. If necessary, Arthur's last defence would be activated. Fryer still wrestled over whether he should have told King Zandis about it – but he was sure he had done the right thing. After all, it was the final secret of the Guardians, one that must never be revealed to any outside of the order.

"What was that?" one of the workers by the portal asked.

"What was what?"

"It was nothing, sir. I thought I saw something out of the corner of my eye but there wasn't anything."

Fryer shouted at the control room. "Activate the force field now! Quickly!" He looked to the detail of soldiers now constantly kept at the ready. "Raise your weapons."

By the time he had turned back to the portal, the force field was active.

A thud at its rightmost edge drew his attention. Fryer's jaw dropped open at the sight of a severed reptilian forearm resting on the ground. As he watched, the palm opened and a silvery ball of metal rolled out.

Before he could react, a flash of light stabbed his eyes, a blast of heat and air threw him across the room. Fryer lay on his back, dazed, every part of his body seared with pain. Summoning all his will, he raised his head from the floor to look at the force field.

It was no longer there.

Tall, armoured figures emerged from the blackness, streams of white light spewing from the weapons they carried.

Unable to hold his head up any longer, Fryer lowered it to the ground. Blackness crept around the edge of his vision and a weariness, greater than any he had known before, engulfed him.

He closed his eyes and slept.

* * * * *

Ayrus Medda awoke with a start. He must have dozed off.

He was sitting against a tree, a kilometre from decent food and a chair, stationed at the top of a small rise on the track leading from the forest. He looked back towards the camp. Something was happening.

Reaching for his spyglass, he saw men rushing here and there, some heading into the hillside complex. He focused on the entrance, his hands trembling as he tried to hold the glass steady. Soon the flow into the complex stopped, and men streamed out, running in all directions.

The creatures had broken through.

He untied his horse from a nearby tree and mounted. Digging his heels into the horse's side too strongly, the startled animal whinnied and reared up before racing off.

He pulled the horse to a stop and pulled a crumpled envelope from his pocket.

Written in Fryer's elegant script were the words: "His Majesty, King Zandis III".

Medda breathed a sigh of relief. He put the envelope carefully away and spurred the horse into a gallop towards Denford.

37.

"The aliens have broken through," Bayl blurted out as soon as Amber opened her door.

"When?"

"Four hours ago," he said. "Medda galloped here as soon as it happened. He's brought a letter from Fryer to the King."

"Then Fryer's still alive?"

"Medda says he thinks not. Fryer was in the complex and he didn't see him come out. Medda had been told to deliver the letter to the King if the worst should happen. His Majesty requests your presence immediately."

That evening, their carriage travelled through a very different city. The streets were deserted. The people who remained skulked about as if they were living on the edge of a precipice. They either had no family or friends outside the town, believed the aliens did not exist or were too stubborn to be moved by anything, including mortal danger.

Amber and Bayl were led straight to King Zandis's private chambers. Medda was standing next to one of the chairs, head bowed. The reason for his discomfort became clear when Amber saw King Zandis glaring at Medda, his nostrils flared.

Before Amber and Bayl could say anything, Zandis threw down the piece of paper he was reading. "Do either of you know what this means?"

They approached, taking in the diagram and writing on the paper.

"Yes, Your Majesty," Amber said. "It is a nuclear warhead."

He stared at her. "We understand," he murmured, "it is a weapon of great power." His face reddening, he picked up the paper, nearly screwing it up. "And yet you did not feel it important enough to mention at our last meeting that there was one within Arthur's tomb?

In fact, you sat in those chairs, knowing about this weapon. Do you want us to be conquered by these reptiles?"

"Of course not, your Majesty," she said. "But you must understand this type of weapon is so destructive that its use on any planet is illegal. It always has been, even in times of war. It would be unthinkable to use it."

"Miss Stefans, on Enodia, we are the law. We decide whether this is too terrible to use or not, do you understand?" He looked down for a moment and calmed himself. "Now, tell me about this weapon."

"Nuclear weapons," she said, "work by pulling matter apart and releasing vast amounts of energy. The result is a violent explosion that leaves the place where it exploded poisonous for a long period of time. The one in Arthur's tomb is one of the smallest but would instantly kill everything for several hundred metres and fatally wound anybody up to a kilometre away. The site of the explosion would be too dangerous to visit for two to three weeks. There would also be invisible poisons thrown into the air that could affect people's health for years to come."

"Would it kill all the aliens at the complex?"

"Undoubtedly, Your Majesty, yes."

"Would it destroy the portal?"

"We have no way of knowing for sure."

"What's your guess?"

"I'm not a physicist, Your Majesty, so my guess is worthless. I have studied human nature extensively, so I can make some deductions on that basis."

"Continue."

"Arthur had decades to consider this. He most likely was a scientist himself or had one with him. If he was sure it would work, he would have used the weapon then. Similarly, if it would definitely fail, then he would not have left those instructions. However, the fact that it was left as a last resort for the Guardians means there must be some chance of it destroying the portal."

"That sounds to us," King Zandis said, "like an elaborate way of saying you're not sure."

"I'm afraid so, Your Majesty. I believe Arthur was not sure either."

"And if the portal was not destroyed, the reptiles would wait the necessary weeks before coming through again, angered by our use of it?"

"Their armour would protect them from some of the poison," Amber said. "They might only have to wait a few days."

"How close to the complex would the weapon need to be?"

"The portal is underground. Large amounts of earth are one of the best protections against these weapons. Exploding it on the surface might not affect the portal. To have the best chance, we would need to be in the main chamber or as close to it as possible."

Zandis smacked his hands on the table and stood up. "Why did none of you tell us this a week ago? This weapon could have been ready to use when the creatures broke through. Now we know about it, we may have no way of using it effectively."

He looked at Bayl and back at Amber.

"You have put us in greater danger than was needed. In future, do not hold anything back from us, even if you think it is not the right option. And that goes especially for you, Groms. Professor Stefans at least has the excuse that she is not a subject of Enodia."

"Yes, Your Majesty," Bayl said, bowing.

"Is there anything else you have not told us?"

Nobody spoke.

"In that case," he said, "we need to find out what the creatures are doing. Groms, you will supervise the scouting with a view to formulating a plan to get the weapon into the base."

"Yes, Your Majesty."

"Professor Stefans, you and Medda will verify that the weapon is in working order. Once that is done, you will continue trying to decipher the aliens' language."

* * * * *

Bayl raised the spyglass and looked down at the forest. The hill gave a good view of its edge. He could see that the creatures had not established themselves beyond its borders during their first night on Enodia.

Although a ring of observers was now placed around the forest to watch for any movement, determining what the aliens were doing within the forest was more difficult. The clearing was well over a kilometre into the body of the trees. Seeing any detail there was all but impossible.

He signalled to four scouts near the bottom of the hill. They spurred their horses, spreading out to approach the forest from different directions. After that, there was little Bayl could do but wait.

He continued scanning but saw nothing more.

Then a distant, faint noise – unmistakably the aliens' weapons – came from the forest.

The scouts would be closing in on the clearing. The noise could only mean they had been spotted. Further sporadic explosions and bursts of fire rang out.

At last, one of the scouts came from the edge of the trees and broke into a gallop.

Bayl let out a sigh and relaxed.

A second scout came into view and both rode up the hill. As there was no sign of the other two scouts, Bayl had to assume they had been killed or captured. He moved the group out of sight, beyond the brow of the hill.

"Your reports."

The older of the two, still breathing heavily, spoke first. "They have the area well-guarded so I couldn't get too close. There are about fifty of the creatures above ground with regular patrols outside the clearing. There was some work going on within the clearing itself but I'm not sure what."

"It looked like they were building something from my angle," the other scout said. "It was difficult to see, though."

"At least," Bayl said. "there's no massive build-up of troops." But whether there were fifty of them or five hundred, with the weapons they had, Enodia's entire army wouldn't stand a chance. "Were creatures permanently stationed anywhere other than the entrance?"

"Not that I could see, sir," the first scout said. The second nodded.

"Well done, both of you. We must take this report to Denford. Split up and take different routes."

He mounted his horse and set off for the nearest road. Things were better than he had feared. There was still a chance.

* * * * *

Her hands trembling, Amber snapped the power cell into place. The warhead was seven centuries old but, with its main component having a half-life of more than 24,000 years, its destructive power was only fractionally less now than when it was constructed so many lifetimes ago. The whole thing weighed less than four kilos, yet the knowledge of what it could do made it feel much heavier.

She turned the cylinder over so that its display could be seen and then placed it on the desk. She unfolded the access panel and pressed the power button on the small keypad. The display sprang into life, its energy levels now reading at full.

"That's good?" Medda said, leaning over her.

"Yes," she said. "If anything about this whole situation can be called good."

"The Founder had great foresight and wisdom," Medda said. "You should trust that all will turn out well."

She turned and looked at Medda. "Deep down, you genuinely believe that this can't go wrong?"

"I wouldn't say 'can't', Miss Stefans. I'm not a zealot. I just have confidence in a plan formed over decades and successfully in motion for centuries."

"But the plan to power the shield has already failed," she said. "Arthur's plans can go wrong."

"It failed by the barest of margins and it was foreseen as a possibility. A second plan was provided. It may be less desirable because of the destruction it will cause, but that makes its success more likely, does it not?"

With a shake of her head, she touched the keypad again. "It's asking for a pass code."

They looked at the paper Fryer had sent.

"Obviously an old document," Amber said.

"Yes," Medda said. "The Guardians have made infrequent copies to ensure accuracy… 2-4-1-1-9."

The control system was simple enough and the ancient instructions accurately described the process of how to set a timed explosion. Amber set the timer to sixty minutes and confirmed it by re-entering the pass code.

The timer began its countdown.

00:59:59

They watched.

00:59:58

"We're assuming – " Amber said.

00:59:57

" – we can interrupt it – "

00:59:56

" – whenever we like."

00:59:55

"So the instructions say," Medda said.

00:59:54

She typed in the code.

00:59:53.

The display froze.

Amber wiped her brow.

"See," Medda said. "We have the weapon that is needed."

"All we have to do now is get it into the complex, get past the guards and destroy the portal."

"The Founder's plan will succeed."

"I hope so," she whispered. "For all our sakes."

38.

A day after the aliens breached the force field and established a foothold, the captured alien was showing signs of recovery. Its fever was subsiding, though by human standards its temperature was low. Even if it recovered instantly, it would take months to progress to the point that even simple communication was possible, time that was not available.

Bayl's scouting had shown they could get the warhead into the complex. But a distraction would be needed. King Zandis was consulting with his military advisers and tomorrow their plan would go into action, deciding the fate of the planet.

Bayl volunteered to plant the warhead.

"You can't do this," Amber said. "You're not a soldier."

"On the contrary," he said. "I have to do it. I'm the obvious choice. I'm young enough and intelligent enough. I've spent several months with you and been exposed to technology far more than anybody else on the planet. Who else could do it?"

"Now isn't the time to get an inflated ego. You could die."

"It's not about ego, Amber, it's about duty. I stand the best chance of getting this done. In any case, the top marksman in the army will accompany me with the weapon the alien soldier dropped. There is a risk. But it has been reduced as far as is possible."

She explained the controls to Bayl, making him run through the process on the weapon itself to just short of confirming the countdown. "You need to set it for ten minutes at least and then hide it where it won't be seen."

"Why ten minutes? Does it need time to prepare for the explosion?"

"This is very important," she said. "When the warhead explodes, if you are not at least a kilometre away you will die, and you need to be double that to be certain of surviving. You have to get away from the complex and escape through a forest. It's going to take ten minutes."

Amber lifted her head. She could hear a low droning sound, out of place on Enodia.

"What's that?" he said.

Amber ran to the exterior doors of the room which led to an outside balcony. Leaning against the stone parapet, she scanned the skies. It had been the noise of a flyer. Sure enough, a distant shape was moving at high speed and banking in an arc to approach the city. It drew close and flashed overhead, causing fear and panic in the streets.

The noise dimmed as the flyer sped off into the distance but Amber saw it turn for another pass. This time, as it flew over the city, it sprayed laser fire on to the buildings below. The few people still in the open fled. The flyer flew on, away from the city.

"Does that mean that we're too late?" Bayl said. "That they're beginning their attack?"

"I don't know. If we're lucky, they've only had the time to build one. We've no time to lose."

* * * * *

Still early morning, the cool of the night had not yet been warmed away by the rising sun. It promised to be a beautiful, bright and hot day.

Amber adjusted the focus on her holo-recorder to get a better view.

Despite the counsel from his advisors, the King had insisted on coming.

And so they stood within the protective cover of a small copse, near the top of a hill overlooking the forest around the complex.

Amber could make out figures moving around the hill within the clearing. But the resolution of the holo-recorder could not give a clear picture of what was happening there.

She shifted her view away from the forest. Images of four of the heaviest horse drawn artillery pieces that Enodia possessed, hidden behind another body of trees, came on to her screen. Next to them, the same number of lighter guns. A token force – nothing more – the King realising that large-scale hostilities would be suicide.

"Good," King Zandis said, lowering his spyglass. "The artillery is in position. It's time for you to take yours, Groms. Good luck."

"Your Majesty," Bayl said, "I will not fail you."

Amber embraced him, holding him tightly for a few seconds. "Be careful," she whispered. "Remember, set the warhead for ten minutes."

"How could I forget?" he smiled as they drew apart. "You've told me often enough. I will be as careful as I possibly can be. It is in my best interests after all."

He turned and descended the hill, accompanied by the army marksman who had been chosen to wield the alien weapon. Amber had given Bayl her own laser-pistol and he wore it strapped to his right side, the nuclear warhead in a cloth bag hanging at his left. The two men travelled directly away from the complex to stay out of sight, then circled away from the artillery.

After ten long minutes, Amber's radio crackled into life.

"Amber," Bayl said, "we're in position at the edge of the forest."

"Acknowledged."

King Zandis gave the signal for the artillery to move into position. The order was relayed via a series of signalmen using flags, positioned to be invisible from the complex or its surrounding forest.

The artillery galloped from their hidden positions to a flat-topped hillock a hundred metres from the edge of the forest. On reaching the top of the rise, they unhitched their guns and readied them for firing. Two minutes later, a puff of smoke escaped from the barrel of one of the larger guns.

At King Zandis's signal, Amber raised the transmitter to her lips. "Go, Bayl. The attack has begun."

"We're on our way."

After the other three large guns fired towards the forest, the crews reloaded. The clearing was at the upper limits of their range. They would be lucky if any of the shots actually hit home. All they had to do was be close enough to attract the aliens' attention. It wasn't a genuine offensive – just enough to give Bayl the chance to get close.

* * * * *

Bayl slipped the transmitter into a pocket and took the laser-pistol from his belt. He had heard the distant sound of the artillery fire.

"We need to go quietly rather than quickly," Bayl said to Lydon, the army marksman. "The important thing is to avoid their attention for as long as possible."

Lydon nodded, turned and led the way deeper into the forest, the sounds of cannon fire carrying in the wind as the full bombardment began.

"Bayl," Amber's voice spoke from the transmitter.

He pulled it from his pocket. "Yes Amber."

"We can see activity in the clearing. It looks like they're preparing to send some troops our way."

"Understood. We're about five minutes away. There's no sign of the aliens yet."

They continued onwards amidst the now constant sound of the barrage. As each shot dwindled to nothing, the next followed a few seconds later. Drawing nearer to the clearing, they heard cannon balls crashing among the trees.

Lydon motioned for him to drop to a crouch, then pointed forwards and right. Two armoured reptiles were walking across their path some fifty metres ahead. Bayl watched, hardly daring to breathe for fear of alerting them. They did not seem to take any notice.

After the aliens had moved a safe distance past, Bayl and Lydon, keeping low, hurried towards the clearing. Once in sight, Bayl used his spyglass to check what lay ahead. He counted far fewer than the fifty soldiers they had seen on the scouting mission. The diversion must be working.

There were still twenty of the reptiles in the clearing – far too many for Lydon and him to deal with. Fortunately, they would not have to.

They circled the clearing, heading towards the rear.

* * * * *

After the bombardment had been going for ten minutes, Amber spotted, through her holo-recorder, the first of the aliens at the edge of the forest.

Although the artillerymen already had their instructions, Zandis ordered the next phase of the plan to be put into operation.

But even before the order reached them, the crews of the large guns abandoned their posts, running the twenty metres to the line of the smaller guns – now, due to the hillock's contours, safely out of sight of the forest edge.

The aliens opened fire upon the abandoned weaponry. The hillside flared up into a wash of streaming laser bolts and, in a matter of seconds, all four heavy guns were hit and destroyed.

A group of the aliens, in their battle armour, advanced at a run from the tree line. There must be around thirty of them. Maybe the distraction was working too well.

The aliens travelled almost to the top of the hillock when they halted and froze. Twenty turned and ran back to the forest.

"Bayl," she whispered into the transmitter. "Twenty aliens have just turned back. They must know you're there."

The other ten carried on to the top of the slope. Coming over the lip at a run, they were hit headlong by four rounds of grapeshot fired at point blank range from the smaller guns. The aliens, knocked backwards, tumbled down the slope. The crews of the smaller guns turned, ran to their horses and fled for their lives.

Seven aliens were pulling themselves back to their feet, the other three left on the ground. When they reached the crest of the hill, they took aim at the fleeing men, who were still galloping for the cover of nearby copses. A few were hit and fell to the ground. The others sped on to safety.

There was a pause, no doubt the reptile soldiers waiting for orders from their commanders. They then destroyed the artillery pieces, returned to their dead comrades and carried them back into the forest.

Amber breathed a sigh of relief.

But the sound of the low rumble of engines screaming overhead made her duck. The flyer sped toward the copse where the artillery men had taken refuge and rained laser fire down upon it.

* * * * *

Now within the paths of the patrols, Bayl and Lydon lay flat on the ground hiding from aliens patrolling to their left, waiting for them to pass by. Bayl could see his objective, the partially dug ventilation shaft that Dr Fryer had needed for his steam-powered generator. Although they did not know exactly how far the shaft had progressed, Fryer's estimates of four days' work remaining meant it must reach virtually all the way down to the underground chamber. Close enough for what they needed.

Bayl felt a tap on his shoulder. Lydon pointed towards the aliens. One of them had an object in his hands that looked similar to one of Amber's technological devices. The alien was turning in a full circle. When he was facing them, he stopped and pointed directly at them.

The aliens advanced slowly, one still looking at the object he was holding, the other looking from side to side, weapon raised.

Bayl raised the laser-pistol and aimed it at the left alien, Lydon aiming at the other.

Bayl mouthed a silent countdown. Then both opened fire. Having seen what it took for Amber to bring down the alien in the portal room, Bayl fired three times in quick succession. Lydon hit the other twice in the chest. Both fell to the ground.

"Make sure they're dead," Bayl said. "I'll start to place the warhead. We'll have to be quick now."

As he reached the top of the ventilation shaft, Amber came through on the transmitter. "Bayl," she whispered, "twenty aliens have just turned back. They must know you're there."

The shaft, located a few metres into the clearing, was quite large at the top. Some discarded mounds of earth gave them protection from sight and weapon fire.

His hands sweated as he pulled the warhead, already attached to a thin rope, from his bag.

As he keyed in the passcode, Lydon reached him.

"They're both dead, sir, but the creatures must have heard that."

"They did," Bayl said. "Twenty have turned back from the artillery, but at least those should be too far away. Keep watch. Try to hold them back."

He stopped. The aliens might now guess what Bayl intended and, if that were so, they had lost the element of surprise. Ten minutes would give them the time to find the warhead.

He adjusted the figure and tapped in the passcode.

"Amber," he said into the transmitter, "I'm setting the timer for six minutes."

"Bayl, it's not enough time."

He lowered the warhead on its rope.

"We've got a couple more, sir," Lydon said, opening fire and giving a grunt of satisfaction.

The rope slackened. The warhead must have reached the bottom. Bayl threw the remainder of the rope and the bag into the hole. As Lydon took careful aim once more, alien weapon fire hit the earth mound.

"We have to go now," Bayl said. "Right now."

A bolt of white fire sped from the marksman's weapon and then he was rising to his feet.

"We'd better hurry, sir. There'll be more any second."

In an instant, Bayl was up and running. The forest was quite sparse, so it didn't slow them too greatly, but they still had to choose routes around larger trees and over uneven ground.

He raised the transmitter again. "Amber, we're on our way out. Tell us when we have thirty seconds."

Half a dozen fire-bolts filled the forest around them, slamming into trees left and right. Bayl didn't dare look round to see if Lydon had survived – for fear of falling – but he soon heard the man's laboured breathing. He was unharmed.

As the forest sped past around him, he heard more bolts from the aliens' weapons hit trees behind him – although there were fewer now.

He ran as fast as he could. His lungs were on fire. His heart felt ready to burst. He willed Amber's voice to tell him the time was up, so that he could finally stop.

"Thirty seconds!" Amber called. "Find the biggest mound of earth you can and hide behind it."

Tears streamed down her cheeks. Why hadn't he left enough time? It was a simple enough thing to do.

"We're taking cover," Bayl said.

Ten seconds.

"Bayl, you can't die."

"I won't. I'm well hidden."

Five seconds.

She lowered the transmitter and looked towards the forest, trying to guess where he must be.

Two seconds.

The alien flyer passed overhead.

A light, as bright as the brilliantly shining sun, exploded from the centre of the clearing. A fireball erupted from the hill and rose into the sky.

"Cover your ears!" she shouted, clamping her hands over her own and turning away. Even then, the thunderous crash and howling wind nearly threw her over.

When she looked back, she saw devastation. The forest by the clearing had been vaporised and, for almost a kilometre, not a tree was standing.

She shouted into the transmitter. "Bayl? Can you hear me?"

There was nothing but static.

The alien flyer climbed up into the sky over the place where the clearing had once been. Now it was nothing but a huge debris-strewn crater.

The flyer circled for more than a minute before speeding away on a course that would take it directly towards Denford.

Christopher J Wright

Part 14. Yorvin/Arthur

39.

"Grandfather, you'll catch a chill out here in the cold." The young woman wrapped a warm fur cloak about his shoulders.

"Thank you, my dear," he said. "The cold creeps up on me, but you know how I enjoy walking out here when the stars come out. The cold nights are the best. The skies are clear and the stars are brighter."

She gave him an affectionate peck on the cheek.

"Yes, but you need to stay warm too. Don't be too long," she said, turning towards the inviting glow of the nearby house.

"You know," he said, "you're the image of your grandmother."

She turned to face him again, smiling.

For an instant, it felt like Sharna was there.

"Yes, I know," she said. "You must have told me a hundred times."

Yorvin smiled back at her. "I'm sorry. I'll be in soon."

He missed Sharna terribly. The long months since her death had been lonely ones. Even the work of guiding Enodia now seemed hollow.

Perhaps it was time to abdicate and let Adran take on the kingship. He was more than ready and, now in his late forties, must be wondering if he would ever rule in his own name. Yorvin had thought about it for months now. Twenty-six years was enough for anyone.

He looked heavenwards, searching out his marker star. Just to the right of it, he knew Sattoria's star sent its light to him – so dim after its sixty-year journey that his failing eyesight could no longer make it out. But he knew it was there and so he maintained his ritual of gazing towards a star that he could not see, lost in thoughts of what was and what might have been.

His daughters, who had been only five and eight when he last saw them, would be thirty-seven and forty now. They would have lives that were completely unknown to him. Were they married? Did they have children of their own?

His thoughts, as ever, turned to Jan. The waves of guilt had lost their intensity over the years, but they still lapped gently at the shores of his mind. He had betrayed her. It was as simple as that. That he knew they would never see each other again, that she no doubt thought him dead, that he'd had to build a new life here – they were all extenuating circumstances. But they didn't change that simple fact.

In nearly thirty years, if she still lived, Jan would be reminded of him. His message to her would be just over halfway home now and he often wondered if it was wise to have sent it. Still, there was nothing that could be done to change that now.

He looked up again, imagining that he could just make out Sattoria. An old man's mind playing tricks. When that light had set out on its long journey, he had been a child. Now, when that same light reached him, he was an old man. He had lived his life as best he could. He'd done everything in his power to help this world that had become his new home.

A change in the wind made Yorvin feel the cold more keenly. He made his way to the house. It was a sturdy, timber structure, one of the new generation of buildings that were finally coming into fashion. Many in the outer villages still preferred their traditional huts.

A fire was glowing warmly in the stone fireplace. Adran sat near it, reading a book.

After most of the fuel cells lost their power years ago, there was a frantic rush to copy the most useful information from the computers on to paper. Even so, only a small fraction of human knowledge was copied in time.

Cobannis managed to rig up a generator, but it was impossible to regulate its power tightly enough. Two of the computers were fried by overloads and they didn't dare try to use the remaining two. As a result, the boost to technology was not as great as he'd hoped. But things had come on hugely and every craft had advanced by hundreds of years' worth of knowledge.

He took a seat near the fire. Adran looked up and put his book to one side.

"Adran," Yorvin said, "I've been doing a lot of thinking and I've reached a decision. Your mother's death has been difficult for us both. Everything seems less important now she's gone."

Adran's expression hardened a little. He was far from being over his own loss.

"The guiding of the tribes is just as important as ever," Yorvin continued, "as are the preparations to power the force field after it fails. Both those tasks need somebody who is fully committed to them and that's no longer me."

He could see Adran working through the implications. "You're not going to step down, are you?"

"Yes, it's time for me to move aside and let you take up the reigns."

"But you're still in good health," Adran said. "You can carry on for years yet."

"You will do a better job. I'll be here to give advice if you want it. The only thing I ask is you follow the plans we've made. The agreed objects must be put in my tomb when I die, and you must ensure the Guardians are established in a way that will last the centuries."

"You know I will," Adran said. "'Though Sarah has been giving me earache about the wisdom of including a nuclear weapon. She explained to me how much damage it can do."

"That's the whole point," Yorvin said. "We can't guarantee that our plan will succeed. We have to give our descendants this second chance."

"Sarah is worried about us relying on it. She says it's still only a theory based on limited knowledge. We have no certainty what effect the weapon would have on the portal."

"That's why you should make sure the Guardians know that it would be the last throw of the dice. But we have to give them every chance we can."

Adran nodded. "An unknown hope is better than none at all. I will rule Enodia as well as I can, Yorvin, and will continue what you have started."

"We'll make the arrangements soon," Yorvin said. "I think I want to walk alone for a little longer, now. The stars are so clear this evening."

He rose from the chair and strolled into the darkness outside. A weight had been lifted from his shoulders. There was much still to be done but his part in it was complete.

He walked across the grass, still awed after all the decades by the beauty of the night sky. As his gaze strayed, once again, to Sattoria, he thought of his two lives and the two women he had loved.

Christopher J Wright

Part 15. Amber

40.

Amber took in the panorama of utter devastation before her. A huge crater had replaced the clearing and its hill. For hundreds of metres, the forest didn't exist. It was close to a kilometre before the bare ground became littered with a tangled mass of tree trunks that stretched for another five hundred metres. Here and there, individual trees had stayed upright in defiance of the gargantuan forces which had just been unleashed.

"By the gods," King Zandis said, complete disbelief etched across his face. "How?"

"That is why those weapons are illegal on every civilised planet, Your Majesty."

"Bayl," she called into the transmitter. Again there was no response, only static. She looked up the weapon's effects on her terminal.

"Professor Stefans," the king said, "we will make every effort to find Groms. But first we need to determine if the portal has been destroyed and whether any of the creatures still live."

Amber let out a long breath, calmed herself. "I understand, Your Majesty. We can't go close to the crater for at least some time. But we might be able to see if it is deep enough to expose the portal. I can scan it from different angles to find out."

"Then do so," Zandis said. "It would seem that all but the creatures in the flyer were in the forest when the explosion took place. We will organise a search for any who escaped. You will tell us immediately if you get news of Bayl."

He assigned two soldiers to assist her. They would be of little protection to her if any aliens had survived. But that was unlikely. Most had been at the complex, with the rest returning to it. She was more worried about the people who had remained in Denford. They were probably experiencing the retribution of the flyer's pilot.

She took a still image of the blast site from the holo-recorder and downloaded it, along with her coordinates, to her computer. If she repeated the process from another position, then the computer would triangulate and, with a few more images, she should get a reasonably accurate three-dimensional representation.

It meant long walks between the positions where she took her readings. But that gave her time to determine that the communicator could be out for tens of minutes – even for a small nuclear device.

It was too long to wait. She resisted the temptation to throw the computer away. Looking at the remains of the forest, she tried to guess where Bayl might have reached before he took cover.

She had no idea. She knew he must have got away from the destruction. But the trees also had been knocked flat for a good distance beyond.

Every minute or two, she called his name into the transmitter, but received nothing but the static. And every time, she realised she was more anxious about Bayl than she was about the portal.

"Amber… Can you hear me?" It was faint, almost overwhelmed by static. But it was definitely Bayl.

"Bayl, are you alright?" she cried.

"We're both fine. We found a safe place to hide, but we're trapped by fallen trees. We need help."

"We'll get you out, but it will take time to find you. I'll be in touch soon."

Amber sent one of the soldiers to relay the news and request a team to assist. She hurried to the next location which she had chosen, where the bearing would triangulate Bayl's signal and fix his and Lydon's position.

When she made contact again, the computer easily located Bayl's transmitter. They had travelled quite a way in their flight from the clearing. Although they were in an area of the forest that had been flattened, they were not too far into the devastation. Hopefully, they'd not been exposed to too much radiation.

It took hours to carve a path through the pile of fallen tree trunks and branches. While the work was continuing, Amber's computer finished its model of the crater.

The portal should have protruded three metres from the crater's surface. There was no sign of it. The nuclear explosion had destroyed it.

At last, Zandis smiled. He demanded renewed effort from the men working to free Bayl and Lydon.

It was afternoon by the time the troops' axes and saws took away the last obstacle to the two men's escape. Bayl had reported after a few hours that he and Lydon had vomited for no apparent reason.

Finally, the last trunk was removed and Bayl and Lydon were free. While they were unsteady on their feet, there were no signs of burns to indicate overwhelming exposure to radiation.

When Amber saw Bayl, she hesitated. But only for a second.

She flung her arms around him. "I'm so glad you're safe," she whispered in his ear.

"I thought," he whispered back, clutching her, "I'd never see you again."

Staring into each other's eyes, they drew back.

"I think his Majesty is waiting," he said. "I'd better let him speak to me."

King Zandis stepped forward, an amused smile on his face. "It is good to see you are safe, Groms. Well done." He turned to Lydon. "And also to you, my man. Enodia owes you a great debt of gratitude."

Lydon looked down at his feet with a mumbled, "Thank you, Your Majesty."

"It seems we are done here for the time being," Zandis said. "We should return to Denford and see what damage has been done."

A detail of troops was left to guard the crater, with orders to send word immediately if anything out of the ordinary occurred.

In Denford, they learned that the alien flyer had launched a retaliatory attack, bombarding the city for nearly an hour. A few dozen citizens had been killed and more wounded early on, but after that, most had found hiding places.

Although many buildings had suffered in the attack, most were intact or repairable – especially those made of stone. When the pilot's rage had subsided, he had flown away, disappearing over the horizon and not returning.

* * * * *

Within a few days, the news of the defeat of the aliens filtered out to the countryside and the city was once again bustling.

King Zandis announced there would be a festival to celebrate Enodia's victory in a week's time, at which Arthur would be re-entombed. Work began on the repairs needed for the event, funded from the King's treasury, concentrating particularly on the Mausoleum, which had been damaged in the attack.

Research into Bayl's health was Amber's priority. Readings taken on her scanner at his hiding place, cross-referenced with the radiation patterns of an explosion, indicated he had taken a high dose. Although the levels weren't enough to kill immediately, they meant his chances of leading a long life were low.

If she could get him to a hospital on Vindor, they might be able to do something – which meant persuading him to leave Enodia. They were more than professional colleagues, more even than friends. But Amber wasn't sure how much more. She wasn't even truly sure how much more she wanted.

The first rule of anthropological field work was to not get involved with subjects. Relationships spanning the cultural and technological differences between Enodia and Vindor were almost doomed to failure. There were too many things one of them would take for granted which the other would find distasteful.

But she realised she did not want Bayl to leave her life, that speaking to him was more than a question of his health.

A few days after they returned to Denford, she and Bayl were walking in the square in front of the Mausoleum, watching the preparations for the festival day the King had decreed.

"How are you feeling?" she said.

"I'm fine. And I was a couple of hours ago, too." He looked at her. "Is there something you're not telling me? Have I been poisoned by the weapon?"

"You and Lydon took quite a high dose of radiation."

Bayl stopped. "Will I die?"

"No, not any time soon. But radiation can set into motion diseases that will surface in months or years. You've taken enough to make that quite likely. You need to go to a hospital on Vindor for treatment."

"You've known this since we got back, haven't you?"

She lowered her head. "Yes."

"Why didn't you tell me sooner?"

She glanced up at him. "I – I – couldn't."

He looked into her eyes. "If I'm wrong about this, forgive me," he said, leaning forward and kissing her.

41.

Amber looked at the sea of smiling faces that stretched for more than a hundred metres. She was sitting in an open carriage with Bayl and Lydon, the marksman, as part of a procession making its way into Founder's Square.

After the shadow that had lain over Denford, and the feverish repair work of the last week, the people grasped the opportunity to celebrate wholeheartedly.

"This was where it all started," Amber said, looking over to Bayl.

He reached out and took her hand. "Only four months ago but it seems like an age. So much has happened."

The horror of the stampede that followed the eclipse had dimmed, but Amber was still uneasy being in the middle of a crowd in similar circumstances. She gripped Bayl's hand.

The procession, led by Yorvin's new coffin, had reached a platform erected in front of the Mausoleum's gates. The coffin was placed on a pedestal in front of the platform, its bearers standing behind it as an honour guard.

In the lead carriage, King Zandis and his Queen were helped down, climbed the platform's steps and sat on two rudimentary thrones.

Bayl, Lydon and Amber stood at the other end of the platform.

To renewed cheers from the crowd, Zandis rose from his throne.

"My people..." he called loudly, causing the cheers to begin subsiding. "My people... We are gathered to celebrate a great victory for our nation!"

A swell of noise greeted his words.

"This was made possible by the wisdom and foresight of Arthur, our Founding King. He foresaw the attack of the alien creatures that terrorised our land. More than that, he bequeathed a weapon of great power to us. We have used that weapon to destroy both the creatures and the gateway they used to reach us."

Zandis waited for the ongoing clamour of the crowd to subside.

"The weapon was kept safe for centuries within Arthur's tomb, ready to be used when it was needed. But now we shall entomb him once more and hold his name in even higher honour than we did before."

The King looked over to Amber and the others.

"However, the victory was not Arthur's alone. There have been acts of courage and valour from those of our own time, without which the creatures might well have won the day. Five, among the many, are particularly worthy of our acknowledgement and honour.

You see only three before you, for two gave their lives in the defence of Enodia. Duke Edrik and Doctor Karl Fryer, one of our leading scientists, nearly thwarted the aliens without the need of the weapon, but lost their lives in the attempt. Senior Advisor Bayl Groms carried the weapon into the middle of the aliens believing he would probably die. Sergeant Lydon protected Mr Groms during that time, killing several of the aliens with one of their own firearms. Finally, Professor Amber Stefans, a visitor to our world, provided key insights and knowledge that allowed us to act effectively. To each of these we award our highest honour, the Star of Adran."

The crowd cheered once more as King Zandis took the medals, eight pointed stars of gold hanging from red silk ribbons, and placed them over the heads of each in turn.

Amber beamed as she lifted her eyes to the cheering throngs. Her time on Enodia had been life changing in many ways. She would have two landmark papers to write, one on the social engineering of the prophecy, another on the glimpse of the only alien civilisation ever discovered. She was also an honoured figure on this world. But most of all she had met Bayl.

As the joy of the assembled throng showed no signs of abating, Zandis raised his hands to quieten them.

"Now, please observe a silence as we take Arthur into the Mausoleum to entomb him once more. As you watch, give honour to our Founder, to Duke Edrik, to Doctor Fryer and to all those soldiers and citizens who gave their lives bravely in this struggle."

Arthur's coffin was lifted on to the shoulders of six bearers and carried slowly through the gates of the Mausoleum. The King and Queen walked behind it, with Amber, Bayl and Lydon following. Various nobles and citizens of station formed the rear of the procession.

There was little ceremony. The coffin was placed carefully within the stone outer coffin and, using ropes, the lid lowered slowly into place. Then the ropes and the wooden assembly were removed and the gate to the room was shut.

Arthur, or Yorvin Bandrell of Sattoria as he truly was, rested once again with Sharna, his queen.

Amber gave thanks to one who had seen danger in a far distant time and had acted to avert it. Silently, she promised that his deeds would be known and recognised far beyond the world of Enodia.

Lingering a while before following the rest of the party, Amber walked in a reflective mood out of the Mausoleum.

"There you are," Bayl said, when she came upon him waiting for her by the gates. "Are you all right?"

"I'm fine," she smiled. "Just being unprofessional and getting emotionally involved with my subjects again. I seem to be doing that a lot lately."

Bayl grinned. "I'm still not sure I like the idea of being a subject. It makes it sound as though you should be prodding me with a stick."

"Well, that can be arranged – if it would make you feel better. And what's this about you being a Senior Advisor to the King? That's not how I remember your introductions."

"Well, we were interested in finding out why you came here. You may consider yourself an experimental subject as well."

"Why thank you," she said, performing a tolerable impression of a curtsey for him, aided greatly by the skirt she was wearing. "See, I think I'm getting the hang of those now." She paused for a moment. "Actually, it doesn't come as a great surprise. Ever since the dig at the spaceship, I've had my suspicions, and you seem to be able to get audiences with the King surprisingly easily."

"In that case my news won't come as a surprise," he said.

"News? You are still coming to Vindor aren't you?"

"Yes," he nodded, "but I'll be doing so in an official capacity. King Zandis has appointed me Ambassador to the Vindoran League. I'm afraid you'll have to put up with me being around for quite a while."

* * * * *

Ten days after the Festival, a Vindoran Navy cruiser arrived at Enodia, taking up station in orbit since it was not designed to land in an atmosphere. Scientific teams and a detachment of marines were sent to the crater and confirmed there was no remaining trace of the portal.

Shuttles were despatched to hunt down the alien flyer. It was found several hundred kilometres away, out of fuel. The alien pilot was captured soon after. Since King Zandis had no wish to hold the first captured alien indefinitely, he gratefully handed it over to the Vindorans. The League would have two live aliens and a working flyer to study. It was going to cause tidal waves amongst the establishment.

The captain of the cruiser also requested the alien rifle be handed over – also for study. Initially reluctant, King Zandis relented when offered ten Vindoran laser-rifles in exchange. These became the new weapons of his Royal Guard.

As a citizen of the League, Amber was instructed, rather than requested, to deliver all evidence of the aliens to the captain. As a dutiful patriot, she immediately complied. She had, of course, taken copies of all the holo-recordings and given them to Bayl for safe keeping, as well as half the books they had taken from the alien world. She knew how governments worked away from the core worlds, where the military sometimes asserted their authority as absolute. She was not going to be cut out of this discovery by a naval officer who thought he knew what was best.

A week after the arrival of the cruiser, Captain Norton arrived on the courier which had originally brought Amber to Enodia. He had come as soon as he heard of the troubles, concerned for Amber's welfare.

And so it was, a month after the detonation of the warhead and the defeat of the aliens, Amber found herself at the edge of Denford between a crowd of sightseers and the courier ship. The sight of spaceships taking off had become more common since the arrival of the cruiser, with its shuttles making frequent trips to Denford. As a result, the departure of Bayl and Amber had not attracted huge attention, with perhaps only a hundred or so turning out to watch.

As Lydon, too, needed treatment for his radiation overdose, he was assigned as Bayl's bodyguard. He walked behind Bayl and Amber, a Vindoran laser-rifle, his newly prized possession, slung over his shoulder. After they boarded, the entry ramp was drawn into the ship and preparations were made for the launch. They took their seats and Amber brought up an outer view on a display screen fitted into a nearby wall.

As the ship began to lift off, the display showed the crowd reduce in size. Then the main engines kicked into action, the gravity compensators ensuring only a slight feeling of acceleration. The crowd on the ground receded. Then the whole of Denford was visible. Once the city had diminished, the view was like looking at a map.

Lydon gripped the sides of his chair tight, his knuckles ice white, his face as pale as a windswept cloud.

Bayl smiled. "It's just like the holo-display of the planet you have," he said, "but this is the real thing? We're really up that high already?"

Amber grinned and nodded, reaching over to touch his arm. "And there's so many more wonders for you to see."

As they reached the upper atmosphere, the circle of the planet came into view.

Bayl gasped at the blues and greens of Enodia against the star-filled blackness around it.

His infectious enthusiasm reminded Amber of the wonder of her own first flight into space.

42.

After Corporal Quince tapped his passcode into the keypad, a diagnostic summary appeared on the display screen. His battle armour made the process more difficult, but it was necessary with the residual radiation still at dangerous levels. The diagnostics confirmed the camera was functioning correctly, still transmitting its signal up to the cruiser stationed in orbit. The power cell would need replacing before too long, but it would last another few days.

He tapped further keys to lock the display, then closed the access panel. There was no need for a squad of marines to be down here checking the cameras. It wasn't the first time he'd thought this and he knew it wouldn't be the last. The captain wanted a physical presence down here and it got people off the ship for a time.

Quince made his way, in the early morning light, over to the next camera, the last before he met up with Edwards. He trudged along, reaching it after a minute or so and began the same diagnostic test.

This wasn't what he'd signed up for when he joined the marines. He had expected a life of excitement, discovering new worlds on the edge of the League, not unending hours guarding a featureless, radioactive crater. They had missed the real excitement by a couple of weeks, and their reward had been two months of mindless tedium. What was worse, there was still another month to go before they would be relieved.

His final camera was functioning correctly, too.

He looked over to the next of the cameras ringed around the edge of the crater.

"Edwards," he said, activating his battle armour's comms system. "You nearly done?"

"Just another thirty seconds to go, sir."

"All right. Finish up there and wait for me."

Another hour down in this hellhole and the shuttle would be here with the next duty squad.

As he walked towards Edwards, circling the crater, he caught some movement from the corner of his eye. His marine-trained instincts snapped into action. Dropping to the ground, he trained his laser rifle downwards. His eyes scanned the area, looking for the movement's source.

At the bottom of the crater, there was an area of shadow so dark that he couldn't see the ground. After a moment, it flickered and disappeared. Quince blinked his eyes and looked again.

Nothing.

Only the rubble-strewn landscape that had become so familiar.

"Edwards, did you see anything just now?"

"No, sir. I'm still working on the camera. I didn't see anything."

"What was it, Quince?" his sergeant said over comms.

"I'm not sure, Sarge. For a second, I thought I saw a shadow down in the crater."

"Probably just an animal. If it stays down there, it'll glow in the dark before long."

"I don't know," Quince said. "If it was anything, I guess they'll pick it up on the ship."

After a last scan of the crater – there was nothing out of the ordinary – Quince pulled himself up and carried on.

THE END

About the Author

Christopher J Wright was born in the north-east of England, raised on a heady mix of seaside video arcades, fantasy novels and science fiction. A measure of numeric competence led to university courses in mathematics and computer science. Afterwards, a career in IT, unsurprisingly, beckoned – firstly in academia, then the computer games industry and, finally, in the real world.

He lives in Northamptonshire with Karen, his wife, close to their three grown children and a growing flock of grandchildren.

Writing was a later choice in life, and would undoubtedly come as a surprise to any of his school English teachers. A judgement on the merits of this decision will be left to the reader.

Christopher J Wright

Acknowledgements

A novel does not get written in a bubble of isolation, and there are many to whom I owe debts of gratitude over the course of the years leading to this moment.

Firstly, I would like to thank Michael J Richards for his skill, honesty and encouragement in editing the final version of this work. It is substantially better, and shorter, because of him, though all remaining flaws are, of course, my own.

Thanks go, also, to my family and friends for their belief in me, and especially to Gemma and Katherine, who read early versions and nudged me onward with their enthusiastic responses.

Fellow writers, both long years ago in the Celestial Sphere group on Absolute Write and, more recently, in Northants Writers' Ink, have also helped hone skills crucial to the polishing process.

As of February 2022, a new cover has been added, courtesy of ambient_studios on fiverr.com. My thanks to them for a stunning improvement on my own limited effort.

Finally, my thanks go to Karen for her unending support and love. This novel would never have seen the light of day without her.

Christopher J Wright
13/11/2020
Edited 19/02/2022

Printed in Great Britain
by Amazon